Ann

"I represent another claimant."

"Another claimant?" Miranda asked. "I thought everything was settled."

The lawyer shook his head. "I drew up a will for Ms. Radinski right after her former lawyers drafted the old one. You were not named in the new will apart from a few odds and ends, like the piano. I have an injunction to remove you from the house."

Miranda sank into the closest chair. "Okay… What's the next step?"

"The locks will be changed after you leave today," Brett said. "You and my client will do the inventory together."

Miranda bit her lip. For a split second she contemplated flying back to Manhattan, but then she stiffened her spine. She was going to fight this.

"I didn't think Miss Virginia had any relatives. Who's this other claimant?"

Brett gestured behind her and Miranda turned. Russ Gerik had walked into the living room. He smiled at Miranda.

Dear Reader,

For years, I'd been fascinated by an old house on my brother's street that was owned by an elderly lady who was considered the hermit of the neighborhood. She kept two ancient cars in the driveway no one ever saw her drive—perhaps because fifteen felines were always draped over the hood or the roof! I took that house as a starting point and created the fictitious Miss Virginia.

I'd also wanted to create a character who was physically challenged. A good friend of mine has Stargardt's disease, which brutally affects vision. Despite being legally blind (and unable to drive in a city not known for mass transit!) she started—and still directs—the Waco Children's Theatre.

When I realized that many people who suffer disabilities or loss of limb because of the war in Afghanistan are thought to be "less than" or just weird, I decided to have my hero lose his hearing. Russ Gerik popped into my brain and whispered, "Use me! Love me!"

Russ became one of my favorite characters, and I hope readers will feel the same about him.

Flo

HARLEQUIN HEARTWARMING

Flo Fitzpatrick
Legacy of Silence

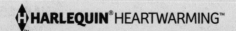

Recycling programs
for this product may
not exist in your area.

ISBN-13: 978-0-373-36686-6

LEGACY OF SILENCE

HARLEQUIN®

Printed in U.S.A.

www.Harlequin.com

FLO FITZPATRICK

was born in Washington, D.C., and spent her formative years moving across countries and oceans as an army brat. She has little memory of living in a château in France but firmly believes the Gothic setting sparked her love of romance and mystery (and *mousse au chocolat!*). A performer, teacher and choreographer, Flo holds degrees in dance and theater. She's spent much of her adult life shuttling from Texas to New York and loves both states for their ability to spawn diverse and often extremely wacky characters.

Flo's second novel, *Hot Stuff,* was nominated by *RT Book Reviews* as Best Romantic Suspense and, along with the paranormal novel *Haunting Melody,* has been optioned for film.

For Linda Haskett, the brilliant and talented creator of the Waco Children's Theatre, who has always embodied the spirit of a child with the wisdom of a prophet—and the loving heart of a loyal friend.

CHAPTER ONE

"I'VE INHERITED A haunted house," Miranda said. She surveyed the front of the Victorian home with a myriad of emotions that swung from sadness to guilt to elation.

Miranda was sitting in front of the house that was now hers—or it would be once she'd jumped through all the legal hoops. The last occupant, whom everyone referred to as "Miss Virginia," had lived alone for the past seventy years—unless one counted the cats that had decorated the porch, fence, roof and the inside of her fire-engine-red Cadillac convertible. Word around the neighborhood was the car hadn't been driven since it was delivered by the dealership in 1959. Miranda's father, Tim, once told her he'd never seen it leave the driveway and no one had ever glimpsed Virginia behind the wheel. Possibly because there were always at least two cats draped around the steering wheel and ten more sunning themselves on the front hood regardless of the season.

Miranda stepped out of the SUV her dad had loaned her and glanced at her watch. She had about forty minutes before the guys from Rocky Ridge Furniture were scheduled to deliver a new bed frame and mattresses to the house where she'd be staying for at least a month—possibly a bit longer. Her first order of business would be hiring a yard service to deal with the unkempt trees and lawn. Miss Virginia had spent her final weeks in a hospital, then at home with a hospice team, and Miranda doubted that pruning or mowing had been anyone's priority. The famous Caddy was still in the driveway, though absent of the felines. Miranda stared at the car for a few moments, blinking back tears and wondering if Virginia had even had a driver's license.

The house itself appeared to be in great shape. Even the roof looked new, and although the shutters needed a good paint job, the windows were storm-worthy.

Dave Brennan, Virginia's lawyer, had dropped off a key for Miranda that morning. It was time to use it. If bats with fangs flew out of the house, she'd simply pitch a tent on the front lawn until she could figure out her next move.

The key turned easily and nothing attacked her as she opened the door so she ventured in a bit farther and did a little tap dance in her sneakers on the hardwood. There was no lingering odor of big or small cats, and the switch in the front hall produced real light when she clicked it on. Not only that but those floors were in pristine condition—possibly because nothing had been moved for years.

After taking a look at the massive amount of furniture, piles of books, records and boxes, Miranda nearly turned around and headed back to the airport. Virginia must have moved all of her possessions down from the attic because Miranda had never seen even half of what was now crowding the room. One item, however, had not been moved. Miranda was thrilled to discover the old upright piano pushed against the north wall. She spent a few minutes shifting some of the lighter boxes so she could find out if the instrument was as neglected as the front yard.

Once the path was clear, she sank down onto the piano bench and lifted the lid to reveal the keys. The chord she sounded was clear, bright and absolutely in tune. The action was even the right weight. She immediately popped back to her feet and, on a hunch, opened the bench, where she discovered a pile of sheet music. Things were looking up already. Images of mornings spent in Virginia's kitchen drinking tea followed by leisurely sessions of playing the piano began flowing through her mind. Perhaps she wouldn't sell. Perhaps she could rent some of the bedrooms to reliable tenants (assuming such beings existed) and stay at the house, something she resolved to do more often. Or she could hire a caretaker.

Miranda resisted the impulse to start playing a musical number from *Phantom of the Opera*. Instead, she dug inside her purse, grabbed her mobile phone and hit Speed Dial number two.

"Hey, Dad." Miranda didn't wait for a hello. "Have you seen this place in the past few years?"

"A bit overwhelming?"

"Well, let's just say I didn't remember it looking like a museum. It wasn't like this the last time I came over. Of course, that was right after I graduated college and Miss Virginia didn't want me to come inside. We had tea and kolaches on the porch." Her voice cracked. "I am *not* a good person. Six years. At least I sent cards. Big whoop, right?"

There was a long pause at the other end of the line. Finally, Miranda's father asked, "Miranda, is this going to be too much? You can stay with Farrah and me until you get things sorted. I just thought this would give you some time by yourself."

Miranda shuddered, imagining the stress of being around her father's self-assured "I've owned my own successful catering business since the day I graduated college" wife of eight months. At forty-one, Farrah Nolan was only fourteen years older than Miranda—too young to be her stepmother and too old to really be a friend. Miranda dismissed that thought, musing that age had nothing to do with her feelings about the new Mrs. Timothy Nolan. Miss Virginia had been in her seventies when Miranda met her and their friendship had been instantaneous and solid.

"Thanks for the offer, but I wouldn't dream of invading your space. Y'all are newlyweds, after all! The good news is the piano is in tune, so I'm a happy singer. And as you might recall, Miss Virginia was a lady with eclectic tastes—I may find riches here…or at least a live cat or two. Are you sure all this is kosher? I mean, my living here before the will has been finalized."

"As far as I know, no one is challenging your inheritance," her father said. "If another claimant does turn up before or during probate, Dave will handle it." He paused before adding, "There are times I'm very glad I teach international law. I'd hate to have to tiptoe around the intricacies of estates and deal with irate relatives. The latter, thankfully, are non-existent in this case. Virginia was quite clear in her wishes. Dave told me that she left the house and all her worldly goods to you, Ms. Miranda Nolan—and added a comment about your kindness to her over the years. You must have impressed the fool out of the lady when you were a kid." His voice caught. "I'm still grateful Virginia took over much of my nonexistent parenting."

Miranda closed her eyes for a moment, remembering the tall but frail woman who'd treated Miranda as if she were her own child.

"It's okay, Dad. You were going through a lot after Mom died. Miss Virginia saw a need and stepped in. She truly was family."

Miranda glanced around the living room and sighed, envisioning the hours of work ahead of her. "I have to say, this is going to be interesting. I'm about to dive into the history of the mid-twentieth century. I'm already in awe of these antiques. You should see the clocks. I've been in the living room less than ten minutes and I've already counted two grandfather clocks, three anniversary mantel clocks and some kind of weird pendulum thing à la Edgar Allan Poe. I can't wait for midnight when everything goes off at once."

"Mark 'em all down, Miranda. You need to provide as much info as you can to help out the executor, who'll be someone from the Brennan firm. Which reminds me, Dave said he'd be happy to send an appraiser or a Realtor at some point, but you might want to contact an antiques dealer if you already have someone you trust."

Miranda tripped over a heavy box but managed to hang on to the phone. "I do know someone but unfortunately, he's in Manhattan. That's okay. I'll get a better idea of who or what I need once I've taken a good tour of the entire house. There are probably hidden passages strewn with pots of gold. Or ghosts in every bedroom and of course the attic."

"Scared?" Tim teased.

"Nah. It's cool. Miss Virginia and I were good friends from the moment we met. If she pops out of the woodwork one night I'll ask her spirit to tea—"

"She loved giving tea parties! For kids, anyway. I remember she'd invite you over and always send you home with a doggie bag full of fantastic cookies and little cakes. The woman was an amazing baker. I wonder if she was one of those culinary marvels who just sweeps into a kitchen and emerges with delicacies or if she had to dive through cookbooks and recipe files."

"Hmm. Now *that* would be a treasure—finding her recipe book. Tell Farrah if anything like that turns up, I'll give it to her. Anyway, I honestly don't mind being here sans companionship, unless creepy critters really do inhabit the woodwork—and I do not mean Virginia's spirit or any other noncorporeal beings. I'm talkin' rats or mites. Or maybe I'll trip over a feline who deserted the old Caddy in search of tuna."

After a moment, Miranda's father coughed and completely changed the subject. He quietly asked "Not to sound like a nosy parent, but how are you feeling about the fiasco with Grant? It's only been a couple of days since you told me y'all broke up. Are you okay?"

He paused. "Are you up to telling me what happened?"

Miranda pushed a box of books off an armchair and then sank down into the soft cushions. "I'm fine. Really. Surprisingly, I'm *more* than fine. The basic story is that Grant Spencer chose the occasion of our closing night party for *Illumination* to announce that he had wonderful news. He's going to direct *Topaz in Delirium*."

"I remember you saying something about that a few months ago. He was sweet-talking the producer every chance he got, right?"

"Oh, yeah. But apparently he took it a step further. After I'd congratulated him on getting the gig he rather casually added that he was dating Cyan Marlowe, the college-age daughter of Tyrone Marlowe, who just happens to be the producer of *Topaz in Delirium*."

"Wait. Back that up."

Miranda could hear the mirth her dad was trying to hide.

"Did you say Cyan?"

"I did."

"As in the inkjet color that always runs out first?"

Miranda laughed. "Precisely. Daddy Marlowe is Mr. Broadway Producer Extraordinaire. It's going to be interesting to see whose ego wins between Marlowe and Grant. Anyway, it struck me that my boyfriend was a toad—which admittedly wasn't until *after* he broke up with me—but it still hit purty durn fast. I decided I'd be better off without a narcissistic, overly ambitious jerk who ruined the closing night party for me."

"Sorry, hon. Sounds like Grant brought tackiness to a new level."

Miranda sighed. "My only lingering question is 'what on earth did I ever see in him beyond good looks, charm and smarts and the theater mania we had in common?'"

Her refined and genteel father produced a distinct snort. "Well, having met the man, I'd add charisma to that list. I thought he was great for you and I'm generally a decent judge of character. I guess we were both deceived."

"Well, I'll just be more careful next time I'm attracted to someone and try to curb my impulsive heart. But I have to admit I'm really ticked Grant's directing *Topaz*—there was a great part in it for me. Ah, well. Nothing to be gained by angsting over it all. I'll hang out here for a while, play Virginia's lovely piano and have a marvelous time sifting through her things. Maybe get some answers as to why she hid in this place for those seventy years."

"Now *that* would be a great mystery to solve. I remember hearing that she worked at one of the old department stores downtown back when they had their own tailors, but by the time we moved here she was taking in clothing at home and wouldn't leave the house. You practically lived at Virginia's 24/7, especially around Halloween."

Miranda sat straight up. "Halloween. Yes. Talk about memories." She closed her eyes, seeing herself as a little girl, dressed in a pink tutu and ballet slippers, ringing the doorbell of this very house and receiving a warm greeting from a tall, elderly woman with exquisitely refined features. Miranda could almost smell the scent of cinnamon-flaked cocoa and the chocolate cupcakes decorated in orange icing that had been sitting on a table in the living room. She could see Miss Virginia, dressed all in black, smiling, as she ushered the ballerina, the superhero and the astronaut inside for what had been Miranda's first Halloween mini-party.

"I was seven at the time. I remember you let the Shapiro twins be my escorts. That's how Miss Virginia and I first met." Miranda glanced at the corner of the room where Virginia's tea table still stood. She could almost see the starched doilies under the plates of goodies and Virginia's steady hand pouring homemade hot chocolate into cups for her Halloween guests. "Dad? Do you remember anything else about her life? Maybe some tidbit a neighbor let slip? I honestly don't recall her talking about her past—she probably knew I was too young to care and most of the time I was rattling on about my dance recitals or school plays or…" Miranda swallowed hard. "What a selfish little brat I was."

"Honey, you were young. No kid wants to hear the life story of anyone over the age of eighteen. Give yourself a break. She understood. Believe me." He paused for a moment then continued, "I heard that she bought the house in the mid-forties—she might've been a war widow. Then again I never heard anyone call her anything but Miss Virginia. And she definitely wasn't from Birmingham."

"That much I knew. She was Czech. I found out the first time she made kolaches for me and I became instantly addicted." Miranda could almost taste the fruit-filled pastries Virginia had baked on a weekly basis. "She was a great cook but I think she also dabbled in art. Or maybe she told me she'd been an artist's model? I'm not sure. She said she had a portrait of a child my age who had my 'impish expression.' But she never got around to showing it to me. I wonder if I'll finally get to see it."

"She also loved music and theater," Tim said.

"She did. I used to perform all my dance routines for her. I have this very clear memory of reciting and acting out the poem *The Highwayman* when I was in sixth grade. She thought it was a Tony-winning performance."

Miranda blinked back tears as the memories flooded in. She had often played piano and sung while Miss Virginia sat in a rocking chair, quietly listening; then the elderly lady and the small child would sit down to formal tea. Miranda inhaled. She needed to end the conversation before the strong emotions finished it for her.

"Dad, I just noticed the time. I'd better get a few boxes moved before the delivery guys show up with the new bed. If they can't inch it back into the bedroom past the clutter they might pitch the frame and mattresses into the yard in disgust. Which reminds me—do I pay them today or did you already take care of the bill?"

"It's paid in full and you don't need to reimburse me. I'll let you go, but remember you're coming over to the house next week. Farrah's invited some folks to meet you. And before you say anything, yes, I'm well aware that you're not up for any matchmaking dinners right now, but Farrah really wants to do this. And I've been asked to remind you that the Trussville Fair is in ten days. As far as I know it's still set up like it was back when we used to go. Lots of artwork and crafts and I think some local bands are playing."

Miranda had winced after hearing *Farrah* and *dinner* in the same sentence but tried not to let her feelings about the get-together leak into her tone as she thanked her father and said goodbye.

She quickly began to move boxes away from the piano, muttering "labels" to herself. She needed a system for cataloguing so she wouldn't end up going over the same box twice as she did inventory for the estate sale. Miranda peeked inside a box that was partially open and found Virginia's sewing basket. Her smile warring with tears, Miranda reverently lifted it out and opened it, eye-

ing the ancient thimbles and the twenty-odd
spools of thread in various colors. She gently
unwrapped a pair of perfectly preserved scis-
sors from their bed of fine linen and just as
carefully put them back.

"No way am I selling Miss Virginia's sewing supplies," she said. These things had been
a huge part of her friend's life. They'd been
her livelihood. Miranda remembered Virginia
carefully searching to find the perfect color
of thread to hem one of Miranda's dance costumes. Even as a child, she had recognized
the older woman's pleasure in stitching that
costume with expertise and love.

Miranda set the box with the sewing goods
back on top of the piano and in doing so,
she upset another opened box. The contents
spilled out onto the floor—more than a dozen
bound notebooks.

"Journals?" Miranda hesitated for a few
moments, not sure whether she had the right
to pry into Virginia's private thoughts. When
a sheet fell out of the book she was holding,
she skimmed it and began to laugh. Recipes.
Farrah would love this. Miranda opened the
notebook at random, hoping to find ingredi-
ents and directions for tea cookies and kolaches.

Instead, she discovered a discourse regarding the fun side of politics in the 1990s including Miss Virginia's opinion that Bill Clinton played one mean saxophone. Miranda grinned, dropped that notebook back into the box and picked up a journal that was obviously far older.

She sank to the floor after reading the first paragraph.

Miss Virginia hadn't really been a miss. She'd been the missus to a gentleman named Benjamin Auttenberg.

May 15, 1960
I ran into Marta Rosenberg tonight at temple. We cried when we saw one another. I did not know she had moved to Birmingham, too. She said she has been attending the temple in the Mountain Brook area. It was so good yet so painful to see her. We were last together in Terezin on that day the Russian soldiers freed us all in 1945. Marta talked of our husbands' deaths and we cried again. She wanted to know if I had remarried and I told her that Radinski was my maiden name. I don't want anyone to know I was Benjamin Auttenberg's widow because I

don't want to be hounded by art dealers trying to buy his paintings. I had enough of those vultures right after the war. I told Marta I simply want peace.

Miranda heard the sound of the delivery truck pulling up out front. She quickly grabbed a tissue from her purse and dabbed her eyes, then replaced the journal in its box.

"I miss you, Virginia. And I'm so very sorry—for everything."

CHAPTER TWO

MIRANDA PAUSED IN the doorway of what would be her bedroom for the next month. She eyed the deliveryman who was currently kneeling on the floor with his back to her, putting the side slots of the bed frame into the footrest.

"Excuse me? Before you get the frame done and the box springs on, would you mind moving the frame a bit to the right? I need just a little more room to vacuum what passes for a rug on that side."

Nothing. He ignored her and continued to click the side railing into place.

Miranda waited for a second, unsure if he was being rude or simply didn't feel like responding. When he moved toward the left side of the footrest without shifting the bed an inch, she coughed, and then repeated her request with a bit more volume.

Nothing. Maybe he was listening to loud

music on headphones and simply hadn't heard her?

She was about to lean down and tap him on the shoulder when Henry—the head deliveryman from Rocky Ridge Furniture—did the same to her. She whirled around.

"He can't hear you, Ms. Nolan."

"Music lover with super teeny headphones set on serious blast mode?" she asked.

Henry shook his head. "Yes and no. He actually *is* a music lover—or I should say 'was.' He lost his hearing about two years ago when he was in Afghanistan."

Miranda was stunned. She tried to imagine what life would be without music and began feeling hemmed in by the room itself. *Would complete silence mean a world walled off from the rest of humanity?* She shivered. "What happened?"

As if the man knew he was being discussed, he turned and stared—or glared— at Miranda. His shaggy brown hair fell over hazel eyes. His nose appeared to have seen a football, basketball or soccer ball bounce off it at some point in the past. The right side of his face bore numerous small scars, but they didn't detract from the kind of quiet attractiveness worn so well by some of the movie stars of the forties and fifties—like Gregory Peck or Gary Cooper. Miranda could have sworn she'd seen him before... She was also aware of a tightening in her stomach. The same tension she always got just before going onstage. Excitement and anticipation and a touch of fear of the unknown.

Henry started to answer Miranda's question but was interrupted by a voice that had a strange mix of richness and a volume that seemed slightly unsure. "Before Henry gets a chance to become melodramatic or bore you with a ten-minute monologue, let me simply state that a bomb went off in Kabul where I was working as an interpreter. I made it out with limbs intact. My eardrums were not so lucky. Nor were the numerous soldiers who never made it out at all. Satisfied?"

Miranda blinked, then calmly and slowly responded, "I suppose you read lips?"

He shook his head. "Not with any great skill. I'm much better with signing. Most deaf folks only read about fifty percent anyway. But your curious 'what happened' is easy to understand. It's an obvious question—and you have fairly decent mouth action." He paused, then continued with a sarcastic edge to his tone, "Most people slur and mumble, which leaves me without a clue as to what they're yammering about. In all honesty, I don't particularly care to know what the majority of the universe has to say. Life is better without the noise of ignorant people."

Miranda flinched, unsure how to respond. "I'm really sorry."

Apparently her mouth action was still "active" because he immediately snapped, "For what? You didn't set the bomb."

Miranda bit her lower lip then tilted her chin up. "'I'm sorry' wasn't meant as a personal apology. Perhaps I should have said, 'you have my sympathy for your trouble.' Would that suit you better?"

He looked at her with some confusion. Apparently his lipreading skills weren't up for snapping out a speedy response—or perhaps he simply wasn't able to understand lengthier sentences.

Henry grinned at Miranda. "Get him, girl! He needs someone to stand up to him. Normally, people duck their heads and leave the room when Russ tries to shame them. Of course, it may help that he probably got about four words out of what you said. He's right. His signing is far better than his lip reading."

"Russ?" Images flickered through Miranda's

mind. She suddenly remembered seeing this man on a stage sitting at an electric keyboard.

Russ was still staring at her.

"It just hit me. You're Russ Gerik—right? You were with a really cool band. Very eclectic musically. Columbiana Patchwork. I saw y'all at a festival over in Gadsden about ten years ago. You were on keyboards and vocal backup and you were amazing." She turned to Henry. "Do you sign?"

"Since the cradle. Both my parents were deaf." He translated her question and subsequent comments.

Russ's puzzled stare shifted to a look of anger oddly mixed with apathy. "Yes. Russ Gerik. Columbiana Patchwork. It's over. So is this—conversation."

Miranda wanted to ask if his hearing loss was permanent. Did he have partial hearing? Was he getting any kind of medical treatment? For that matter, was he getting counseling for post-traumatic stress? But she wasn't up for another confrontation, so she turned her back on Russ and addressed Henry. "Before I get told off again would you mind asking him to move the bed a few inches over? I'd prefer being able to vacuum back there before the dust bunnies start going on Easter egg hunts."

Henry smiled. "No problem." He immediately began signing Miranda's request. Russ shifted the bed with ease, then, with an odd smile, he signed something to Henry.

"What did he say?"

"Loosely translated, 'Fine, and it's not going to matter anyway.'"

"What does that mean?"

"No clue."

The doorbell rang before Miranda had a chance to ask anything else. She wove her way through boxes, chairs, floor lamps and at least three side tables before finally reaching the front of the house.

She pulled the door open. Two young men dressed in white shirts and black trousers smiled at her. They were both extremely clean-cut blonds with blue eyes. "Miranda Nolan?" asked the taller of the two.

"That's me."

The man handed her a card as he said, "I'm Brett King. Associate at Henniger and Waltham. Sorry to do this, but I'm here to issue an injunction."

"Excuse me?"

The shorter man scowled. "Good grief,

Brett! Think you can ease into this just a bit? Hi, Ms. Nolan. I'm Cort Farber. I'm an associate at Brennan and Driscoll, the firm handling Miss Radinski's estate."

"The firm that *was* handling the estate," King stated firmly

Cort coughed. "Handling, Brett. As in present tense. Remember? We were both just in court establishing exactly that."

Miranda blinked. "I'm so sorry. I'm beyond confused here. Two different firms vying to be executors? Do I get to choose or something? Do y'all get commissions?"

Cort sighed. "I wish. Look, may we come in?" He handed Miranda his card, as well.

The cards seemed legitimate, as did the attorneys. She opened the door a bit wider and gestured toward the disaster on the right that was the living room.

"I'm not exactly set up for business calls right now but if y'all can find a chair that isn't covered in Miss Virginia's belongings or cat hair, go for it."

"We're not staying long so don't worry," Cort said. He glanced around the room. "Wow. You've got your work cut out for you. It's like a high-class thrift store in here. Did you know Miss Virginia had thirteen cats in this house? She found homes for all of them before she passed away. Once she went into the hospital she knew she wasn't going to be able to live here again." He shook his head. "She must have had incredible persuasive powers."

"I hadn't seen Miss Virginia in six years," Miranda said, "but I can tell you she always had the ability to charm people into doing things they were originally determined not to do. Which is odd, really. She was such a hermit and— Sorry. I'm rattling on. So, what exactly is the deal here? Why do I have two firms?"

"You don't," Brett quickly replied. "I represent another claimant."

Miranda's jaw dropped. "Another claimant? I thought everything was settled."

Brett appeared a bit irritated. "This is all extremely disorganized and I apologize. I've been out of town for the past two weeks so I didn't realize Ms. Radinski had passed away. My paralegal—who's about to be canned for incompetence—didn't call me. I drew up a will for Ms. Radinski right after Dave Brennan and Cort drafted the old one. You were not named in the new will apart from inheriting some of her possessions like the piano and a few personal odds and ends. The point is, I have an injunction removing you from living in the house."

Miranda sank down into the closest chair. "Okay… This is just…terrific. I don't get a whiff of this until I'm moving in? Couldn't someone have contacted me while I was still in Manhattan so I could have saved a trip?" She sighed. "Oh, never mind. So, what's the next step?"

Cort shot Brett a glance that was less than friendly. "We're so sorry about the bad timing. Dave thought we'd have this straightened out before you flew down. Sadly, that didn't happen. Now, what Brett failed to mention is that our firm has no intention of allowing this second will to stand. Dave and I are challenging its validity. I was here with him the day Miss Virginia signed the will naming you her sole heir—"

"Cort, you're stalling," Brett said. "Get on with it."

"If you'll quit interrupting and let me get a full sentence out, it would help! Ms. Nolan, the Brennan firm is contesting this so-called new will. You can't live here for the time being, but you'll still be cataloguing the possessions. The catch is you have to do the inventory with the second claimant. I personally think it's ridiculous, but Judge Winston Rayborn, the nutcase who issued the injunction, thinks this is a fair and reasonable solution."

"The locks will be changed after you leave today," Brett added. "The keys will be provided to you and my client once you've made arrangements for doing the inventory. Paralegals from our offices will pick the keys up each time you finish. That way no one can sneak back in. It's tricky and annoying but that's the judge's ruling."

Miranda bit her lip. She'd gone from inheritor to homeless to accused thief, all within the past ten minutes. For a split second she contemplated flying right back to Manhattan, but her spine stiffened and she realized she was going to fight this. She wanted Virginia's house.

Cort gave her a reassuring wink. "Don't worry about it. We're going to deal with this and you'll be living here in no time."

Miranda finally had enough presence of mind to say, "I didn't think Miss Virginia had any relatives. Who's this pesky other claimant?"

Brett gestured behind her. Miranda turned.

Russ Gerik had entered the living room and was standing beside the piano as though it were his. He smiled at Miranda.

CHAPTER THREE

"BROOKS, YOU ARE the most incredible agent in the history of show business, but this is nuts! I just got here," Miranda groaned. "On the other hand *here* didn't end up being where I thought it was."

"What are you babbling about?"

"Never mind. I'm currently at my Dad's—which means I'm also at Farrah's—instead of sleeping in my brand-new bed at Virginia's house. Two days so far." She shuddered. "She's trying to teach me to cook."

Brooks howled. "I'd buy tickets to see Ms. Miranda Nolan in the kitchen! But this is more important. I swear. So book a flight and get up here—like yesterday. You're perfect for this role. Wendy Konstanza is casting and she specifically requested that you read for the part of Miami Montreville, superspy. I gather she caught your stellar performance in *Illumination* and was impressed. And Miranda, this is a one shot deal. They're not doing callbacks. You're looking at a major film and consequently a major career booster. You won't *need* a house in Birmingham—you can buy an apartment in Manhattan if this comes through."

Miranda was still reeling from the news that one of the best casting directors in the business wanted her to audition. "Konstanza asked for me? Really?"

"She did. So quit whining, take a red-eye and be ready to knock 'em dead Thursday. I'm emailing you sides and as much character analysis as the skimpy sheet provided," Brooks Tanner practically growled into the phone. "Someday I'm going to revolutionize the entire industry by demanding that in-depth casting breakdowns become the norm."

Miranda chuckled. "Dream on, darlin' dream on. Agents from the days of vaudeville have tried and failed. Okay. I'm already on-line. I'll see what I can find for cheap flights and get there tomorrow sometime. Give me the details and maybe we can squeeze in a little agent/actress coffee while I'm in town. Wait. Scratch that. Let's make it a meal at China Tan's. I need hot 'n' spicy anything with peanut sauce on it." She chuckled. "And a fortune cookie reading, *Nice Job! Movie Yours!*"

"It's a date," Brooks said. "Now go pack. I'll see you tomorrow."

Sixteen hours later Miranda was in a Manhattan studio smiling at five men in suits who were apparently producers and the only other woman in the room—Wendy Konstanza. Miranda had just taken a big breath and was ready to read her lines opposite the bored production assistant when a curve ball came sailing past home base.

In the less than twenty-four hours since Brooks had called her, the producers of *The Agency* (precisely which agency not specified and hopefully non-existent in the real world) had begun to consider options for the character Miranda was reading for, a spy with the unlikely but entertaining name of Miami Montreville. The original script (and the sides) had called for Miami to die.

But the producers and screenwriters were obviously thinking "sequel" and hadn't decided whether to let Miami miraculously survive what any sane person would consider certain death.

Now, instead of a scripted death scene, Miranda was plunged into the land of "wake up, realize you're alive and escape," which translated into "improvise, Miranda." The character breakdown hadn't included much of the plot for *The Agency* apart from, "Miami Montreville, female spy, dies in Indonesia while on a mission." Miranda wasn't terribly familiar with the geography of Indonesia but she knew Jakarta was a big city and big cities have restaurants and shopping malls so she figured those would be great places for a resurrected spy to duck into and find a cell phone some poor tourist had carelessly left on the table. Miranda idly wondered if plans were being made for an actual location shoot in Jakarta, hopefully during winter months, but she shelved that thought for later.

All was going well. Wendy liked Miranda's improv and the guys in suits gulping coffee nodded a lot during Miranda's attempts to come up with outrageous lines spoken into an imaginary cell phone.

Then came the final twist.

Wendy held up her hand. "Miranda? Nice job. But we'd like to see a little interaction with another human." She gestured to her assistant, who opened a door and ushered in an actor. Miranda nearly shouted, *He's not human! He's a rodent!*

Grant Spencer stepped inside the studio. He appeared to be as stunned as Miranda.

"Hi, Grant."

"Miranda."

Wendy glanced from one to the other. "You two know each other?"

Miranda nodded. "We do." She hurriedly added, "We actually just finished doing a show together, although it was my impression that Grant was about to start directing *Topaz in Delirium.*"

Grant's color changed from red to white to red again "I am. But it's stalled for who knows how long, so I'm free."

"Ah." *Why is it I can come up with terrific lines for a superspy, but "ah" is the only thing that drips out of my mouth when I want to be brilliant?* She trusted that her improvisational skills would kick in again once she and Grant were given the basics of the next scene.

They did. She and Grant were used to playing opposite one another on stage and both were professional enough not to let any personal issues sneak into their performances. Wendy seemed pleased again, as did the suits. An hour later, Miranda finished calling out goodbyes and began briskly walking down Eighth Avenue to meet her agent.

"Miranda!"

She turned. "Grant."

"I wanted to ask how you're doing. I was worried about you after our talk during the *Illumination* party...uh, a couple of weeks ago. You kind of disappeared."

Miranda looked directly into Grant's pale blue eyes. "It was less than a week, Grant. And I didn't disappear. I flew down to Birmingham, and now I'm here. I fly back tomorrow."

"Why?"

"Why, what?"

"Why are you going back down to Alabama? I thought your stepmother drove you crazy."

"She does."

"So why are you heading back?"

"Why are you being nosy?"

He inhaled sharply. "Whoa! That was rude."

"No. It was honest. If you must know, I'm doing inventory on the estate of a good friend who recently passed away. And, I'm meeting Brooks in about twenty minutes, so I see no reason to hang out in the street making small talk. Good luck with getting a part in this movie and I trust you wish me the same."

"Oh."

"Bye."

She whirled around and briskly crossed West Forty-Sixth Street at Eighth then headed down Ninth Avenue. She was absurdly pleased that Grant's last word had been a mere "Oh." So much more vacuous than "Ah," which at least signaled the speaker was thinking of something brilliant to say.

Miranda arrived at China Tan's with seventeen minutes to spare. She ducked into her favorite art gallery, A. J. Rinaldi's, which was conveniently located next to the restaurant.

"Miranda, great to see you!" the manager exclaimed before enveloping her in a huge hug.

"Hey, Jason. You, too! I know, I know, it's been ages but I've been working nonstop and just haven't had the chance to come by." She loved A. J. Rinaldi's. The gallery sold enough high-end artwork to pay for its midtown address, but the manager, Jason Devere, and the other employees were friendly and just as willing to help clients choose one of the less costly pieces

The staff was not only friendly, they were

knowledgeable. After Miranda finishing ooh-
ing and aahing over a sculpture she knew
she'd never be able to afford, lightning struck.
"While I'm here, I wanted to ask if you've
ever heard of an artist named Benjamin Auttenberg? He was imprisoned in Terezin, the
concentration camp in the Czech Republic.
He died there in 1945."

"Auttenberg?" Jason's interest was apparent. "Talk about a blast from the past. I
haven't heard anyone mention Auttenberg in
years. There's a lot of mystery surrounding
him—as there is with most of the artists who
were imprisoned."

"Please tell me."

"Well, you already know that Auttenberg
was a Czech artist. I believe he and his family
lived in Prague before the war, which wasn't
far from Terezin. His works had begun to
sell not long before he ended up in the camp,
along with his wife and child. Rumors have
floated for years that he continued to paint
while he was at Terezin. The only thing that's
certain is that he was killed in the camp just
before it was liberated. I've heard from some
dealers that a few of his paintings ended up in
the hands of private collectors. And of course,
there were the Nazi generals who were forced

to hand over a piece or two after the war, although those were actually the works he'd done back in Prague. They were stolen directly from his home before it was burned to the ground. The most interesting rumor is that his wife transported his Terezin artwork to America, but Mrs. Auttenberg was never located."

"Until now," Miranda muttered.

"Meaning?"

"You may need to take a trip to Birmingham, Alabama, sometime in the near future."

"Why?"

"Because I've supposedly inherited a house from Miss Virginia Radinski. I use the term supposedly because there's an issue regarding her will—make that two wills." A vision of Russ Gerik immediately flashed through her mind, followed by an anticipatory tingle. She'd be working with him once she was back in Birmingham.... She determinedly brought her focus back. "Anyway, I found out three days ago that Virginia wasn't a miss. She's the widow of Benjamin Auttenberg."

Jason appeared astonished.

"Seriously? This is amazing! It would be even more amazing if you found any of his works there. Have you spotted anything in-teresting?"

Miranda shook her head. "Haven't had a chance to take a look at any art that isn't al-ready on the wall and what I've seen was by artists I know aren't Auttenberg. In the brief time I was in the house, I spotted one Renoir print and two seriographed Tarkays."

Jason grinned. "I'd call that interesting. Two?"

Miranda smiled. "Two very fine Tarkays, which are hanging in Virginia's living room. Even if I don't get the house, I'm hoping the judge will decide those prints go to me. I haven't yet hit the attic, so there might be something hidden away in a secret panel or guarded by a presence from beyond. One never knows."

Jason sighed. "It would be worth dealing with ghosts and goblins. If you truly have inherited her possessions there'd be a pretty price in an original Auttenberg. Or if you're not inclined to sell, you'd still have a piece you'd enjoy owning the rest of your life. Aut-tenberg is a great fit for your taste."

"Well, if I do find anything—and it's actu-ally mine—I'll give you a call before I make any decisions. Thanks for all the info." She inclined her head toward the front door, where a middle-aged couple with determined expressions glared at Miranda and Jason. "Looks like you have real live paying customers."

Jason glanced at the entrance. "I do. They're here for that pricey sculpture you admired. If they like it, I'll be able to afford my apartment for at least a year on my commission alone."

They grinned at each other, and Miranda gave Jason a quick hug. "I'm outta here anyway. Meeting Brooks next door."

Brooks was waiting for her at a small booth in the middle of China Tan's. Dishes of rice, spicy bean curd, walnut chicken, veggies, crab rangoons, egg rolls and wontons with peanut sauce were already on the table.

Brooks quickly kissed her cheek. "I've ordered for us both. Hope you don't mind. I have a meeting in an hour."

"Of course I don't mind. You know what I like and I'm starving, so I'm a happy woman."

"Well?" he asked.

"Well, what?" Miranda filled her plate, poured peanut sauce over everything but the egg rolls, took a bite of wonton and sighed with sheer pleasure.

"Audition, Miranda. Remember? The one you left about thirty minutes ago?"

"It was lovely. *I* was lovely. The only non-lovely part was running into Grant. He's up for the role of a suave spy agency director who gets shot in the first reel."

"Ouch!"

"To what? The demise of his character?"

Brooks chuckled. "Well, I was thinking more in terms of you seeing Mr. Spencer again. Couldn't have been easy."

"Not a problem. I'm fine. Truly. The bust-up wasn't all that dramatic. Plus, I've been concentrating on how to avoid getting into a huge fight with my fellow claimant or lega-tee or inheritee or whatever word works. I'm also discovering some very interesting things about Miss Virginia's life before she came to Birmingham."

She told Brooks about the house and about Jason Devere's revelations regarding Benja-min Auttenberg.

Brooks listened attentively. "Intriguing. Although I wonder why she would hide price-less pieces of art?"

Miranda shook her head. "They might not be hidden. They might not actually exist."

"So, what's the skinny on this other claim-ant?"

Miranda paused. "He's…as intriguing as the house."

Brooks's left eyebrow shot up. "Oh?"

"Uh. Yeah."

"Come on, girl, give it up."

Miranda told her agent all about meeting Russ her first day at the house "I have no idea how he ended up in Virginia's second will and I'm extremely curious to find out. If he was that close to her, why didn't he and I meet years ago?"

"Because you've been in New York or on tour for six years?"

"Good point. Anyway, Russ appears to be very smart." She paused. "There's a warmth and humor behind his sarcasm. I could see it in his eyes, which are a fabulous dark hazel. But what's truly sad is that he can't hear his own voice. It's like hot liquid honey. Really rich baritone."

Brooks grinned. "You do realize that your own lilting alto just savored every bit of that honey and now you're turning the color of your hair?"

His cell phone rang as Miranda was hiding her face in her napkin pretending to mop up a trail of hot 'n' spicy sauce. "Hang on, Miranda."

She politely stayed silent while he was on the phone—finishing up two crab rangoons and her bowl of wontons and thinking about topics that could steer the conversation away from Mr. Gerik.

Brooks hung up and clinked his teacup against hers. "You don't need a fortune cookie today. You got it! Congrats!"

"What?"

"I'm glad you're sitting. That, my pet, was Wendy Konstanza. She loved you. The suits loved you. She said you were the ultimate superspy! She's sending contracts to my office this afternoon and filming starts right after the Fourth of July."

CHAPTER FOUR

"Nowadays, most of the casting for Broadway, film and television is done by casting directors," Miranda explained. This was the fourth man who'd asked if she'd been on Broadway and/or TV and/or movies. She felt as though she were on a late-night talk show and wondered precisely why so many gentlemen were displaying such an interest in show business. The questions had been the same. How does the audition process work? Does one need an agent? Do you know anyone famous? What's the pay like? Do you get residuals for any TV show you do? Are you really going to be in a spy movie?

Bachelor number four, a Mr. George Miller, smiled as he placed a business card into her hands. "I can't help with theatrical productions but if you need a real estate agent, I'm your man."

Miranda smiled, stifling a scream, and hoped Farrah's seating arrangement wouldn't place her next to any of the men who'd offered her their cards and services. So far she'd spoken to a real estate agent—"Watch out for Brewster's Realtors—totally shady." From the accountant—"I'd be happy to help you this tax season. Stay away from Brewster's Consultants—totally shady. Here's my card." A landscaper—"No, of course I don't do the yard work *personally*. I have people for that. Oh, by the way, stay away from Brewster's Landscaping. Totally shady." And an engineer—"You'll need top-notch inspection services before you sell, but stay away from Paulsen' Professional Inspectors—they're crooks. Here's my card." Miranda had been happy to know that Brewster wasn't the only shady character in Birmingham. Each of the four gentlemen had mentioned that he was single and interested in Miranda—as a potential client or a date. She wasn't sure in which order the interest was strongest and she didn't care. Miranda felt as though she'd entered a bizarre land where speed dating had merged with advertising. She didn't like it.

Miranda glanced around the Nolan living room, seeking escape. The other three wannabe suitors were huddled together about six feet away. Miranda could hear snatches of "he should have been picked in the first round draft. What the heck were they thinking?" and assumed football was the primary topic of conversation. She grinned for the first time that evening. She was definitely back in Alabama, where football was always the primary topic of conversation. Miranda spotted two couples conversing in the far corner of the room, but she hadn't been introduced and didn't feel comfortable intruding.

Farrah waved at her from the opposite side of the room, where she was chatting with Tim, Dave Brennan and the unanticipated duo of Cort Farber and Brett King.

Miranda shook hands with George, murmured something about having to discuss plans for an upcoming trip with her father then headed over to the fireplace to join the attorneys. Her dad and Dave were enjoying a heated discussion that appeared to be centered around the stupidity of hiring a new offensive line coach for the Crimson Tide, so she addressed Brett first. "Mr. King? I'm surprised to see you. Aren't you deep in the enemy camp here?'

He chuckled. "Nah. Cort and I went to law school together. We happened to be having lunch together when Farrah called. I wangled an invite."

Cort winked at Miranda. "I had to offer him something. He was extremely depressed after hearing that his favorite greyhound lost at the races. Not to mention he's still sulking because our firm won a different contested will and I take great delight in repeatedly telling him he's going to lose Miss Virginia's case, as well. We've got a much stronger claim."

Dave broke off his chat with Tim Nolan, frowned at his young associate and turned to address Miranda "I can't discuss the inheritance with Mr. King at my shoulder, but I wondered if you and Mr. Gerik had been able to make any plans for the inventory process. I'd also like to apologize for the whole business turning chaotic thanks to Judge Rayborn. He's quite the character. Likes folks to think he's eccentric but there are many in the legal community who say he borders on nutcase. When I'm around his friends I stick to the word *charming.*"

Miranda grinned. "I'm in theater, Dave. I've met more than my share of offbeat characters—in scripts and off stage. As to the inventory, I'm going to sort everything into piles and tag it all with stickies that read *recycling, charity, keep for now* and the ever enjoyable *dump as fast as you can.*" She paused before adding, "Of course, this needs to be ironed out with my adversary."

"Ah, yes. When are y'all getting together?" Dave asked.

"Tonight at nine. Just a prelim, but I can't wait to get a closer look at the house." Miranda didn't mention that her anticipation at starting on the inventory kept centering on Mr. Gerik, rather than the objects at Virginia's.

Farrah suddenly interjected, "What kind of price do you think you can get for the house?" She smiled at Brett. "Assuming she ends up the winner."

The response came from George Miller, who'd managed to plant himself behind Miranda. "A good one. The market is bouncing back, and that house is a gem. Two-story, four bedrooms, three baths, a huge living room plus a parlor, which we now call a bonus room. There's a usable attic, gorgeous trees all around the property and a deck in the back that only needs a little sealant to get it into shape. There's even a storm cellar. I'd suggest an estate sale first..."

George glanced at Brett, which made Miranda wonder what the Realtor knew about the two wills.

"Whoever inherits, that is. You know, I'd imagine there's a ton of antiques in that place," George continued. "I've heard the piano alone is worth several thousand. Do you or Gerik have an appraiser yet?"

The lust in his voice made Miranda queasy. She spoke up before George could continue his verbal tour of the Radinski property. "I'm sure we can find one when the time comes. Now—no offense, y'all—can we change the subject? This all seems rather ghoulish to me since Miss Virginia has been dead less than a month. And from the very little I've read in her journal, she did not have a pleasant life."

"What do you mean?" Cort asked.

"Oh." Miranda immediately wished she'd kept silent but said, "Well…to begin with, she was in a concentration camp in Czechoslovakia. Her husband was killed there. Horrible."

Tim winced. "No wonder she was so reclusive and seemed to prefer the company of children. Most of them don't learn how to hate until they reach adolescence."

"That's a gloomy thought," Dave said.

"It is, isn't it?" Tim glanced at his daughter. "I feel woefully ignorant. I honestly didn't know there were camps in the Czech Republic."

Miranda nodded. "You're not the only one who was clueless. I didn't, either. I looked up Terezin online after I saw the name in her journal. It was very close to Prague, and it housed a lot of artists and musicians. Sounds almost nice, doesn't it? Yet the death rate at that place was…" She swallowed. "So many talented people who lost their lives…" She smiled wanly. "I'm so sorry. I didn't mean to bring this up. Miss Virginia's spirit seems to be accompanying me everywhere."

Farrah quickly became the good hostess. "Well, let's hope her spirit leads you to some of her old recipe books. Tim has told me about the baked goods she used to share with everyone in that neighborhood. If you could find her kolache recipe I'd be the only caterer in the city who could deliver authentic Czech pastries." She smiled. "I know there's no way *you'll* attempt to bake them." Her tone changed almost imperceptibly, but Miranda swore she caught a whiff of superiority as Farrah added, "Miranda is the world's worst cook. I'm hoping to get her to the point where she doesn't have to exist on takeout once she's back in Manhattan."

Miranda gritted her teeth but casually said, "Might as well give that up as a lost cause. My schedule is usually too wacky for me to attempt making home-cooked meals. But Farrah, you'll be pleased to know that I already found one recipe book in the short time I was in Virginia's house. I'll do my best to make sure you get it, even if I have to beg Russ Gerik to sell it to me. At any rate, I definitely don't have use for it apart from reading, salivating and remembering devouring some of those goodies years ago."

Farrah frowned. The men didn't seem to notice any tension and began discussing Birmingham's best restaurants. The debate over which local barbecue joint served the juiciest ribs and the closest to homemade biscuits was still raging when Farrah announced that dinner was ready and asked the guests to be seated in the formal dining room.

Dave Brennan offered Miranda his arm and led the way to the table. He pulled out a chair for her and quietly said, "Farrah Myers Nolan is a very fine chef and her catering business is taking Birmingham by storm. She appears to truly adore your father. That being said, she doesn't know the first thing about dealing with a grown stepdaughter. My wife, Nancy, could certainly give her a few tips on mothering. I credit her with raising all five of our kids to be reasonably productive members of society who still feel free to come to us for advice and support. The most important thing—what Farrah needs to learn—is that you shouldn't push."

Miranda sank back against her chair. When Dave took his own seat next to her, she whispered, "Feel free to repeat that advice to my dad so he can deter Farrah from planning further 'let's find a date for Miranda' parties. I'm not interested. Right now, I want to focus on doing the inventory with Mr. Gerik."

Dave nodded. "Look, I haven't met this Russell Gerik but if you're at all uncomfortable looking through Virginia's possessions with him, let me know and I'll send over some eager paralegals or even new associates who'd be more than happy to play chaperone and hoist a box or two in order to impress me." He gestured at Cort, who was seated across from them.

"Is he hiring me out again?" Cort snickered. "Honestly, it makes me feel so cheap."

"I think you're safe." Miranda grinned.

"I've only met Mr. Gerik once, but I didn't get the impression I'd be working with the big bad wolf. He wasn't exactly laying on the charm but he wasn't howling at me, either. And I have to admit I'm looking forward to learning more about Miss Virginia."

"What else did you find in that journal?" Brett asked.

Miranda didn't want to use Miss Virginia's past as dinner party conversation, but she had to say something. She politely answered, "I did find out she was married to an artist. That's about it."

Farrah apparently had no problem with discussing the details of Virginia's life. She raised her voice slightly so the rest of her guests could hear. "His name was Benjamin Auttenberg? Have y'all ever heard of him?"

There were negative head shakes from all the guests. Miranda closed her eyes and wondered whether she should gag her stepmother with a napkin or an apron.

"Who was he?" George asked.

Miranda tried to find a way out of providing any more information, but Farrah jumped in with, "According to an art dealer Miranda talked with when she was in Manhattan, Auttenberg was on his way to becoming quite a name in the art world before he was sent to the concentration camp. This dealer also said that there are rumors some of his works still exist and if any were found, they'd be worth a fortune."

Miranda flinched. She quickly began to describe some of the other items she'd seen at the house, including a wooden bird whistle, numerous wind chimes, an Amish pie safe that had been hidden under never-worn coats and Miranda's favorite—a picnic basket that screamed *church social circa 1912*.

"I think those qualify as odds and ends, so they could be legally mine, even if Mr. King's client wins the house. Although, I don't know where I'd put them when I get back to New York." Miranda smiled. "My apartment is teensy."

"You could always stay here, you know," Dave suggested. "Birmingham isn't a cultural wasteland and you'd be near your dad, which would make him very happy."

"Well, I do have a pretty good career going up north. But it's a thought. I could always keep the house as a refuge from big-city insanity. Then again, I happen to love big-city city insanity—most of the time. Right now I'm so tired I don't care where I land."

MIRANDA REMEMBERED THOSE words when she
arrived at Virginia's house later that night to
meet Russ and the poor paralegal who'd been
tasked with opening the door and either staying for the inventory session or coming back
in a couple of hours to lock up again. Miranda
hadn't lied—she *was* exhausted. Dave had
been a pleasant dinner companion and she
was grateful for his attempts to steer Farrah
off topics that often slid toward the embarrassing, but she hadn't been thrilled with most
of the other guests. Half of the bachelors had
treated her as though she were a new species
of plant life because she'd been on Broadway.
The other half were so busy trying to sell her
their services they didn't care what she did
for a living—as long as she spent her earnings with them. And Miranda was still dis-
gusted that Farrah had blithely talked about
Miss Virginia as though she'd been some
reality-TV star.

   At least all the guests had left shortly after
dinner. Farrah had even tactfully retreated to
the kitchen to clean up so Tim and Miranda
could have a father/daughter chat. They'd
missed out on those when Miranda had been
a child. Tim had been so devastated by his
wife's death he'd often ignored his daughter,

burying himself in his work. Then it had been Miranda's turn, performing nonstop starting her freshman year at college.

Miranda turned the corner onto Miss Virginia's street and immediately realized that her night wasn't going to be spent dealing with Russ Gerik and a bunch of boxes. Three police cars lined the curb outside of Virginia's house. Miranda slowed her dad's car and parked two doors down. Russ was standing in the yard, accompanied by a large canine who appeared to be enjoying the night air.

One of the policemen waved at her. He politely waited until she'd crossed the lawn and joined him near the entrance of the house before asking, "Are you Ms. Nolan?"

"Yes. I'm Miranda."

"Great. Please stay out here, miss. Officer Hernandez will join you while we search inside."

CHAPTER FIVE

OFFICER HERNANDEZ LOOKED as though he'd be more at home running touchdowns than babysitting frightened crime victims, but he greeted her with a cheery "Nice night…but not for this, right?"

Miranda took the first calm breath since she'd seen the lights flashing on top of police cars. She managed a smile, then glanced at Russ, who was sitting on the curb calmly scratching the dog behind its ears.

"I'm assuming someone broke in?" Miranda asked. Her voice shook just a little.

"You're assuming right," he replied. "Thankfully no one was home. Things can be replaced, but people? Not so much."

Officer Hernandez continued to make small talk, asking Miranda if Miss Virginia's old car—which still sat in the driveway—had been driven in years, what her favorite musical groups were and finishing with the all-important, "Auburn or Alabama?"

Miranda smiled. "I'll never tell. I've watched too many feuds break out over the answer."

Miranda was not surprised to learn her first impression had been right. Hernandez had played football for Auburn the year before he entered the police academy.

"What position did you play?"

"Wide receiver."

"Wait, I know you! I mean, I've seen you play. What's your first name?"

"Ted."

"Ted as in Ted *Touchdown* Hernandez? That's you, right?"

He nodded.

"Wow. You were awesome. Weren't you going to go pro?" she asked. "Or is that a sensitive subject?"

"Nah. It's fine. Everybody in the state was betting on whether I'd be picked up by the Cowboys or the Falcons. They both wanted me. Sadly my shoulder didn't cooperate with the master plan. It got knocked out of whack too many times that final season and the bowl game finished me off."

"Were you disappointed?"

Hernandez smiled. "At first. But I love being a cop. I get to help people, my employment expectancy is longer, my brains and bones might stay intact—and my mama is proud." He paused, then shook his head. "I'm also one of those people who believes we get signs from the universe telling us what we really need to be doing." He shot her a sharp glance. "You can tell me to back off, but I could swear there was a note in your voice when you asked about disappointments. Wrestling with your own decisions, perhaps?"

"You, Officer Hernandez, are an insightful soul. I'm not sure I'd even call it wrestling at this point, but let's just say I'm starting to wonder what to do if this house becomes mine."

Before Miranda had a chance to confide her concerns, the two officers who'd entered the house waved and motioned for Hernandez, Miranda and Russ to join them. Russ hadn't said a word to either Miranda or Hernandez and Miranda suddenly felt frightened again, but *for* Russ. He appeared calm, but he might have been terrified. Russ wasn't stupid. What if he'd been inside, unable to hear? She shuddered, stopping herself from traveling down that road. And where the heck was the paralegal?

"We can go in now," Hernandez said. "If you're up to it?"

Miranda straightened her shoulders. "I'm okay."

Hernandez glanced back at Russ and signed, *You?*

Russ answered, "I'm fine. Let's get this over with."

The trio headed inside the house, but Miranda paused at the doorway. "How did the burglar get in? Do y'all know?"

Hernandez checked the lock, then signed as he spoke. "This lock could have been opened by a ten-year-old with a credit card. You guys need to rekey. Get a strong deadbolt."

"I thought the lawyers had changed the locks."

Hernandez shrugged. "Well, if they did, they went for cheap."

"The paralegal put the key under the geraniums pot next to the front door," Russ said. "He left a message on my phone telling me where to look. Apparently, he had better things to do. So, even a decent lock wouldn't have mattered."

A quick interrogation began, initiated by a tall, bald-headed cop who identified himself as Officer Burroughs and introduced his partner as Officer Williams. Miranda gave her name and her reason for going to a house she didn't yet own at 9:00 p.m. Russ stayed silent although Hernandez had signed Burroughs's questions.

After Miranda explained about the two wills and the scheduling problems, Burroughs laughed. "The judge was Winston Rayborn, right?"

"Yep. I gather he's known for coming up with interesting Solomon-like solutions?"

All three officers nodded and grinned. Burroughs added, "For someone fondly referred to as a nutcase."

"So, I assume you never had cause to bust open the lock to the attic?" Officer Williams asked.

"No! Seriously? It's broken?"

Williams nodded. "We found a window open on the right side of the attic. It looks like your intruder left through the window and shimmied right down the old sweet gum tree that's about to take over the roof." He pointed and added absently, "That thing needs a good pruning."

Burroughs pulled out a notebook. "Do you think you'd be able to tell if anything's missing?"

Miranda held back the laugh she feared would lead to hysterics. "Missing? Have y'all *seen* the rooms downstairs? I have no idea what some thief might have taken."

Hernandez turned to Russ and signed, *How about you? Any ideas on what might be missing?*

Russ shook his head. "From what I remember, the attic has some old Hanukkah items, rocking chairs, about fifty very small lamps and a couple of old mannequins that still had dresses on them. There were some trunks, too, but they were locked pretty tight so if they're not broken then I'd imagine no one else got into them. I didn't see anything else in plain sight and I have no idea if Virginia stored anything valuable up there." He paused then added. "I'd imagine the thief was hoping to find an original Auttenberg."

Officer Burroughs raised an eyebrow. "What's an Auttenberg?"

Russ explained to the policemen that Virginia had been married to the late artist Benjamin Auttenberg and that his works were worth a fortune, assuming any had survived. Miranda felt a knife twist in her stomach. How had Russ known about Virginia's marital status? *Because she told him, you dummy. She trusted him more than she trusted you.*

The officers promised to do all they could to find the intruder, but they weren't optimistic since no one had a clue whether or not anything was missing. The only thing tampered with—the broken padlock on the attic door—had been wiped clean of all fingerprints. Rounding up all the wannabe felons in Jefferson County wasn't an option. Ted Hernandez suggested that Miranda or Russ call their respective lawyers first thing the next morning and ask for better locks and an alarm service. He gave Miranda a friendly hug, shook Russ's hand, told them to call if they found anything useful and then followed his fellow officers out the front entrance.

"Well, should we get to work?"

She whirled around. Russ and his grinning canine were staring at her. She crouched and began petting the dog, who immediately reciprocated with moist kisses. Miranda glanced up at Russ.

"Can I have a minute to breathe? I'm still nervous knowing this house was broken into."

"Too fast! Plus, you seem to be mumbling," Russ growled. "Hand gestures would be nice. Word has it you're a good actress. You might consider facing me directly and doing a little pantomime."

She straightened up. "Sorry." She repeated her statement and pointed to the house miming someone smashing windows or jimmying the door, then put her hands to her face in an imitation of the child in the movie *Home Alone*. Finally she put both hands over her heart and began to pant.

She wasn't sure how much Russ had understood since he stared at her without speaking for a good thirty seconds.

"I got about three words," he said. "Basically you're scared."

She nodded. For a few moments there was silence. Finally Miranda gestured down at the medium-size yellow and tan canine, who appeared to be a mix of Labrador, shepherd and some sort of terrier.

"Name?"

A reluctant smile crossed Russ's attractive features and Miranda's heart began pounding harder than it had when she first realized someone had broken into Miss Virginia's house. "You'll appreciate this, I'm sure. Miranda, meet Prospero. Spero for short."

"A lover of the Bard? Or just *The Tem-*

pest?" She mimed the burst of a storm as best she could while slowly asking the question.

Russ obviously understood either the lip movement or her actions.

"Both. And Spero the dog truly *is* a magician in many respects."

Miranda wanted to ask if Spero was a service dog but wasn't sure if that would be offensive. As if Russ had read her mind he said, "Spero's trained to help me manage my hearing loss."

Russ reached down and patted the dog on his head. Spero's tail thumped wildly in response. The dog began to excitedly nuzzle Miranda's knee in an unabashed attempt to receive more affection. She gave it readily, squatting back down and hugging him. Just the act of feeling warm fur and inhaling the faint doggie odor made her feel safe and comfortable.

She looked up into Russ's hazel eyes. "What kind is he?"

Russ's small smile grew a bit broader. "No one knows. Including his vet."

"Well, he's a sweetie."

"He is."

They lapsed into an uncomfortable silence. Miranda moved first by giving a thumbs-up and pointing to the house, which she hoped he'd figure out meant, *Are you up for this? Inventory? Tonight?*

"I'd give that a yes if you mean am I ready to work. We're here. We might as well get started. The sooner we finish this, the better."

He held the door open for her. Or, Miranda thought with amusement, for Spero, who trotted ahead of Miranda and made himself at home on the nearest chair.

Russ pulled a notebook out of his backpack, then grabbed the nearest box, opened it and began to write.

It was going to be a long night.

CHAPTER SIX

MIRANDA AND RUSS spent the next forty minutes opening boxes, taking quick peeks inside, then labeling the outsides with the stickies Miranda had brought. Russ jotted notes regarding larger items such as furniture and mirrors and oddities like the umbrella stand and the hat rack filled with Fedoras from the 1940s.

Then there was what Miranda considered the most incongruous item for a ninety-five-year-old former seamstress to own. Miranda started laughing when she uncovered a state-of-the-art laptop computer from under an antique quilt covered in cat hair. Russ was buried nearly waist deep into a box so she tapped him on the shoulder.

"What?" he growled.

"Look! I had no idea she was this high-tech." She stopped. There was no way Russ was going to lip-read that last comment, so

Miranda lifted the computer to where Russ could see it. "Cool, huh!"

The corners of Russ's mouth turned up just long enough for Miranda to take advantage of the slight thaw in his icy attitude. He even responded. "Virginia was an avid on-line shopper. I believe she was on a first-name basis with customer service at the three largest booksellers."

Miranda smiled. He might well shut her down in an instant but she had to try. "How did you meet Virginia?" she asked, attempting to find actions that would fit the question. She reached out to shake his hand as though greeting someone.

Russ grasped her hand in his and a shock zapped through her body. The kind of electric tingle one gets after scraping one's feet on carpet. Except that they were both standing on hardwood. Russ immediately dropped her hand as though he'd felt it, too. His next words started tumbling out like random clothes from a dryer.

"I...she...we met..." He paused and took a deep breath. "I was giving an afternoon lecture at her synagogue. Five years ago. The topic was the nature of linguistics, which was my specialty when I taught at Samford. Ironic, considering my current circumstances." He closed his eyes for a brief second then continued. "Anyway, Miss Virginia introduced herself at the reception afterward. We immediately hit it off. She asked very insightful and intriguing questions about the politics of language and culture. We spent a good hour talking until the rabbi was ready to close down. She asked if we could go somewhere for coffee or tea and continue the discussion." He looked at Miranda. "She explained that she didn't get out much. She wasn't able to drive at night, cabs were expensive and she said she'd always been a 'stay at home' person."

"That's putting it mildly," Miranda muttered. "Can we say one step from agoraphobia?"

"What?"

She waved her hand in the air and shook her head. "Nothing. Go on?"

"Our tea turned into dinner and that dinner turned into regular visits. I'd come over here sometimes after I'd taught my classes. Or if there was an event I thought I could encourage her to attend, like a concert or play or a showing at a gallery, I'd drive." A broad smile suddenly brightened his face and Miranda's pulse quickened. "I practically converted to the Jewish faith since I drove her to quite a few Friday-night services at the temple."

Miranda grinned, remembering the day she'd met Cort and told him that Virginia had been able to charm the few people she allowed into her life into doing just about anything she wanted.

"We got to be friends," Russ said. "Good friends."

Miranda couldn't stop herself. "But still— why you?"

"What?"

She pointed to him and then waved her hand around to indicate the whole house. "Why you?"

"Oh. You want to know why Virginia wrote the second will replacing you and making me her heir?"

Miranda grimaced but nodded. "Well, yeah."

His eyes suddenly pierced hers. "Perhaps she felt the house should go to someone who was there for her instead of someone who couldn't be bothered to visit for six years. Someone who didn't even make it down for the funeral."

Russ's statement held no malice. Just cold

facts that hit her the way a frozen drink causes a brain freeze. She swallowed. She started to protest that she hadn't known about Virginia's death until after the memorial service. But that excuse sounded feeble even to herself.

Miranda turned around and headed for Virginia's kitchen. Russ didn't follow. She attempted to remove cups and saucers from the cabinets in an effort to keep from crying, but her hands were shaking so badly she was afraid she'd drop the non-shatterproof antiques.

She stiffened. "Stop it, Miranda. You were *working* nonstop for six years. You sent letters. You called every chance you could. You were not an evil person." She wasn't going to let Russ get into her head, even if his statement had hurt her like a claw hammer ripping off a bandage. She took a few moments to do some deep breathing and then returned to the living room. Forcing a serenity she didn't feel, she grabbed a box at random and sank to the floor. She almost put it back with the other boxes when she realized it was loaded with notebooks.

Two of the books turned out to be filled with recipes. Great. Something else to remind

her that she often acted like a brat around
Farrah and that she'd hurt her father by not
attending their wedding the year before, because, naturally, she'd been working. She'd
just been cast in *Illumination* and couldn't fly
down for one night. *Pile on that guilt, girl.*

She tried to keep her expression neutral
as she methodically printed the dates of the
books onto labels. After about ten minutes
she glanced up. Russ was staring at her.

*What now? Is he going to tell me Virginia
not only changed the will but warned him to
make sure all the cats were safe before I entered so I wouldn't be tempted to turn them
into tennis strings?*

"What?" she asked, thankful he couldn't
hear the combined quiver and anger behind
the one word.

He shoved a journal at her. "You might
want to read this."

She glanced at the first page and blinked
back tears. Virginia had carefully noted the
names and the date right below a photo that
depicted three children.

November 1, 1994
Amber Shapiro, age twelve. Jillian Sha-

piro, age twelve. Miranda Nolan, age seven.

Last night I met someone who will be a special friend. She is the same age as my precious son the year he was murdered in the camps. She knocked on my door with two other children, all of them dressed in their Halloween costumes. I invited them in for pastries and hot chocolate and to meet other children in the neighborhood. Americans are odd in this way. Children meet in their schools, sometimes in their churches, but often do not know their own neighbors. This night I was amused to see the mix of costumes. There were spacemen and superheroes and witches and blue creatures they called Smurfs. There were goblins and other characters from cartoon shows. But this little girl stood out because she and her ballerina costume were both so pretty.

She came inside with her older friends but instead of joining the children who were eating cookies she walked up to me with no fear and said, "Want to see me do a pirouette? That's French for spin. I have to warn you, it's not very good yet but I can do one without falling down."

I told her I would love to see her pirouette. She very carefully set down her bag of Halloween treats and solemnly got into position. When she finished, she curtsied and I applauded and truthfully said she was wonderful!

"Do you want to be a ballerina when you grow up?" I asked.

She shook her head. "Nope. First off, I'm going to be too tall. I love ballet but I also love to sing and act. I'm going to be a triple threat."

Miranda couldn't help but smile even as her heart constricted. More than twenty years had passed and she remembered that night with absolute clarity. She positioned herself so her back was comfortably resting against the sofa, then closed her eyes. She could hear Virginia's gentle voice, a voice that had retained a slight accent even after fifty years in America.

"Triple threat? My, my! That sounds quite scary but very important. What is your name, young lady?"

"Miranda Nolan. What's yours?"

"People call me Miss Virginia."

"That's pretty. It's also a state. I learned that in school. Its capital is Richmond but I visited Williamsburg last year with my dad and it was neat. We had the best gingerbread ever and we watched these guys making lutes and violins. I want to go back someday."

"What grade are you in, Miranda?" Virginia had asked.

"Second. We're learning cursive and I'm terrible. But I'm going to be a Native American princess for our Thanksgiving play at school." Miranda still recalled how upset she'd been when she told Virginia, "My teacher wants me to do a dance to 'This Land is Your Land.'"

"Are you worried you can't do it?"

Miranda had been scornful. "Oh, no! I can do it. It's a really easy dance! It's just… Well, Native American princesses didn't do ballet back then and that song wasn't written until the 1940s. I looked it up. I'm not stupid just because I'm seven."

Virginia's composure had never broken although now, as an adult, Miranda realized the elderly lady had doubtless needed to stifle a laugh or two over Miranda's serious attempt to resolve her dilemma—the desire to perform versus anachronisms and reality. Virginia had quietly steered the young Miranda into a solution that helped set Miranda's career in theater in motion.

"This is a fantasy play, Miranda. It is not historically accurate. After all, I do not think the Pilgrims and the Wampanoag tribe sat down to a turkey dinner with stuffing, mashed potatoes, cranberry jelly and pumpkin pie with whipped cream."

Miranda had giggled. "Bet they would've liked that more than eels and gooseberries! My teacher said that's what they probably ate. Icky!"

Before she and Virginia could continue the conversation, one of Miranda's friends had called out, urging Miranda to try a cupcake. Miranda had again curtsied with the grace of a budding ballerina, then thanked Miss Virginia and run to join her friends.

Miranda opened her eyes and continued to read the journal.

As they were leaving I asked if I could take a picture. Miranda and the twins all posed for me in their costumes. Amber and Jillian went outside, but Miranda stopped and again carefully set her bag on the floor. She hugged me.

"Will you come to my Thanksgiving play, Miss Virginia?"

"I will. But only if you come back and perhaps show me a preview of your wonderful dance."

Miranda beamed at me. Her young blue eyes sparkled. "I'll do more than that. I promise to come and visit and show you my dances from my studio, too. And sing if you'll play the piano. I'm taking lessons but I'm not very good. My teacher says my talent is in my feet and voice, not my hands."

Miranda couldn't stop herself. She glanced up at Russ even though her eyes were now moist. She'd kept that promise to Virginia—to come entertain her neighbor throughout her own childhood. High school had slowed down the visits but Miranda had still dropped by to sing or dance or ask Virginia to run lines with her. During Miranda's years in college the visits became far fewer and once Miranda moved to New York, they'd stopped completely. Miranda's failure to make it home and see the woman who'd been like a mother must have hurt. No wonder Virginia had made Russ her family.

Russ was still staring at her but his expression seemed to have softened slightly. He appeared puzzled.

Miranda squared her shoulders. She rose and handed the journal back to Russ. She didn't know how to sign but she figured this was an easy phrase. She tapped her watch.

"Time to go."

CHAPTER SEVEN

"YOUR TIMING IS PERFECT. I have teachers for acting and music. I have a designer. I'm directing the show, but I do *not* have a dance teacher. Are you sure you want to spend the next few weeks with a bunch of rowdy kids?" Bonnie Hamil, owner and director of the Masquerade Children's Theater, grinned. "The age range is from five to eighteen, and the talent runs from zero to awesome. It's just summer camp, so we're not doing anything elaborate. Think back to your days with us when you were in junior high. Not much has changed but the space—and of course the pay is pitiful. Miranda, seriously, we'd be grateful for your time and expertise. Still interested?"

Miranda nearly shouted, *You better believe I'm interested!* while doing a happy dance around the room, but chose to simply say, "I'd love to help. I need something to occupy my brain and get me out of the house so I'm not forced to listen to Farrah explain the intri-

cacies of fondue or a good salmon mousse."
She shuddered. "I really hate salmon. And
my time is wacky since I have to wait for
Russ and his work schedule before we get to
the inventory. Bonnie, this is perfect. Just to
double-check—you finish before July Fourth,
right?"

"Yes. Our big production this year will be
on the second. So, I'll see you a week from
Monday?"

"Definitely. Again, thank you."

"Hey, I'm the one who should be thanking
you. Wow! A real, live Broadway actress and
movie star helping out at our camp. Our little
performers will be thrilled!" She assumed a
look of innocence. "Having your credentials
plastered all over our brochures looks im-
pressive and should also help with our grant
funding." Her expression changed to pure imp
"It proves to the money people that a local
children's theater can attract solid citizens
as instructors."

Miranda hugged Bonnie and repeated her
thanks before heading out. The year-round
children's theater had always focused more
on process than product, which Miranda
liked. The summer program was about the
right amount of time to teach some basics

to the beginners and challenge but not exasperate the advanced kids. The small show at the end of the session was more for fun than anything else.

She got into her car and gazed for a few moments at the old warehouse, which was currently being renovated by Masquerade. Bonnie had told Miranda that once the work was complete, the company would have its own tech and costume shops and better equipment for each classroom, including Studiofoam panels for the music room and mirrors for the dance studio. She'd added, "Just be glad that you'll be teaching on the stage since it's a real wood floor and not concrete like every other space here."

Miranda was proud of herself for achieving two of her scheduled tasks before lunch. She'd called Dave Brennan's office that morning to arrange for a security system to be installed at Miss Virginia's house and been assured by a concerned Cort Farber that the matter would be handled immediately. He'd also said that Russ had spoken with Brett. Both law firms usually hired a local security firm, Tomlinson Alarms, who could install the system that day to ensure the house stayed secure during the probate process.

Next on the agenda had been getting re-acquainted with Bonnie Hamil at the children's theater. Farrah had awakened Miranda at 7:00 a.m. to tell her that a friend of a friend had heard Miranda was in town and word was that Bonnie was in desperate need of a dance instructor for the summer theater camp. Miranda had immediately phoned Bonnie and set up a meeting.

Miranda opened her combination organizer/GPS tracker to make certain she had the correct address for her next visit. There were three schools in Birmingham that taught ASL classes. One advertised classes that started every two weeks. It was only about four miles from Tim and Farrah's house and offered a Super Crash Course, which would be held over the next three weekends. Miranda chided herself that she was crazy to even think about learning a language when she had inventory to deal with and teaching duties, but she still clicked on the address in the tracker. "I can check it out. No harm in that. And it's good for the brain to learn new things." She smiled wryly. "Miranda Nolan, you are lying, lying, lying to yourself. For shame. Learn new things, my foot. You know exactly *one* person who communicates this way and that person doesn't care one single whit if you learn ASL, Urdu or Swahili, which makes you the prize cuckoo bird of the century." She exhaled. "Fine. Let's do it, then."

She started the car, rolled down the window and was about to back out when she heard the sound of brakes screeching, followed by the slam of a car door. Miranda glanced out at the street and was immediately horrified when she spied a small Border collie standing in the middle of traffic. The dog had obviously just been shoved out of the car that was peeling off, sailing through a red light.

Miranda jumped out of her car and ran into the street, holding her hand up to stop the slow-moving traffic. The terrified puppy stared at her but remained frozen, refusing to move from its spot in the center of the road. When Miranda knelt down and put her arms around the dog, it finally managed a feeble tail wag. No collar and no leash. As cars carefully made their way around the pair, Miranda got creative and let her shoulder bag drop to the ground. She looped the strap around the dog's neck like a makeshift leash in order to persuade the collie to accompany her to safety.

"Scratch that. You're not exactly a moose."

She tossed the bag back over her shoulder and scooped the dog into her arms. There was no protest.

Miranda opened the door to the SUV and gently placed the puppy inside. The dog quickly made herself at home in the passenger seat—after doing the obligatory three-circles-in-a-row routine. She looked up into Miranda's eyes, then batted her with a small paw. "Well, you are a little charmer, aren't you?" Miranda crooned. She spent a few moments hugging the pooch and receiving lavish kisses in return.

"All righty, sweet girl, I'd say this changes my plans for the rest of the day," she said. "Let's see. What needs doin' here? Hang on a second. Let me check my phone and see if the vet my dad and I used to use is still in business." She punched in the name Dr. Tyler and was pleased to note that the clinic hadn't moved. "Cool. We're off to the vet's to make sure you're okay, then we'll buy you a new collar, leash and name tag—once I figure out what to name you. Bless phones that do everything but drive the car!" She patted the puppy's head then gently released the paws that had encircled her neck, closed the

passenger-side door and trotted back around
to the driver's seat.

The dog happily shifted position so she
could watch her rescuer as Miranda inserted
the keys. Then the puppy cautiously sat up
and stared at her new buddy as though fear-
ing she would disappear without constant sur-
veillance. Miranda gave her a reassuring pat.

"I am crazy," she muttered to herself. "I'm
adopting a dog. What do I do when I get back
to Manhattan?" She glanced at the puppy.
"Doesn't matter. I'll take you with me and
hire dog walkers and pet sitters any nights I
can't make it home before midnight. I'll even
quit going on tour. I never liked that anyway."
She smiled. "I have so missed not having a
dog for the past six years. You, Miss Puppy,
lucked out today with your timing."

The dog barked once in obvious agreement.

Three hours and two hundred dollars later,
Miranda and Phoebe—named after the character Miranda had played in *Illumination*—
were back in the SUV on their way to Miss
Virginia's house. In the show, Phoebe Flan-
nigan had also found herself alone on a highway—after being dumped by her cheating
boyfriend. But by the end of *Illumination,*
that Phoebe had found true love and happi-

ness after learning the difference between lies and charm. Phoebe the dog appeared to have already made the distinction and determined precisely who her best buddy was. She was gazing at Miranda with that expression of sheer adoration and trust only a dog can muster with complete honesty. Amazing, considering Phoebe had obviously been mistreated. Miranda had always heard that Borders were one of the smartest breeds and Phoebe already seemed to know that Miranda had rescued her and was ready to give her all the love and care she needed.

Miranda checked her watch. She was due to meet Russ in less than fifteen minutes, which wasn't quite enough time to take Phoebe to her dad's house. Miranda didn't really want to let her spend the day with strangers anyway. Hopefully Russ wouldn't mind having an extra canine at the house.

She parked the car in front of Virginia's. Four men were standing under the large shade trees in the front lawn, engaged in an animated conversation. Miranda recognized Brett and Cort and George Miller, the determined Realtor. The fourth man wasn't familiar but the large red logo on his shirt blaring Tomlinson Alarms was a decent clue that he was there to install the new alarm system. A fifth man stood on the porch with Spero by his side. Russ.

Miranda attached the new reflective leash to the new reflective collar, grabbed her bags and eased Phoebe out of the car. The dog immediately began barking at the men and Miranda realized she'd gotten a perk as well as a friend. Phoebe already made her feel more secure than any alarm system ever could. Miranda was sure if she let the puppy loose, Phoebe would begin herding the quartet into a tight circle. But when Miranda told her to sit and stay, Phoebe calmly did as asked, eyeing each man in turn as though measuring friend or foe. Only when Phoebe had decided no threat was imminent did she turn her attention to Spero, who was already manically wagging his tail, eager to make a new pal and begin a grand chase around the yard.

Miranda wasn't as confident as her dog that the group was trustworthy, but she said, "Gentleman. Nice to see you. What's up?"

George crowned himself spokesman for the quartet. "Mr. Tomlinson has just installed your new system. Brett and Cort and Mr. Gerik—" he gestured toward Russ, who was keeping his distance "—supervised. I happened to drop by in the middle of installations to ask if I could tour the house and we've been talking football for the past twenty minutes."

"Ah." Miranda made a mental note to find a better word to express, if not displeasure, at the very least, uneasiness. She opted for "Um." She inclined her head toward the man who'd done the installation. "What do I, uh, that is, what do Mr. Gerik and I need to know about alarm codes, Mr. Tomlinson?"

"Simple. You punch in the code to activate. You punch it in to deactivate." He handed her a card. "Here's the number. If you or Gerik wants to change it, give our office a call and we can do that over the phone. Brett and Cort have the code, as well." He continued to explain exactly how the alarm system worked and what his company would do in an emergency situation.

Miranda barely glanced at the card. She wasn't sure what the point of an alarm system was if everybody and his associate had the number, but she thanked him and Brett and Cort for handling the details.

George assumed his most charming air and tone. "If you have time, Miranda, I really would love a brief tour. I've seen the pho-

tos and read about the essential details, but
knowing the ambiance and the general layout
would be a huge help when I list the property."

Miranda inhaled and inwardly debated letting Phoebe loose with the word *kill*. She remained pleasant, merely saying, without a
smile, "Excuse me, Mr. Miller, but neither
Mr. Gerik nor I have retained you or anyone
else to sell this property. If I'm not mistaken
we don't have the right to do so. The property is in the process of being contested by
both of us. If and when that property is legally mine, I'll let a Realtor take a tour. If Mr.
Gerik wins the estate then you're free to seek
his business. At any rate, I'm busy right now.
The puppy is hungry and we're going inside
to grab a snack and do some work." She addressed all four men. "Thanks for your help
today. Bye, y'all."

The group took the broad hint. Brett and
Cort sped away in their respective company
cars after asking what time they needed to
send the paralegal to pick up the key. George
hopped into a spiffy new sports car and Mr.
Tomlinson headed for his van after inform-
ing Miranda the alarm system was currently
not active.

Phoebe had been as patient as one puppy could. The instant the men left she angled her chin toward Russ and Spero. It was obvious she wanted an introduction. Miranda loosened her grip on Phoebe's leash to let her know it was now okay to relax and the pup immediately began to perform the classic doggie wag-and-sniff ritual with Spero so they could become instant buddies. Russ looked at his dog, at Phoebe, then at Miranda. "New friend?"

"Yep. We found each other earlier today literally in the middle of the road."

Russ exhaled in exasperation. "Slower, please? Or better still—this worked before—mime it, all right?"

Miranda pantomimed a car speeding, a car braking, a car door opening and pointed to Phoebe as she flung her arms down.

Russ's eyebrows rose. His voice sounded hoarse with anger as he asked, "They tossed her out?"

Miranda nodded.

"I'm holding back some words I haven't spoken since Afghanistan. It's pretty astonishing what savages some people can be."

"I totally agree."

He bent down and gave Phoebe a big hug,

nearly getting knocked down by his own dog, who wanted in on the action. "She looks young. Definitely a puppy."

Miranda nodded and held up four, then five fingers. "Vet thought maybe four months. Five at the most."

"What's her name?"

"Phoebe."

He looked confused and she realized that Phoebe probably wasn't easy to lip-read. She attempted her own awkward hand alphabet, which Russ amazingly picked up on.

"Phoebe?" he asked.

Miranda nodded and Phoebe promptly gave Russ a sloppy kiss, then snuggled against his chest. Miranda suddenly envied the dog.

"Let 'em both off the leash," Russ said. "Spero's very good and I've never known a Border collie who strayed from the flock, no matter their age."

Miranda did as asked. The dogs wagged tails and met wet nose to wet nose, then ran around the yard a few times to make certain their rhythm was in sync. Miranda turned to Russ and began to mime eating. "Lunch?"

His eyebrows lifted. "Three's a bit late, isn't it?"

"I've been busy." She pointed to Phoebe.

"Rescuing the pooch, here. Before that I was getting myself hired to teach at the children's theater." She had no idea how to mime what she'd just said.

Russ sighed. "There are numerous notebooks in the house. Let's go inside and perhaps you could write out whatever you're trying to say?"

She nodded and then motioned to her car and mouthed, *Dog and people food.*

"Need some help toting?"

"Sure."

Once inside the house, Miranda fed both dogs and made a couple of sandwiches for herself and Russ, who didn't seem bothered by eating in the middle of the afternoon.

Russ finished his lunch. He looked at Miranda, who was pouring sodas for both of them, then looked at Phoebe—now sleeping comfortably on top of Spero's back, then back at Miranda. He gave the first unguarded smile she'd seen since she'd met him, barely a week earlier.

"By the way, Spero was also a rescue. Best dog I've ever known. Good job."

She blushed. "Thank you."

"You're welcome." He turned serious.

"Now, I suppose we need to do some work. We've got two hours until we're booted from the premises."

CHAPTER EIGHT

MIRANDA PROUDLY SIGNED, *Great class! See you next week,* and *thank you* to the instructor, Dr. Vinny, then picked up her bag and slung it over her shoulder. The ASL class at The Cooper School was advertised as an intensive workshop designed to cram as much information as the students' brains would allow within three Saturday sessions. *Intensive* was an understatement. Grueling, exhausting, mind-blowing and just all-out maniacally insane were the correct synonyms. Miranda had asked herself five times during the past five hours why she'd been crazy enough to take this class. So she could communicate slightly better with someone she wouldn't see again after the Fourth of July? Five times her inner self had declined to answer.

Dr. Vinny had begun the lesson with a dazzling array of images, using a combination of on-screen technology and props, which included small plants, dollhouse furniture and Dr. Vinny's large mixed-breed cat who was obscurely named MacDougal.

After bombarding the students with visuals and touchable objects—MacDougal, a benign feline who didn't mind having his ears scratched being one of the more desirable tactiles—Dr. Vinny divided the class into four pairs to practice. Miranda's partner was a child of perhaps six or seven with badly trimmed dark brown hair, huge brown eyes and two missing front teeth. His name tag read Jesse.

Jesse signed what appeared to be *You're pretty!* and Miranda promptly fell in love.

She tried to sign back, *You're handsome!* but learning the signs for small plants, doll furniture and MacDougal hadn't let her master returning compliments. So she smiled, pointed at his face, gave him two thumbs up and winked.

Jesse grinned.

Dr. Vinny kept the pairs together until the end of class. No words were spoken. By the time the lesson was over, Miranda was signing what Dr. Vinny called the tourist questions such as the all-important *Where is the restroom?,* the shopper's required *How much is that?,* the hopefully never needed *Call the police!* and her favorite, *Where's the best bakery?*

After Dr. Vinny had signed that class was over and passed out materials for home use, Jesse politely escorted Miranda into the hallway.

"I'm so tired! And ready for that bakery! Not to mention the bathroom."

Startled, Miranda whirled around to face one of her classmates. The woman appeared to be in her mid-forties but was aiming for a younger look with her skinny jeans, midriff-baring top, multiple ear piercings, more cosmetics than Miranda had worn in her last show and a red tattoo on her arm too messy to distinguish.

The woman had clearly been addressing Miranda, so Miranda smiled and replied, "I saw a ladies' room down that hall. The bakery is still a question." She paused, then said, "You obviously don't have hearing issues. May I be nosy and ask why you're doing the intense weekend workshops?"

The woman pointed to the small child who was still clinging to Miranda's hand. "Him."

"Ah. Your son?"

"Nope. Foster kid—one a' three but the

other two can hear. Jesse Castillo. 'Course the kid's way aheada me in signing. He gets some lessons at his school and he learned some in the hospital after his accident a couple years ago. He ain't totally deaf, though, and, ya know, he can talk. But he never says a word. I don't get it. Maybe he ain't all that bright?"

The woman dug her cell phone out of her purse and punched in a number while continuing to talk. "Anyways, the state pays for fosters to take these classes if they have a disabled kid so I figured I'd do this workshop thing 'cause I ain't got no time for night school."

Miranda glanced down at Jesse, wondering if he'd lip-read anything his foster mother had said. Fortunately, MacDougal the cat had joined them and Jesse was too busy hugging the kitty to pay attention. The woman was almost yelling into her phone. "Yeah. We're done! I was fixin' ta grab a bite at Chunky's. Wanna meet me?" She paused for a second then nodded vigorously. "Great! Lemme take care 'a some business and we're outta here." She dropped the phone back into her bag.

Miranda was puzzled. "If you don't mind

my asking, why did you agree to take a special-needs child if you don't have time?"

"My stinkin' ex signed like a whiz. He had a deaf brother. Then the rat up and leaves me a month after we get the kid! And Jesse's not a wack job—he's not gonna set fire to my apartment or nuthin' crazy. But this class was too hard! I don't know how I'm gonna get through the next couple of sessions. I'm just not catchin' on."

"It should get easier. And perhaps you and Jesse could practice at home?" Miranda winked at the little boy. "He's a sweetheart. I don't know if you noticed but he and I were paired off in class and I quickly discovered he's really smart. I'd say he's well worth the time and effort you're putting in." She paused, then held out her hand to Jesse's foster mother. "By the way, I'm Miranda Nolan."

"Willow Terence."

"Cool!" Miranda said. "That would make a great stage name."

"Well, ya know, it's really Wilhelmina but I just hated that. Some of my friends called me Willie—I hated that even worse—so I came up with Willow. My ex said it fits 'cause I'm so thin," she said with more than a trace of bitterness.

"Well, I like it. It's very pretty."

"Thanks. Hey, can you look after the kid for a minute or two? I really need to use that john. I guess I shouldn'ta had a super large coffee, but this thing started so early I figured I needed all the lead I could handle. And I could sure use a cigarette break, too."

Miranda nodded.

Willow took off down the hall, leaving an anxious Jesse with Miranda. For all he knew, his foster parent might not be coming back.

Miranda quickly signed, *Where is the restroom?* Jesse got it. His expression signaled understanding and a hint of amusement.

Miranda wanted to chat with Jesse but didn't know enough signing to entertain him while Willow was off using the facilities. After a moment, she decided to try a slightly different form of communication. Miranda signed, *dancing,* then went into dance-teacher mode and demonstrated a basic tap-shuffle step; finishing with a huge *ta-da,* throwing her arms out wide as she dropped to one knee.

Jesse's eyes lit up. He attempted the shuffle step and dropped to his knee with a flourish. Miranda showed him a shuffle ball change about three times then signaled for Jesse to give it a shot. He nailed it on the first try, then shyly tugged at her hand and pointed to her feet. He wanted more.

Miranda was in the process of teaching him a simple four-count riff when Willow returned with what appeared to be an extra pound of cosmetics on her face. "Come on, kid," she said, grabbing his hand. "We're gonna meet up with Rick at Chunky's for a burger then it's home to see what the others have been up to."

Jesse bit his lip. He had no idea what she was saying but he was aware they were leaving, especially when the woman pointed to the exit sign, turned and began to head down the hall. Jesse pulled his hand from Willow's grasp, gave Miranda a huge hug, then followed his foster mother out of the building. He stopped just before he opened the door, dropped to his knee and gave a fine imitation of the *ta-da!* finish Miranda had just showed him. She applauded and the two waved wildly at each other before he opened the door that led to the parking lot.

Dr. Vinny appeared behind Miranda and scooped up MacDougal. He signed, *Cute kid.*

Miranda nodded. "How does one sign *want to kidnap all in a good cause?*" she asked.

"I get it," he replied. "Willow is not the

first foster mother I've seen dragging in here because she doesn't want to lose that monthly payout. Jesse's social worker told me that the Department of Human Resources is looking for another home for him and it can't be too soon. In all honesty, I'm always amazed that some of these people pass whatever qualifications are required to become a foster in the first place. She's probably fine, but there doesn't seem to be much bonding going on between those two."

"It breaks my heart to see a child, hearing or non-hearing, in a situation where there's little affection."

"Agreed. So, Ms. Nolan, do you mind if I ask why you're taking the class?"

"I have a friend—" she pursed her lips "—well, that's not quite true... I'm not sure what to call him..."

Dr. Vinny chuckled. "Your face is already starting to match your hair. No signing or lip-reading required to understand you've got growing feelings."

She smiled and signed, *Good!* then explained the situation regarding Russ and the estate.

"Well, we're glad to have you, Miranda, no matter the reason. If you'd like, I'll make sure you and Jesse stay partners for the next two weekends. There's a clear affinity between you. It should help both of you progress even faster."

She signed, *Yes. I like.*

Dr. Vinny scooped up MacDougal and carried him back to the classroom and Miranda headed out to the parking lot. She was proud at having mastered a bit of signing and frustrated that Jesse would be going home to a lonely, silent world.

Once she arrived at her dad's house, Miranda avoided stressing about Jesse's family life by focusing on Phoebe and teaching her some advanced commands. She'd already mastered sit, stay and roll over the day Miranda had rescued her during their wait in the vet's office. Miranda had spent some time setting up an obstacle course in the large backyard and she'd been playing Frisbee with the dog on a daily basis, even though Phoebe was a far better catcher than Miranda was a thrower.

After Phoebe made it clear she was ready for a nap, Miranda spent a few hours doing online research regarding Benjamin Auttenberg. She found a site devoted to the paintings he'd sold before his internment at Terezin, then dug deeper into the blogs for any information about possible works he'd finished while at the camp.

She hit gold when she found a photo of a piece simply titled *Performance* which depicted the children of Terezin frozen in a moment from the theatrical production that had been designed to convince the International Red Cross that Terezin was a cultural mecca rather than a residence of death. The blogger was light on explanations as to how he'd managed to snap a picture of the painting, but while Miranda was no art expert she felt certain the work was similar enough to Auttenberg's earlier pieces to be genuine. Even the poor quality of the photo couldn't conceal the emotion and the strength of the work.

A few sites appeared to be nothing but discussions of estimated prices for any of Auttenberg's undiscovered works. Miranda's friend Jason had been correct. An original Auttenberg could send one's children, grandchildren and great-grandkids to Ivy League colleges.

She skimmed one or two limited biographies of Benjamin Auttenberg, but was disappointed that none of the websites revealed much apart from basic facts. He'd been born in Czechoslovakia in 1917, married (no name for his wife and no wedding date provided), had a child (also no name and no date of birth provided) who died May 3, 1944, after the family had been at Terezin for three years. Benjamin Auttenberg died on May 3, 1945; a year to the day after his only child. Miranda's throat tightened. Virginia had been a young mother, around age twenty-five when her child had been murdered in a concentration camp. "No wonder she wanted to hide," she told Phoebe, who perked up from a sound sleep upon hearing Miranda's voice.

Some of the online forums were filled with nothing but wild theories as to how Auttenberg's widow had smuggled his work into America after the war and where at least two paintings, with no titles, might have been hidden. One blogger claimed to know for certain that Mrs. Auttenberg calmly walked out of Terezin with a suitcase filled with artwork while another raised the bizarre scenario of Mrs. Auttenberg tucking them away in some desolate castle near Prague then coming back and uncovering them forty years later.

Miranda could have spent the next two weeks digging for information but was practical enough to realize online sources were productive to some extent and extremely addictive, but not always the most reliable.

She finally shut the computer down and shook her head.

"That's it. I'm exhausted. Miss Virginia?" she called softly. "Please know that I intend to keep your possessions safe. But I refuse to turn into a crazed treasure seeker. I only hope one of your journals provides an answer because I'd dearly love to find even a single piece created by the man you loved and lost."

CHAPTER NINE

MIRANDA HAD ALWAYS enjoyed going to the Trussville Fair with her dad, an outing that had turned into an annual event for the pair since the day Miranda had been old enough to walk by Tim's side. They'd spent their time divided between Tim's beloved model-train exhibits and the local artists' tent and finished up the day with slices of homemade cake and tall glasses of iced tea.

This year, as soon as Miranda stepped onto the grounds, she knew she'd made a mistake. She was resentful that Farrah was with them and embarrassed at that resentment.

Just as Miranda had resigned herself to a long morning checking out expensive kitch-enware, she spotted the tent that housed the artwork. Feeling slightly contrite at wanting to desert Tim and Farrah as soon as they'd stopped at the first booth Miranda said, "Dad. Farrah. Why don't I meet y'all by that funky little antique-dolls stall in about an hour? I'd like to see what Jefferson and Shelby counties' finest artists have produced."

"Don't give me that lame excuse, young lady. You're heading for the only place with the good A/C. We now feel officially dumped." Tim grinned at his daughter. "Seriously, no problem. But let's meet at the model-train booth instead and give us an extra half hour. Farrah is indulging me in my favorite hobby." He hugged his wife, who beamed with delight. "Of course, I'll escort her to the kitchen exhibit first so she can burrow through the mass of fluted baking pans and something called a spring-form pan."

Farrah nodded and said, "Would you like me to get one for you? They're perfect for baking cheesecake."

Miranda smiled. "Nah, that's okay. I'd never use them. When I get the craving I tend to head for the nearest deli."

"I'd be glad to teach you. Really."

Miranda's smile remained intact even as she inwardly screamed, *Do you not get the fact that I hate to cook and I have no desire to learn? I'm not domestic. Never have been. Don't want to be. Give me a stage. Give me a song. Give me tap shoes. Give me takeout and delivery.*

"I appreciate the offer, but I think finishing the inventory at Miss Virginia's and teaching children's theater will have me hopping for the next two weeks. Then I'll be in Manhattan shooting the film 24/7 and it'll be back to food-service tables on set and takeout at home."

Tim winked at Miranda as he gently steered Farrah toward the kitchen-supplies booths. "Ninety minutes then and we'll meet you at the model trains. Enjoy the artwork."

Miranda ducked inside the tent and sighed with pleasure as the silence and, yes, the cool air hit her. A young man was seated behind a makeshift desk, dressed in a conservative gray pin-striped suit that would have been more at home in Dave Brennan's law firm than a booth at the Trussville Fair. He nodded at Miranda, waved her over and quietly said, "If you need some help with anything, let me know. Not everything is for sale. If there's no tag, it's exhibition only."

She thanked him and surveyed the surroundings for a long moment, mapping out how much time she could spend in front of each piece. She totally forgot that plan when her focus was drawn to a black-and-white illustration depicting what appeared to be a

Middle Eastern city. There was a loneliness about the work that was unexpected and arresting.

She allowed herself to indulge in the time it took to notice each small detail. The artist had sketched modern buildings and escalators in new malls trying to exist alongside rusted lanterns, empty benches and ruins dating back a thousand years. There were no people. The effect was not only that of loneliness but of sadness, yet there was a tranquil ease that permeated the drawing.

Someone tapped her shoulder. Miranda turned and looked up into the hazel eyes of Russ Gerik. A shiver cascaded down her spine that had nothing to do with the air-conditioning.

"What do you think about this one?" he asked.

She answered as best she could, using lip action mixed with the signing she'd learned at the Cooper School and a few gestures. "It makes me want to cry. But…it's solitary and abandoned and oddly cold for somewhere in the Middle East. Yet the overall effect, to me anyway, is peaceful. I love it. Which is weird."

A dark eyebrow lifted. "You're very perceptive." He paused. "You're also signing a little. When did this happen?"

"Oh." She signed, *I'm taking some week-end workshops. First was yesterday.*

Russ stared at her for a very long moment. "Why?"

Because I wanted to have a real conversation with you. Miranda couldn't say that aloud. She couldn't sign it or mime it, either. She desperately tried to think of an answer that wouldn't scream, *I like you!* Good grief. She had just nailed a role in a major motion picture largely through her skills in improvisation. She even intended to work in some improv with her theater kids to loosen them up during the first class. Camp. Children's theater. She had it. Again mixing mime with signing she explained, "I'm going to be teaching dance at Masquerade Children's Theater starting tomorrow. Their summer camp. I wanted to be able to sign a little for any kids who were non-hearing."

It wasn't a complete lie. She had suddenly been hit with the brilliant idea to persuade Willow Terence to let Jesse take some classes. It would impress the fool out of Willow's social workers, and Bonnie Hamil had told Miranda the theater liked to include as many

new children as they could. Adding children
with hearing or visual impairments might
also help with grant money for the theater.
She made a mental note to call Bonnie as
soon as she got home to see what they could
do, including setting up transportation. Something Miranda was willing to provide if nec-
essary.

Miranda couldn't tell if Russ believed her
or had even caught half of what she'd said,
but he didn't challenge her. He merely used
her own fallback word. "Ah."

She quickly leaned down to make out the
artist's inscription on the illustration she liked
so much—*K. Durani. I don't know the name.
I guess he's local?*

"*Was* local." He paused. "He was one of my
students." Russ closed his eyes for a moment
before opening them and saying, "He's dead."

"What? You knew him? And he died?
That's so sad."

Russ's eyes reflected a pain that was fresh.

"He was more than a student. He was a
friend."

Miranda sensed he wanted, even needed,
to say more. *Tell me? Please? What was his
first name?*

"The *K* stands for Kamyar. Kamyar Yusuf

Durani. His family emigrated from Afghanistan before he was born. He was a good linguist and an amazingly gifted artist. He joined the army and was sent to Kabul."

Miranda pointed and signed, *Is that where he made this?*

Russ nodded. "This particular piece was his dream of how the city might look one day—free and calm, with the modern world living peacefully alongside the ancient. I don't know if you've checked the bottom, but he called it *Silent Sunlight* after the old Cat Stevens song. I always felt like it was the perfect choice."

Miranda instinctively knew the answer to her next question but she couldn't let it go unasked. To do so seemed disrespectful. *What happened?*

"He died in the same blast that took my hearing and the lives of twelve good men. He was twenty-three years old. In one of life's supreme ironies, he'd sent *Silent Sunlight,* along with several other of his works, to his family days earlier." Russ reached out and gently traced the wooden frame. He closed his eyes and let his hand drop, then turned back to Miranda. "It's always been my favorite. Kam's father agreed to loan it out to the festival, but the Durani family doesn't want to sell it. Maybe they'll donate it to a museum one day. It's good enough and it ought to be seen."

Miranda nodded and signed, *It is that good. I agree.*

The pair stood in silence for a few moments. Miranda finally touched Russ's hand to get his attention and tried to mix signing and gestures in with her speech. "I don't want to sound nosy or bring up bad memories, but how did you happen to be working as a translator in Kabul? Were you in the military?"

He frowned. "Slow down. Please. Sign more if you think you know enough words. What are you asking?"

"Sorry." She repeated her question about his work and avoided extra comments, mentally embracing Dr. Vinny for the fast-track class.

"Oh. I was an interpreter—an independent contractor. The military hires folks who can speak the language, especially those who also understand and speak the local dialects. I was too old to fight, but I wanted to do my part. And by the way, I didn't work as a translator most of the time. There is a difference."

I didn't know that, Miranda signed.

"Most people don't," Russ said. "An interpreter hears the spoken word. A translator reads and well—translates—the written word. I primarily acted as an interpreter, although I had to dig through and translate written documents on plenty of occasions."

Miranda motioned for Russ to wait while she dug into her purse for her small organizer, then quickly scribbled, "So you obviously speak Pashto."

"And Farsi. Along with several other languages."

"I'm impressed. So the Army snapped you up?"

"Smart outfit, right?" he smiled. "It helped that I have a doctorate in Cultural Anthropology and that I was familiar with the local culture. I also earned undergrad degrees in Middle Eastern Languages and Anthro from Ohio State. Totally useless for any halfway normal career but perfect for spending a couple of years in Afghanistan chatting with tribal leaders who don't trust anyone outside of their own villages."

Since Russ seemed somewhat amenable to talking about his life, Miranda dared to take her questions a step further. *You actually wanted to go over there?*

"Yeah. I believe in what we're doing to try and free those people."

Miranda winced but declined to voice her objections to "what we're doing." This was no time to debate U.S. foreign policy. Instead she signed, *What were you doing before you hired on as an interpreter?*

"Teaching. Cultural anthropology over at Samford University. That's how I met Miss Virginia, remember? Her temple had invited several members of the Samford faculty to do a series of lectures and I was one of the guest speakers. The formal title that particular day was 'Linguistics in the Modern World.' And, Curious Girl, before you ask—" he flashed a brief smile "—I was in Afghanistan for about eight months before that suicide bomber decided to destroy the lives of a bunch of young soldiers and one thirty-five-year-old interpreter. That was two years ago last month. I haven't taught for more than three years now." He stared at the tent's dirt floor for a long moment.

Miranda hurriedly wrote, "If I express sympathy for his death will you bite my head off like you did the day I met you? Since I wasn't the one who caused the explosion?" She hoped he wouldn't think she was being rude.

His eyes opened wide. So did his smile. "I did do that, didn't I? Bite your head off..." Russ said wryly. "I guess it's my turn to apologize."

Miranda smiled back. "What was that old song by Elton John? 'Sorry Seems to Be the Hardest Word.'"

He seemed confused, so Miranda put her hands over her heart. "The meaning of the word *sorry*. We say 'I'm sorry' for so many things. Sometimes for things that aren't our fault. Or we use a tone that's sarcastic." She tried to frown and wrinkle her nose to express sarcasm, then held up her hand. "Wait. This needs to be written. Otherwise it makes no sense."

She wrote, "How does one express that our hearts are feeling sympathy for something we had no part in causing?"

Russ patiently waited for her to finish. He read her words then stared at her. "Would you like to know what's one of the worst things about being deaf?"

Miranda signed, *Yes. Please tell me.*

"I'm unable to hear the tone in someone's voice. It's easy to lip-read 'I'm sorry,' but it's much harder to tell if it's being said with sincerity. I do have partial hearing in my right ear, but the only thing that comes through is muted sounds—almost like vibrations from a stompin' bass guitar—or sirens. I can hear trace sounds of sirens. Something I'd prefer never to hear again. Anyway, I can't hear words. So having even that slight bit of hearing doesn't help when it comes to conversations and the intent behind certain words."

"What about sign language? For emotions?" Miranda switched back to writing. "The crash lesson I took focused on basics or emergencies. Nothing emotional past 'I like you.'" She handed the notebook to Russ.

He shrugged. "It helps a bit—signing. Less than you'd imagine, though. Generally one signs a different word to express the precise meaning, so it helps to look at someone's face while they sign. I wish my lip reading skills were better."

"You seem amazing to me," Miranda said.

He winked at her. "Now you're just being kind. But thank you." They smiled at each other before Russ added, "Did I tell you there's more than one form of sign language? The majority of Americans who are hearing impaired learn American Sign Language. But I've run into folks who used British Sign Language and communicating with them feels like playing charades. Annoying and confusing." He flashed another quick smile. "Wait. Speaking of sorry, should I apologize? Is my former teacher's tendency to lecture popping out with all this talk about different ways of communicating?"

"Oh, no. Please, go on." *I could listen to you for hours,* she thought.

"Okay. Tell me if I get too long-winded. Let's take your example. If I said 'I'm sorry' but was being sarcastic, I might sign the word 'mean' then follow up with 'I'm sorry.' But if I wanted you to be *sure* I was being sarcastic I'd probably sign 'I'm sorry' while shaking my head furiously or jumping up and down and yelling 'not!'"

Miranda laughed and Russ joined her. The tension that had existed between them during the hours they'd spent at Virginia's eased another degree.

Russ gestured toward *Silent Sunlight.* "I still have a couple of pen and ink pieces Kam drew while we were in Kabul. Actually, I have one or two he did back when he took my Intro to Anthropology class. If you'd like I can bring them over to Miss Virginia's sometime when we're dealing with…all that." He pulled a card from his pocket. "Which reminds me. Would you call with your schedule once you start your theater classes? My own hours with the furniture store can get pretty crazy, but it would help if I knew when you were free to work." He paused for a long moment. Finally, he mumbled, "I have a phone that types out the messages." His mouth turned down at the corners. "Or just let me know tomorrow night when we're tearing through boxes again."

"I'd very much like to see more of Kamyar's work," Miranda wrote. "And I'll give you my schedule as soon as I know how much after-camp stuff needs doing. We're in class from nine to two each day but I think Bonnie Hamil has some extra rehearsals planned."

She was aware of Russ's discomfort and his anger at being unable to hear, but she figured it was best to ignore it. He didn't appear to dislike her, at least away from Virginia's house. Miranda wasn't sure where this tentative friendship might be headed, but as she and Russ left the tent together she was certain of one thing. She wanted to find out.

CHAPTER TEN

MIRANDA TURNED TO face the front of the empty warehouse, where an audience would eventually sit, and stuck her right arm straight out. "Stage right." She dropped her arm, then stuck her left one straight out. "Stage left." She pointed forward. "Downstage." She turned and pointed behind the group of six- and seven-year-old eager wannabe actors, singers and dancers who were learning the basics of stage directions before graduating to dance steps. "Upstage. Got it?"

Heads nodded in understanding. Miranda smiled. She knew quite well the group no more had this than she had three heads. The ten- and eleven-year-old kids who'd been in the last class had been equally clueless. The junior high class hadn't been much better. These younger kids could barely tell the difference between right and left, much less how those directions figured into where they needed to move when on stage. She gestured for her students to stand. "We're going to drill it now, crew."

Miranda spent the next four minutes calling out directions and watching excited kids run from one area of the stage to the other. When she was satisfied that the majority knew where they were going she introduced the children to the world of ball changes and heel stomps. She was absurdly proud of Jesse Castillo, who'd caught on to the directions faster than any of the other children even though he had to lip-read her words or follow her signing with intense concentration. Miranda had arranged a private lesson with Dr. Vinny to make sure she knew enough signing to indicate stage directions and the various words used to describe dance movements. Once the children had begun to learn actual steps and were practicing, Miranda let Jesse dance barefoot to feel the vibrations from the wooden stage, and she clapped in time to the music, standing where he could see her and follow those claps.

She grinned at her charges. "Okay. We're going to learn how to do a three-step turn, go over it until y'all are perfect, then we'll add some heel stomps and step ball changes. If you're *really* wonderful, which I know you will be, in a week or two I'll teach y'all the Most Extraordinary Super Duper Unbelievably Amazing Kick Line in the Universe and add it to whatever song we do for the camp show."

Miranda was even prouder of Jesse when she demonstrated the step ball change and watched him understand the concept of the weight shift long before his fellow dancers, including many of the older children. He was having the time of his life and she was grateful to Bonnie for checking addresses and finding that two of the older students lived in the same apartment complex as Willow Terence. Their parents were more than happy to provide Jesse with a ride so he could be part of the camp. Miranda also blessed whatever divine inspiration had led her to The Cooper School.

Miranda was having the time of her own life, as well. She'd taught dance before when she was in high school and later, as part of her undergraduate work. She'd taught part-time at a community college in Queens one year. She'd choreographed for summer stock in Maine and New Hampshire, but she'd never experienced the kind of enthusiasm and sheer joy she saw on the face of nearly every child involved in the Masquerade Theater.

Camp was scheduled to end at 2:00 p.m., but since this was the first day, Bonnie had asked each of the instructors to come up with a short performance, starting at one-thirty. The kids loved having the chance to watch their teachers on stage and generally strived harder after seeing what advanced performers were capable of. Miranda glanced at her watch. One twenty-five.

"Okay. Time for y'all to sit back down in the audience and chill, my awesome dancers. Just be nice and applaud for me, will you?" She grinned.

Heads bobbed in agreement. Two children yelled, "We love you, Miss Randi!"

Kids from all classes suddenly scurried in and plopped onto the floor of what passed as the theater house, then settled down to enjoy watching their teachers. First up was the music instructor, who shoved the old upright piano out of the wings and onto the stage and entertained with a medley of tunes from *Mary Poppins*. The two acting teachers followed, delighting the kids with a very funny scene from the Broadway version of *Matilda*.

Miranda had provided the music teacher

with a copy of "Hold On" from the musical *The Secret Garden*. It was a piece she often used for auditions, so she felt comfortable singing without having had a chance to rehearse. Even though she'd probably sung the song more than a hundred times, she still loved it. She glanced into the audience. The kids apparently felt the same, since they were giving her a standing ovation midway through the second verse. Miranda almost laughed—the last time she'd sung onstage had been during the final night of *Illumination,* for a sophisticated Broadway crowd who'd paid over a hundred dollars a ticket. Now she was giving her all for one hundred kids wearing shorts and tees, their sweaty faces beaming with pride that *this* was *their* teacher!

She was about three measures into the third verse when she noticed a face that was definitely not smiling. Russ. He was staring at her with his jaw thrust forward. He looked at the children who were standing, then back at her. The theater was a small space and Miranda could see Russ's slightest movements. He began to blink rapidly, then he swallowed hard, determinedly squared his shoulders, inhaled and whirled around so fast she half expected the kids' baseball caps that were hanging on pegs just inside the entrance to be blown out the door.

Miranda desperately tried to remember the words to a song she'd known since she'd been as young as the kids in the audience. She felt dizzy and disoriented. The song actually felt slower, as though she were singing through syrup. She was fighting for the high notes while experiencing the sensation that her voice and her body were being controlled by a sadistic ventriloquist who refused to let her off the stage. The theater was air-conditioned yet Miranda could feel rivulets of perspiration inching down her spine.

She made it through the last chorus, barely registered the applause and cheers from the campers and faculty, then politely but impatiently waited for the remaining acts to finish. After the design teacher wrapped up a five-minute demonstration on how to build a "flat," Miranda waved to the kids who were lining up to get their belongings and catch their rides and pulled herself together enough to receive the fist bumps from the older kids and the hugs from the younger crowd. Only then was she able to race down the hall to the makeshift office used by Bonnie and the theater's administrator, Mrs. Cassidy, a tall woman with perfect posture, iron-gray hair pulled into a bun and an iron will to match. Seventy-odd years ago one of her parents had given her the unlikely first name of Candy.

"Candy. Uh, hi. Weird question, but was there a delivery made here earlier? Like maybe twenty minutes ago?"

Candy threw her a sharp look. "There was. I'm sitting on half of that delivery and happily filling out a database on top of the other."

"Ah. I see. That very lovely desk-and-chair set."

"Yes, indeed. Rocky Ridge Furniture was having a sale and Bonnie and I have always done business with them. Mind if I ask why you're interested?"

"Oh. No reason. Just curious," Miranda said.

"Right. Curious spelled *R-U-S-S-E-L-L?*"

Miranda chewed her lower lip. "That obvious?"

"Only to me, hon. And perhaps I'm more observant because Mr. Gerik asked where you were when he was setting up the desk and chair for me. I told him dance classes were in the new theater space and if he wanted to pop in he could check it out and say howdy."

"Well, he did—but he didn't stay long."

"He did have work to do," Candy said. "Then again, he did tear out of here like he was the fox and the hounds were after him. He didn't look happy. What did you do to him?"

"Nothing! I didn't even know he was in the building until I was halfway through the third verse of 'Hold On' and then I saw him and next thing you know, poof! Gone."

"Well, shoot. If I'd realized you were as crazy about him as he is for you, I'd have hog-tied him and kept him here for you!"

"What? Crazy about *me?*"

Candy snorted. "Honey, I may look like a prison warden, but I'm a romantic to the core and I'm telling you, that boy has more than a passing interest in you. Even with the great estate rivalry of the century."

Miranda shook her head. "I'm not buying it. I mean, it hasn't been pistols at dawn but he's normally pretty standoffish. Although we did have a very nice conversation this past weekend at the Trussville Fair. Neutral territory and all. Neither of us mentioned Virginia's name or anything to do with wills." She smiled. "I really enjoyed talking with him, though I'm not as certain he felt the same."

"Well, Russ was always a tough nut to crack—even before he lost his hearing. He's not the most trusting guy in the world. I've known him since he was a teenager."

"Really? I had no idea. How and where?"

"Russ attended the high school where I was the principal's secretary. He was and is smart as a whip. He was in the band, he ran track, played tennis, loved art classes and did very well on the debate team—I seem to recall a trophy or two. All that. But he was never terribly happy."

"Why?"

"His mother left his dad when Russ was twelve. Took off to Nashville intent on becoming a county-singing star. Nice, huh? Just that age when a kid is about to enter adolescence and needs a mom to help him figure out the female species. What's really crazy is that Nashville isn't all that far. But I don't think Russ has seen the woman in twenty years. His dad died about six years ago so he really doesn't have family."

Miranda winced. "That's awful."

"I agree. Now go away and let me get some work done. I'm a fast typist but I'm not superhuman, and I'd like to have this database finished by tomorrow morning. By the way—

break Russ Gerik's heart and I'll break your legs."

"Well…I'm off, then. I actually have to meet the man at Virginia's in about forty minutes." She winked. "Enjoy the new desk and chair."

Miranda quickly headed for the exit, waving at the kids who were piling into cars in the parking lot or waiting inside the glass doors of the theater for their rides to arrive. She drove to her dad's so she could grab Phoebe and walk the dog over to Virginia's to give the pup the minimum exercise required for a Border collie.

Miranda and Phoebe made it to Virginia's in record time but Russ was already there, sitting on the porch. The door behind him was open.

"The cops should be here in approximately one minute," he said.

She signed, *I seem to remember we set the alarm the other day.*

"We did. I'm assuming someone either knew the code or figured it out."

Miranda nodded. *This doesn't make me happy. Who the heck is breaking in and what is he looking for? An original Auttenberg maybe?*

"I got about half of that," Russ growled. "I thought your signing was better. But I did glean enough to know that something needs to be done before this joker gets bold and decides to break in while we're here working."

Miranda started to respond but was interrupted by the arrival of two police cars. She was glad to see that Officer Hernandez was driving one of them. After he'd introduced Miranda and Russ to the other three responding officers, Hernandez suggested the group head inside for a check of the premises. Russ took a moment to reassure Spero and Phoebe that the visitors were friends and they could relax.

Once the pertinent question of "What time do you think this happened?" had been asked and unanswered—neither Russ nor Miranda had the slightest idea—Hernandez signed, *I assume y'all have had a bit more time to figure out what all's in the house. Maybe you'll have some idea if anything was stolen?*

Russ shrugged. She shook her head. "Yes and no. We've been able to do some inventory of Virginia's belongings but nothing valuable has turned up. I mean her recipe books are nice but not exactly worth all this effort to break in. And we haven't found any priceless paintings or expensive antiques. Of course someone else obviously believes that something valuable is here but they apparently aren't aware of where it's hidden, either. Assuming it exists. And the only thing of value I can think of would be artwork. Which we're not totally sure even exists, either."

Four police officers stared at her. Hernandez chuckled. "That was the most convoluted answer I've heard since the guy cooking meth in his basement tried to explain he was frying bacon in the kitchen and that's why his entire house, *except* the kitchen, blew up."

Miranda tried to explain. "Well, yeah, it is somewhat complicated but no one is really sure that Miss Virginia even had any of her husband's paintings. If she did, she hid them and no one knows where, including Russ and me. And I'm probably not doing the best job of explaining since I'm still feeling a bit sketchy about this whole breaking-in business. Scratch that. Let's say extremely sketchy. My knees are weak and my stomach isn't exactly stable."

There were nods all around. "Very understandable," Hernandez said gently. He turned to Russ and signed, *Ideas?*

Russ answered, "Your guess is as good as

mine. I was at this house at least once a month before I went to Afghanistan and although I wasn't able to visit as often later, I'm sure if Virginia had kept anything worth stealing, she would have mentioned it to me."

Miranda took a deep breath. "Okay. Now that explanations or guesses are over, why don't we give y'all the guided tour? It should be a bit easier now that most of Virginia's things are in the living room. Well, some stuff is in the attic. We haven't started up there yet."

"Did she have any electronics?" Officer Burroughs asked. "High-tech computer or sound equipment? That's usually what thieves are after since it's easy to sell. Or drugs. Oxy is a big draw for kids breaking in and lots of elderly folks have a cabinet full of major pain meds."

Miranda turned to Russ and mimed popping pills then asked, "Virginia?"

He shook his head. "The only pain meds were specifically for the cancer. And the hospice team was here when she died so they would have cleared out any old medications."

Miranda's throat tightened, lost for a moment as she imagined Virginia's last months on earth. Had she wished for more time than her ninety-five years? Or had she simply hoped to meet her husband and child again after losing them both nearly seventy years earlier. With some effort, Miranda brought her attention back to the officers. "She did have a new laptop but that wouldn't get a thief more than a couple hundred bucks at best. And Miss Virginia's lawyer told me her jewelry is in a safe-deposit box, and she had very little anyway." She paused. "Oh! Dave Brennan!"

"Who?" asked Hernandez.

"Miss Virginia's attorney. Well, one of them anyway. Dave is handling my part of the contested estate. He needs to know about this latest break-in and he also might have some idea of where she hid her stuff. Plus he needs to know…"

"What?"

She hesitated for a moment. "I hate to accuse people. Really."

"But?"

"Four people knew the alarm code. The associate from Dave's office—that's Cort. There's an associate from the firm handling Russ's claim, uh, Brett King. Then we have the very—oh, I'll be kind and say 'overly enthusiastic'—real estate agent, George Miller and Mr. Tomlinson, the guy who installed the system. Out of that quartet, three probably have more knowledge about the contents of this house than I do and all of them know there may be some valuable paintings hidden inside."

Miranda didn't mention the obvious. Russ also knew the passcode. She had only his word that someone had broken in. He'd been first on the scene for each incident. Could he possibly be trying to gaslight her into giving up the inheritance? She refused to let that thought stay in her mind. She quickly joked, "Perhaps Miss Virginia's ghost is checking up on how we're dealing with her things?"

Hernandez shot her a sharp glance. "Call Brennan. Now. And Russ needs to call his attorney, as well. If nothing else, they need to know what's happening here. If you're right about the artwork being the 'why' perhaps the break-ins really are all about Miss Virginia's past."

CHAPTER ELEVEN

"I UNDERSTAND, because I was brought up here, that the South has a charming way of doing business that is often laid-back and somewhat informal, but that law office is so casual it's going to get us murdered one afternoon in the middle of labeling!" Miranda slammed the receiver back into its cradle. Phoebe and Spero, sitting attentively at her feet, barked in agreement.

Miranda glanced at Russ and the four police officers who'd patiently waited for her to finish her call to Dave Brennan. "Folks, they might as well have put up a billboard reading, *This way to the Treasure!* and announced a fun day for any and all comers wanting to poke around Miss Virginia's house. With tour guides dressed in Scarlet O'Hara crinolines for effect."

Russ growled, "Slow it down!"

"Sorry." She signed what she could, which wasn't much since half of what she'd said was pure garbage. Miranda finally gave up, grabbed a notebook and wrote down what she'd said, adding, "Yes, it was meant to be somewhat sarcastic."

"So, what exactly did Brennan say?" Russ asked.

Miranda stared at him for a long moment. Then she grinned. "I am so stupid but ultimately brilliant. Let's give text messages a shot, okay?" She dumped the notebook in favor of her phone. "Texting? Yes?"

Russ smiled. "Yes."

"Great." She continued her tirade, speaking aloud to the police but texting part of it on her phone and holding it out so Russ could see. "First, Dave Brennan said he was sorry someone had broken into the house. He was absolutely positive that no one associated with his firm would do such a thing and since half of Birmingham knows that Tomlinson Alarms uses the number of a house and the initials of the first and last name of the person who ordered the stinkin' alarm system, anyone on the street could have been zipping in and out of here with wild abandon every hour on the hour."

A long pause while Russ read her text,

which had ended up even less coherent than her statement.

Russ grimaced. "He did *not* say that."

"Well, close. It's the basic meaning anyway. But—this is important—the associates, paralegals, secretaries, clerks and probably the janitors at Brennan's firm and at Henniger and Waltham had all heard rumors that something valuable might be on the premises."

"You haven't found anything yet, correct?" asked Officer Williams.

"Zippo."

Hernandez waved his arms. "We're wasting time, folks. We all agree that the ultimate target is the artwork. Now let's see if we can find any trace of this joker's presence."

The search was on. Miranda and Russ were allowed to accompany the police in case either of them noticed belongings out of place or items that had vanished. Spero and Phoebe trotted behind the group—alert and ready to provide whatever canine assistance was required.

The search took less than forty minutes. It was thorough but ultimately unproductive. Miranda and Russ had managed to organize and label about half of the boxes since the last break-in. Out of the odds and ends from

Virginia's cabinets, the only items that might be of value were the three boxes of Lladró and Hummel figurines, which Miranda had packed, sealed and labeled. It was obvious no one had tried to open any of them.

Russ waited in the living room with both dogs while Miranda escorted the police to the door. She shook hands with Ted Hernandez and said that she'd get the alarm code changed as soon as possible.

"That's a good start, but something tells me it won't do much to deter your art-loving visitor. Then again, it can't hurt and doesn't cost a thing."

"Well, thanks. I'm truly grateful to you for getting here so fast and for everything you've done," Miranda said. She tried to smile. "Wanna move in for the next couple of weeks and guard the place?"

Ted winked. "It's going to be fine. Just let me know if you find something worth stealing. I'd wager that Miss Virginia put the small things she considered truly valuable in a vault somewhere, but forgot to mention that in her will. Either of them. You might ask the lawyers if she has some kind of secure storage facility and if so, if either you or Russ could legally access it."

"Great idea! I'll do that. Cort is smart, but I think he's too busy dealing with the fight over who inherits to figure out exactly what Russ or I would get. Apart from the house that is. I don't know about Brett."

She headed back to the living room and was immediately greeted by both dogs, who clearly thought she'd been gone long enough to start up the big puppy dance of greeting.

"Well? What's the plan of action, Ms. Nolan?" Russ asked.

Food. Read jrnals. Call lawyers. Ask about storage unit? she texted. She paused then added, Have nervous brkdwn. Want orange tea? Want to help?

Russ chuckled. "With the breakdown or the tea?"

The latter. I can do the former solo, she signed.

Russ did his bit by turning on the stove for the water. She waited until he faced her again before texting, Faster we find art, safer for us. Yes?

Russ nodded. "Absolutely. I have to admit I'm almost relieved that neither of us is living here right now. It could be really dangerous."

Miranda shivered. She felt cold, even in

a house that had no air-conditioning. She texted, U think thief would harm?

Russ didn't answer. After a long moment, he shrugged. "Honestly? I don't know. One doesn't think of art thieves as being violent but maybe we're all too conditioned by tales of elegant cat burglars in movies and mysteries." He added, "I'm becoming more convinced though that there really is something in one of her diaries. Perhaps we should get a better system going and start sorting by dates? Want to print more labels?"

Miranda nodded. Anything to stay busy.

She walked back into the living room and headed for the desk that currently held Virginia's laptop and printer. Miranda had noticed during the last session with Russ that there were about twelve boxes holding diaries, so she typed in years from 1946 to 2014 and hit Print. As she mindlessly stared at the printer, lightning struck, but the flash had nothing to do with journals or art. Without waiting for the labels to finish printing she ran back to the kitchen and grabbed the cell phone she'd left on the counter. Russ was pouring hot water over the tea leaves. She tapped him on the shoulder.

"What?"

Miranda pointed at her cell phone then signed, *Voice*. She didn't know the sign for *recognition* so she typed it in, followed by the words *software and Dragon*.

She texted, Do U know? Need larger phone? Galaxy. IPhone. IPad. + Wi-Fi. U Speak. Dragon types out. Sftware out for 10 yrs or more.

Russ stared at her for a moment then burst into peals of laughter. Spero and Phoebe jumped up from their respective spots on the couch and began to bark in excitement.

Miranda was horrified that she'd somehow offended him. She'd thought it was a pretty good idea.

Russ wiped tears from his eyes and patted Spero to calm him down. "Sorry! It's just that I've been deaf for two years and no one has even thought to mention this device. I'm not familiar with it but then, I'm pretty low-tech." He chuckled. "So, here comes inheritance rival Miranda Nolan who presents me with an option that could help my life beyond imagination. I don't know why that strikes me as funny but it does. Thank you!"

She blushed and found a notebook. "Hey, you're welcome. I just hope it works and it really does help you. If so, I'll buy a computer notepad thingee and a Dragon for Jesse."

"Who?"

Russ appeared interested, so Miranda spent a few moments telling him, via the notebook, about her signing partner and how much she liked him and how proud she'd been that Jesse had jumped right into the dance classes without fear and even made some friends on his first day.

Russ frowned. "I wish the kid wasn't in a foster situation with someone who isn't exactly savvy about special-needs children. Hopefully it's only a temporary placement."

Miranda nodded before writing, "Perfect solution would be adoption by someone who's adept at signing AND will love him for the cool, funny and smart child he is."

"I agree." He glanced down at his watch. "Okay. Let's be civilized and drink tea, then dive into more boxes. We've got ninety minutes. Not that it matters about some paralegal bringing the key since apparently this place gets more traffic than the diner down the street. I think we need the doors completely rekeyed since it appears someone has copies. Hernandez said he didn't see indications of a forced entry."

Russ brought the tea into the living room and set Miranda's cup down on an end table by the sofa. The dogs settled again on the couch, Phoebe using Spero's back as a pillow. Russ took a sip from his own mug, then paused, staring at the wall behind the sofa.

"What?" Miranda signed. "Problems?"

He shook his head. "The opposite. I just need to stop every now and then and simply breathe in the atmosphere of this house. It's a fascinating place—beyond Miss Virginia's antiques. The house itself is an anomaly on this block. It's a mix of Gothic Revival and the Craftsman cottage bungalows, so it should have been built over in the Norwood historic district near Highland Avenue. I did a little research and discovered the house was built in the late 1800s. The big surprise is that it didn't get demolished in the 1950s when everyone was going for ranch or cottage."

Miranda blinked. *You love this house, don't you?* she signed. *I don't mean just for memories of Virginia, but the house itself.*

"Yes."

Miranda nearly signed, *Take it! It's yours! You deserve it! Just let me have Virginia's diaries, sewing basket and piano!*

Russ had turned his back and was drinking his tea before Miranda could act on that urge. By the time he'd set his glass down and said they'd best get to work, she'd had time to realize it was a little crazy to give up her inheritance. She loved this place, too. Besides, Russ might think she'd made the offer out of pity and despise her for even considering it.

The pair spent the next hour and a half tearing open boxes and organizing the diaries by year. Neither Russ nor Miranda said a word. About forty minutes into the labeling process Miranda realized the silence was comfortable.... It was also the norm for Russ. She closed her eyes and tried to feel what that must be like. The never-ending, constant quiet. Her imagination was good, but even as focused as she was, sound still crept through. She could hear birds outside. She could hear street noises. She could hear the rustle of the fans in the room and the soft yips and snores emitted from Phoebe sleeping at her feet. Miranda wasn't sure she would've been able to handle losing her hearing with the grace displayed by Russ and the people she'd met at The Cooper School, including Jesse. Russ could be gruff and impatient but she had to assume that was partly because they were on opposites sides of an estate battle.

She opened her eyes. Russ had moved across the room and was standing by Virginia's piano. He let his hand trail across the keys then noticed she was staring at him. He smiled wryly. "Asleep?"

She smiled, grabbed the phone and crossed the room to hand it to him.

No. Wndring how long to take to read all this once we've dated and reboxed evrythng. We don't really have time snce also trying to figure out where all Virginia's stuff needs to go. I mean stf we're not keeping.

He hesitated for a moment. "Actually that brings up something I've wanted to ask about. But I realize you're pressed for time with the camp, so I'm not sure you want to take on anything else." He took a deep breath before adding, "I also wanted to apologize for running out at your concert this afternoon."

She shook her head and signed, *Not a concert. Just a fun thing for kids. No problem.*

"Well, it was rude of me. I could have at least waved." He glanced down at the piano keys. The pain of missing music must be excruciating for him.

She tentatively signed, *Does it help at all having songs in your head?*

Russ nodded. "Obviously it's not like hearing live music but it's better than total silence."

This is probably stupid to ask but do you still play keyboards at all? I mean, just to keep up the technical skill?

Russ hesitated so long Miranda was afraid her question had been too personal, or that he hadn't understood her. Finally he said, "I do play. I guess I haven't lost all hope that one day I might be able to hear at least a chord or two. After all, one never knows what medical device some brilliant scientist might create. At any rate, I'm sorry I ran out on your performance."

Her heart lurched with pleasure at hearing an apology that wasn't needed and because Russ had felt close enough to her to be able to share that moment of honesty.

She smiled, sensing it was time to lighten the conversation. *It's okay. Candy gets impatient when office furniture is waiting.*

Russ smiled back. "Believe me, she would have stalked me throughout the halls of that warehouse to get her beloved desk set up!"

Miranda laughed. *So, what did you want to ask me?*

"Ah, yes. Back to that. I could really use your help with something."

Miranda pretended she wasn't astonished and signed, *What do you need?*

"Kam Durani's parents have asked me to put together a show of his work. There's a gallery in the Highlands area that's keen on featuring local talent...." His expression darkened momentarily. "I said I'd love to make all the arrangements, but there's a problem and it's slightly embarrassing."

"Go on."

"The owner and I used to date. She's... well, let me be kind and merely say Darci's a piece of work. Temperamental and pretty daffy, even though she's brilliant when it comes to art. She doesn't sign and doesn't want to learn. She's also extremely impatient and I need an interpreter who not only understands art but...seems to be able to talk to all kinds of people. I have to warn you, it could be awkward being around her since she tends to be inquisitive but I really want this show to be a success and she does run the best gallery in Birmingham. Plus..." He ducked down and began to play with Spero's ears. They were joined by Phoebe who wanted in on the affection. "Um, I'd like for you to meet the Duranis and...uh..."

Miranda waited for a finish to that thought but apparently Russ had nothing else to add. She nodded as she wrote in the notebook "Love to help. Been around temperamental divas all my life. I'll survive." She didn't feel the need to say she was beginning to welcome any excuse to be with him. And she *was* truly interested in seeing more of Kamyar's work. She wrote down that latter reason, handed the notebook back to Russ and tried to avoid asking herself why she wanted to be around Russ Gerik so badly that she was willing to deal with an impatient ex-girlfriend.

He smiled. "Can we meet here tomorrow, after your classes? Adding to my embarrassment, I hope you don't mind driving—my car is in the shop."

"That's fine."

A few minutes later the paralegal arrived with the key. Miranda looped Phoebe's leash around her neck, waved to Russ and headed back toward her temporary digs with Tim and Farrah. Five minutes into the walk it struck her that Russ might have bitten back the fact that he wanted Kamyar Durani's family to meet her so they could provide an opinion on the girl who might steal his inheritance.

CHAPTER TWELVE

RUSS HADN'T TOLD Miranda much about Dr. Yusuf Durani and his wife, Abra, apart from the fact that Yusuf had been a colleague of Russ's at Samford University and how much the Duranis had adored their son. Miranda had assumed she'd be meeting a couple in their mid-sixties, both dressed in black, who'd barely speak to Miranda, simply show them Kamyar's paintings and usher them out of the house as fast as they possibly could.

The attractive woman who greeted them at the door appeared to be in her late forties. Yusuf Durani seemed older but Miranda surmised that his neatly trimmed white beard might have added a few years. There was a warmth emanating from both Yusuf and Abra that made Miranda feel at home.

Introductions were made quickly and Russ and Miranda were escorted inside, out of the freakish ninety-degree temperature that was still raging despite the dark. Abra sighed.

"We left Kabul when we were in our early twenties and one would have thought we'd be accustomed to heat, but there's something about the high temperatures in Alabama—often starting in May—that sap my energy. It's simply not right."

"I totally agree," Miranda said. "My dad doesn't understand how I've withstood New York winters for six years and I patiently explain that one can always layer on the clothes. In the heat, you can only lose so much before arrests should be made for indecency! Although I do have to admit that Manhattan in the summer can be and often is nothing but disgusting and smart people leave the city in June."

Russ glanced down at his new Dragon. Miranda had spoken slowly enough for the voice recognition to pick up every word. Yusuf was eyeing the gadget with interest. Russ handed it to him.

"What is this?" Yusuf asked.

Miranda answered for Russ, who hadn't said a word to anyone once the first introductions had been made. "Meet Puff."

"Puff?"

"As in 'the magic Dragon.' Remember the old song by Peter, Paul and Mary? It's voice recognition software that captures sounds and translates them into words on the screen. It hit me last week when I was texting Russ that this kind of device could simplify his life." Miranda smiled at Russ, who had remained silent during her explanation.

Yusuf was clearly fascinated with Puff and Abra flashed a wide grin. "I'm amazed," she said. "It's a high-tech toy named after a children's song."

"Well, I think it's brilliant," Yusuf said. "And so are you Ms. Nolan for suggesting it. Russ, why don't you keep Puff in your hand while I show you my own latest high-tech gadget in the master bedroom. Ms. Nolan can keep Abra company while she makes the lemonade."

"Call me Miranda, please, and I'd love to help squeeze lemons but I'm curious—what high-tech gadget?"

Yusuf beamed at her. "It's an intelligent-design alarm clock that forces you to answer questions you've downloaded before it shuts off. It's very exciting!"

Abra rolled her eyes. "It's the most annoying thing on the planet. The clock beeps incessantly until you answer all the questions. You can even program it to light up like a seventies disco. Strobe lights and a tiny mirror ball that twirls until you smack it to shut it down. Amazing."

Miranda laughed. "I think that would make me crazy. I'd probably toss it across the room in a rage."

Abra smiled at her. "Are you one of those people who just naturally wake up at the same time every morning?"

Miranda chuckled. "Wet nose."

"I beg your pardon?"

"Mine is named Phoebe. She's new. Russ has an older model named Spero."

Abra snapped her fingers. "Ah! Of course! Doggie clocks." She fluttered long lashes at her husband. "Could we perhaps try that instead of being quizzed at 6:00 a.m.? After all, Yasmin has been begging for a puppy for the past year."

"Yasmin? Miranda asked.

"Our daughter. She just turned fourteen." Abra tapped her head of partially gray hair. "I swear this was all brown until her birthday a week ago."

Miranda grinned. "I get it. I'm dealing with about six her age at the children's theater. Fourteen is an absolutely hideous age. For all concerned—the teens *and* the adults they torment. They should be forced to carry a sign that reads, 'I'm fourteen! Danger! Run away while you have the chance!'"

Abra led Miranda toward the kitchen as Yusuf and Russ headed the other direction. "I don't know how you do it with more than one at your camp. I keep thinking I should lock Yasmin in a closet until she's twenty-one. Or thirty."

"It's easier for me. They're all pretending to be what they call 'hashtag impressed' for the fifteen- and sixteen-year-olds in the same class. Plus they're learning the same things and staying really busy and I only have them a few hours each day. I'm also not the one who has to say 'no, young lady, that eye shadow makes you look like a Halloween mask' or 'no, you may not go out with the dude on the motorcycle who has the tattoo of the parrot plastered on his shaved head.' I stick to things like 'Yo! Troops! Point your toes, spit out the gum and quit looking at the floor.'"

They'd reached the kitchen at this point, laughing most of the way.

"How can I help?" Miranda asked. "Am I slicing lemons?"

Abra shook her head. "No. It's all done except the pouring." She opened the refrigerator and grabbed the pitcher from the first shelf. "I really thought Yusuf and Russ could use a little alone time." She shot Miranda a sharp glance. "I don't normally spill my inner thoughts but I feel certain I can trust you. You won't go running out of the house or despise either man for being unable to express his true feelings." She exhaled, then quietly said, "It's not good. They pretend they're fine, but there's so much self-reproach on both sides I'm afraid it's going to explode one day and I keep hoping they'll talk it out before that happens. Russ avoids us. I truly believe part of that is his way of hiding from the guilt."

"Guilt?"

"Oh, yes. Yusuf feels guilty because it was his idea that Russ take a break from teaching for a year or two and become an interpreter for the military. This was *after* Kamyar had joined the Army. Yusuf had encouraged him to go which adds to his belief he's to blame. I truly believe Yusuf thought Russ could look after Kam, but how could he keep our son safe when suicide bombers were waiting to kill themselves and everyone around? Russ is strong and brave and brilliant, but Russ is not a superman. So Russ lost his hearing and Kam lost his life and now Russ doesn't even want to see us." Abra blinked back tears as her voice grew hoarse. "I'm sorry. Again, I probably shouldn't be saying any of this but I felt you needed to know. You may call me crazy and I hope I haven't embarrassed you. If you want to tell me to squirt those lemons in my eye and shut up, I'll understand."

Miranda reached out and took the pitcher of lemonade from Abra's trembling hands. "What I understand is that there's a world of hurt on all sides and no reason for guilt on *any* side. I gather Russ would have gone to Afghanistan regardless of whether he knew anyone in that unit or not. The only person who should be guilty is the fanatic who decided to use hate to destroy too many lives."

Both women sank down into chairs at the small café-style table. Abra closed her eyes for a moment, then opened them and reached for Miranda's hand. "Thank you. I knew you were a good person the instant I met you. You and Russ are perfect for each other. You can help keep him grounded."

"Oh, no! I mean, we're not together as a couple. Didn't he tell you about the wills?" Miranda told Abra about Miss Virginia's death and the conflicting wills that had forced her and Russ to work on the inventory together. "The upshot is that our attorneys are fighting and Russ and I are working and being civil—and discovering we have a lot in common apart from our love for Miss Virginia. Anyway, I'm helping him because I wanted to see Kam's artwork and apparently the owner of the gallery, uh, Darci somebody, can be tricky to deal with. I gather she requires a faster translation than even the Dragon can provide. We're meeting her tomorrow after I'm through at the children's theater."

Abra ignored Miranda's attempt to define her relationship with Russ. She sniffed. "You're together. You and Russ that is. You know it and I know it and soon Russ will know it, and he will learn to trust. As for Darci? Well, I'm not a believer in gossip but I will say I'm glad to hear she's engaged to some divorce lawyer in town. I actually like her. She's very funny. But she and Russ were not a good fit. I think that lasted about a month before they called it quits."

Before Miranda could ask what Darci was like, the back door to the kitchen opened with a bang and a tall, attractive young girl dressed in hot-pink capris and a hotter pink T-shirt stormed inside.

"Muh-ther! Why can't I join Lacy and

Sarah for a sleepover!" The girl didn't ask. She demanded.

Abra chewed her bottom lip. "Yasmin! Show some manners and behave like a civilized person. I would like for you to meet Miss Miranda Nolan, a good friend of Russ."

The girl continued to glare at her mother. Miranda quickly said, "Nice to meet you, Yasmin."

Yasmin mumbled a hello but didn't look at Miranda. Instead she repeated, "Sleepover?"

Abra's tone was stern. "You are not going because that so-called sleepover is in Gadsden and the last I heard the only person even resembling a chaperone will be Sarah's seventeen-year-old sister, who's been grounded more times in her young life than a plane with engine trouble."

"But I'm so *bored!* There's nothing to do!"

Miranda smiled at Yasmin. "What do you want to do?"

The teenager finally turned her attention to Miranda. "Go to sleepovers with my friends. But since that's obviously *out,* I'm kind of clueless. I just know sitting around here learning to cook isn't my idea of a fun time. Tossing new recipes at me 24/7 isn't going to change that one single bit."

"You got that right," Miranda muttered. She glanced at Abra. "Sorry. But I'm with your daughter on this one. I also hate to cook, but my new stepmother is always urging recipes and gadgets on me. And if that came out as rude, it's your turn to tell me to squeeze the lemons and keep quiet."

Abra smiled. "Don't worry. It was an honest response. I love to cook so I don't understand why everyone in the universe isn't happily slicing and dicing and downloading every recipe imaginable. I'm well aware that Yasmin doesn't share that particular interest—I suppose it's my own feeble attempt to find a way to bond with my daughter." She winked at Yasmin, who shrugged but seemed somewhat calmer. "Yasmin's a cheerleader, so she was very busy throughout the entire school year. But school is out and she won't go to cheer camp until mid-July."

Miranda eyed mother and daughter and made a quick decision. "Just a thought—I'm teaching dance for the summer camp at the Masquerade Children's Theater. Which is a misnomer since half the campers are over the age of thirteen and they get very touchy when called children. Anyway, our designer was telling me he needs more teens to help in the shop since the little kids shouldn't be doing the nailing and gluing." She turned to Yasmin. "Do you think that's something you might enjoy?" She grinned. "No cooking involved."

Yasmin whooped, "Whoa! Yeah! That would be really cool. I mean, I don't have the kind of talent Kam did—" she swallowed "—but I love to put stuff together and slap paint on walls and I'm amazing with a hammer and nails. Mother, please, could I?"

"If your father approves, and I see no reason why he wouldn't, I have no objections," Abra said solemnly. "I'll even volunteer to drive you."

"Fantastic! I'm going to ask him now!" Yasmin started to fly out of the room in that manner only befitting tornados and teenagers.

Abra quickly stopped her. "Wait! Let Miranda ask him first. She can explain what this entails." She glanced at Miranda. "Do you mind?"

"Not at all."

Miranda followed Abra's directions to Yusuf's office. The door was partially open. She was about to knock when she heard Yusuf exclaiming, "I don't care about the model trains,

Russell! I care that this is only the third time you've come to see us since you've been back. Two years. You barely said a word past introductions and you let your friend do the talking and now all you can do is rattle on about how the McWane Science Center is hosting a train show in July? Talk to me!"

Russell took the time to read Yusuf's words on his Dragon before responding. "I'm sorry. I am." His voice sounded as though he were choking. "But I look at you and I look at Abra and I see Kamyar standing in front of me on that last day. He was so annoyed because the unit's new cook had been asking everyone where he could find bacon to mix with the powdered eggs. Bacon! Kamyar said no wonder America couldn't make headway with the people in the Middle East if the Army kept sending idiots who didn't understand basic Muslim traditions. Then he started laughing because this same cook had asked Lenny Goldberg if he needed him to find a kosher ham!"

Miranda could almost see Yusuf's smile. "That's a good memory, Russ. Laughter. Believe me, it's the only way Abra and I have lived through the past two years. Kamyar brought so much joy to us and to Yasmin. I look at her and I see her brother in her eyes. I hear him in her laughter." He paused, then continued with a voice that had suddenly become hoarse. "For my part, I am truly sorry that you cannot hear her. I am so terribly sorry that your world is one of silence."

Miranda tiptoed back down the hall. This was not the time to intrude…or to eavesdrop.

"Well?" Abra asked.

She grimaced. "I decided to let Yusuf and Russ continue their private conversation."

"Ah. So, Miss Nolan, you're tactful as well as creative."

Yasmin spoke up. "Well, I'm not tactful. I'm busting in." She whirled around and headed toward her father's office before Abra had a chance to hold her back.

Abra shook her head. "Probably for the best. I'm not sure how long a private conversation between my husband and Russell needs to be at this point. But you! Miranda, you're a miracle worker. In two minutes you've managed to come up with a project that will keep my daughter busy and stop her from whining about that bacchanalia the girls euphemistically refer to as a sleepover. Bless you."

"Well, I hope it works out. The theater does

need help since we'll be doing a production at the end of camp. It's a tight schedule."

Abra inclined her head. "This will be great."

Before either woman could continue discussing the mysterious business of parenting, they were joined by Russ and Yusuf.

"I've just been accosted by a flying teenager who was thrilled to tell me that her mother believes she should spend her time at a theater slapping paint onto boards and doubtless all over herself. Is this true?" Yusuf asked, his eyes twinkling.

Abra nodded. "It is."

"Well, that's good, because I said yes."

"Where is she?"

"In her room firing up the computer. She's going to study up on stagecraft. I believe she plans to take over the designer's job five minutes after she arrives at the theater."

There were smiles all around as Abra poured lemonade and offered dishes filled with fruit and nuts, yet Miranda still felt that an undercurrent of words had yet to be spoken. Was it Russ's sense of culpability for something he had no control over? She glanced at Yusuf and Russ. Something was definitely in the wind that had nothing to do with Yasmin turning into a theater rat.

The silence suddenly turned uncomfortable. Miranda quietly asked, "Are you both okay with this exhibition? I'm sensing an elephant in the room."

"It's not the exhibition," Yusuf said. "I'm proud that our son's works will be seen. It's…" He nodded at Russ and signed, *Tell them what you told me.*

Russ inhaled. "I've been offered a job."

"Well, that's a good thing!" Abra said, smiling. "Delivering furniture is not what you were put on this earth to do. Back at Samford?"

Russ read her words on the Dragon. He shook his head. "No. This is with a defense contractor, but not the one who hired me a few years ago. This outfit works out of Washington. They deal with military intelligence and our friends at Langley."

"The CIA? Seriously?" Miranda asked.

"Yes. They want me to work as a translator." He smiled briefly.

Miranda slid the Dragon back to Russ. "What do they want you to translate?"

"Classified documents that would lead to… various classified operations," he said.

Miranda's expression darkened. She paused but finally had to ask, "Including drone strikes?"

"That's part of it," Russ said. His mouth tightened. "You don't approve?"

"Honestly? No. I didn't approve of the war in Afghanistan or in Iraq and I believe that drone strikes only serve to keep the anger and hatred alive while too many innocent people die."

"You're wrong," Russ said with more than a trace of anger. "We've taken out a boatload of terrorists and crazies that way while saving our soldiers."

Abra joined the argument. "They've also helped demolish wedding parties and entire villages by mistake. Russ, I know you believe you'd be helping the war effort, but I'm with Miranda. I don't see it that way. Not that our opinion makes a difference in what the military decides to do." She paused. "Would you be able to do this job from Birmingham or would you have to move to Washington or Virginia?"

Russ read Abra's words on the Dragon before responding. "I can work from Birmingham. The company would send the information on a secured computer and I'd translate. And before everyone here gets their proverbial knickers in a twist, I only received the offer yesterday. I haven't decided what to do. So, can we change the subject? I'd rather not get bogged down in politics right now."

"Of course," Abra said. "Miranda? Tell us about the children's theater Yasmin plans to own by the end of the week?"

Miranda gratefully launched into a monologue about the classes, the camp, the funding needs and how marvelous the kids were. The tension in the room almost visibly dissipated.

Before long the pitcher was empty and the chatter was hitting topics that included children's theater and Broadway, Abra musing about getting a part-time job and Miranda saying she'd be happy to ask her stepmother if she needed an extra hand at her catering business. Yusuf eventually stood. "This is delightful but are you two ready to see Kam's works?"

"Absolutely."

The artwork was stunning. Miranda found herself veering between admiration and awe for the pieces themselves and sadness and anger that a young life had been taken. Kamyar Durani would never create more of this beauty.

An hour later, Miranda and Russ left the Durani house. Neither spoke during the entire trip to Russ's house. Miranda wasn't sure if they were both unwilling to break the spell of emotions swirling from the impact of Kam's artwork or if residual friction about Russ's new opportunity kept them silent.

Finally, just as Russ was exiting the vehicle and thanking Miranda for the ride and her upcoming help with the exhibition he spoke. "I know you're antimilitary, but I got the sense that's not the only reason you think the translating job is not a good opportunity. Am I right?" He handed her the Dragon.

"I'm not antimilitary," Miranda protested. "I'm antiwar. Especially this one. But since you're asking, yes, I don't believe it's in your best interest."

"Why?"

She inhaled, braced herself and said, "Because, in my opinion, this job is just another way to hide."

Russ looked her straight in the eyes. Miranda waited for a response but he simply took the Dragon from her, opened the door, climbed out of the vehicle and walked away. He didn't look back.

CHAPTER THIRTEEN

DARCI BECKER WAS STUNNING. Miranda took one look at the perfectly coiffed dark brown hair and the porcelain complexion and inwardly groaned. After a long day of teaching that had primarily consisted of showing kids of all ages how to jump, spin, shuffle and pound the floor with their heels while singing "Revolting Children" from *Matilda,* Miranda felt like—and was fairly certain she resembled—the used side of a scouring pad. The finishing touch was her partially blue hair, courtesy of paint flying from the shop where flats for the upcoming productions were being assembled. Miranda had been amused but pleased that Yasmin Durani had been an instant hit with the designer, who recognized a workhorse when he saw one and had bestowed upon the girl the responsibility for creating four flats depicting the sun and the sky.

Darci Becker was extremely curious as

to the precise nature of Russ Gerik and Miranda Nolan's relationship. Miranda worried the woman's head was going to spin off her neck since she kept turning from Russ to Miranda and back again like a demented fan watching a championship Ping Pong match.

Russ had nailed it when he'd told Miranda that Darci was impatient and intolerant regarding his inability to hear. She rattled off her suggestions for the Durani exhibition too fast for the Dragon recognition software to catch her words. Miranda was forced to repeat whatever Darci said, slowing down the woman's nonstop patter in an attempt to say something semi-manageable for Russ and the high-tech equipment to understand. Miranda was amazed Puff hadn't started blowing smoke and fire while screaming "Error! Error!"

Darci didn't seem to care whether Russ caught any of what she was saying. She wasn't being deliberately nasty; she was merely indifferent to his uneasiness and annoyance. Either way, neither Russ nor Darci was happy with the time it was taking and ten minutes into the tour of the Becker Gallery, Russ had had enough.

"You two go on. I'm going to hang out in

front of the 'new, new' Impressionists and see if I can be impressed," he growled.

Miranda followed the fast-moving, fast-talking Ms. Becker while she considered the merits of straying from her lifelong adherence to nonviolence in favor of smacking Darci and telling her to quit behaving like a spoiled pre-adolescent and show some empathy for other people. "Other people" in this instance being Russ, who had obviously clamped down on his own temper by remembering that he needed Darci in order to achieve a wonderful exhibition of Kam's works for the Durani family.

Miranda held off from ranting or physical violence by remembering the same thing. It was quickly apparent that the Becker Gallery was a fantastic venue. It was spacious yet intimate. The colors on the wall did not distract or detract from the artwork. Miranda wasn't thrilled with the paintings Russ had called the new, new Impressionists but the arrangement of the works and the background made her want to stop and give each painting a second or third glance.

Even the benches had been carefully placed so they wouldn't turn into obstacles for art lovers who wanted to tour while other guests took the time to sit and chat. The gallery's peaceful quality—amazing since the owner and designer, Ms. Darci Becker, was anything but calm—would offer the perfect backdrop for pieces like *Silent Sunlight*.

Miranda also conceded that Darci's organizational skills could whip a small country into shape. The two women discussed the details of transporting Kamyar's works and the way she intended to publicize the exhibition, beginning with a gala opening just before the Fourth of July weekend. Darci told Miranda who would print the invitations, who would cater and who would play music. Miranda came close to asking if Darci intended to include a color code for the women's dresses but thought that might come across as sarcastic and while she had no desire to make Darci a best buddy, she didn't want her for an enemy.

Darci was a smart, interesting person. She was actually starting to make Miranda's "likable acquaintance" list until she began the barrage of questions about Russ. Russ had called her inquisitive. Miranda would have said nosy.

"So what's it like working with Russell on inventory while fighting over ownership?"

"*We're* not fighting," Miranda replied.

"There's no point in fighting. The lawyers are fighting."

Darci's smile held a hefty dose of skepticism. "Give me a break. I already know Russ would kill for that house. He told me about the situation with the wills when he emailed to set up this meeting. He's an emailing guru, but I have to wonder about his common sense. Two master's degrees, one doctorate, speaks more languages than most people even know exist, and he nearly gets himself blown up. Now he delivers furniture and writes emails. A terrific way to spend his life, don't you agree? Although, I guess if he gets the house he can stop delivering furniture and just hunker down and write emails all day."

Miranda hadn't spent four years in a college drama department and six years in professional theater circles without learning a thing or two about divas. They wanted confrontation regardless of reason and they would continue to hound and harass until that confrontation exploded and the opposition surrendered. However, Miranda was also aware that she needed to maintain a degree of diplomacy in order not to jeopardize the exhibition.

"No offense, but why did you bother to ask? I mean, about how we're getting along?"

Darci's elegant eyebrows rose. "I wanted to see how much *you* want that house—which you've been very good at hiding. I find that quite intriguing."

Miranda took a breath and counted to a fast ten. "Well, *you* may find it intriguing but it's not. I want the house—I adored Miss Virginia. So, apparently, did Russ."

"Yeah. Right. Whatever. So, how long have y'all been dating?"

"We're not dating."

"Oh, give it up, girl. I see how you look at him and how he looks at you."

I don't know how you can see anything, Miranda thought. *You're too busy rattling off whatever comes into your mind to notice what other humans are doing.*

Aloud she repeated, "We're not dating. We're doing inventory and arranging for Kam's exhibition. Period."

Darci switched to a slightly new tack. "Inventory. Now that truly is interesting. I heard you all were searching for an Auttenberg which, if found, would rock the art world to its greedy core. Don't worry, Miranda, I may be a fast talker but I'll keep mum on that possibility. Although from what I hear it isn't exactly news. I think half of Birmingham knows. You do realize that everyone and his brother wants to get his hands on an Auttenberg—including me? I stand a better chance of snagging it if one of you guys finds it. Believe me, I'll give you a great price."

Miranda was glad to leave the topic of her relationship with Russ—whatever that was—but she wasn't thrilled to know another party was keeping tabs on the hunt for an Auttenberg. Virginia's house was becoming even more vulnerable to treasure hunters. If someone was determined, he or she would find a way in even if it meant short bites at the apple. A thief could set the alarm ringing but do a quick search before the police arrived. She tried to push that thought out of her mind.

"So, Darci, since you doubtless know a ton more about Auttenberg than I do, has there been any talk in art circles about what he might have painted in the camps? I know his earlier work—before he was imprisoned—was saved. A buddy of mine who manages a gallery in Manhattan told me that five of Auttenberg's paintings are in museums and he'd heard that a private collector owns two. But anything Auttenberg painted at Terezin is a mystery. I did see a very poor photo of a piece called *Performance* on a blog but there's no word on where that ended up."

Darci nodded. "There's talk, but it's purely speculative. I know dealers who spend half their time scouring websites for the latest theory as to where works of any of the concentration-camp artists might be. I may become one of them. This much is certain, Miranda, if an Auttenberg does pop up in that house, you're set for life. Of course, that works for Russell, too." She smiled before making a U-turn back to the topic of Russ and Miranda. "If *you* win, I'd suggest you immediately sell and get a loft in Manhattan. I'm not quite buying this tale that there's nothing going on between you and Russ, but take a friendly warning. He wasn't exactly ready to settle down before he went tearing off to Afghanistan and I can't see that changing, especially with a woman who's in theater." She laughed. "Not to mention how ticked off he'd be if you inherit!"

Miranda didn't want to continue this conversation but she tried to keep things light. "Well, I could always sell to him, couldn't I? As a consolation?"

Darci laughed. "I'd buy tickets to watch that negotiation!" She sighed. "I do have to admit Russell is a catch. Honestly, if he ever gets to the point where he isn't impersonating a hermit, I might consider giving him another run—even with his messy hearing issues. But you, Ms. Nolan, might as well forget any hopes of landing Russell Gerik. It's too funny. Here you stand…a singer, just like his mom, plus you're his opponent in the biggest estate debacle of the decade."

With the conversation going off the rails, Miranda realized that out-diva-ing the diva wasn't going to work. She was already tired of trying to figure out what game Darci Becker wanted to play, and she was in no mood to argue or spend the next hour avoiding verbal traps. But those last comments about Russ couldn't be left standing.

"Um, excuse me, Darci, but aren't you engaged?"

"Oh, I'm *always* engaged," she said, smiling. "Engaged isn't married."

"O-kay. Well, not to sound defensive where Russ is concerned, but 'giving him another run' sounds like hauling a horse to the racetrack and slapping on the saddle. I can't see Russ taking to the bit all that readily."

"I don't know about that. I'm pretty good

at lassoing ponies who try to escape into the hills."

Any response Miranda might have made to this outrageous and nonsensical statement was derailed by the sound of the *1812 Overture* blasting from Darci's cell phone. Miranda bit her lip as she listened to the cannons and brass section blaring the finale. Trust Darci Becker to choose a ring tone that evoked armies reigning victorious.

Miranda's own cell phone began ringing in the midst of Darci's unabashedly loud conversation. "I told you not to call when I'm doing business. Do I call *you* in the middle of surgery? Oh, you're going *into* surgery so we're canceling? Who the heck schedules surgery on a Friday night?"

Miranda had programmed her own phone to play the last eight measures of the sweetest song in *Les Misérables*—"Castle on a Cloud," sung by the child Cosette. She smiled at how their choice of music matched their differences in temperament. "Hello?"

Miranda wished she could change places with Darci's caller when the person on the other end turned out to be Farrah.

"Miranda? I'm just calling to remind you about the get-together this evening."

"Get-together?"

A sigh from Farrah. "You forgot, didn't you? I knew it. I *told* Tim you'd forget."

"Sorry, Farrah. It's been a very long week and a very long day and it's turning into a very long hour."

"Well, it's not too late. You've got about ninety minutes before anyone arrives. That should be plenty of time for you to get home, do your makeup and find something pretty to wear."

"Hold up a sec. The *one* thing I do remember is that this was supposed to be a small get-together as in you and me and Dad and maybe your catering partner. Did I miss something?"

Silence. "Well, yes, it did start out that way, but I found this great new recipe book at a flea market and I had to try it out. Next thing you know I had all this food! I can't let it go to waste. I've been frantically calling people. I'm making these marvelous little cheese appetizers and an Italian crème cake. I just know you're going to stuff yourself silly."

"Farrah, I'm in the middle of trying to work something out for a gallery showing and I'm with someone."

"Well, bring her."

Miranda inhaled and prayed for patience.

"Not her. Him. You and Dad were briefly introduced at the Trussville Fair. Russ Gerik. Miss Virginia's other legatee in the estate battle."

"Oh, wow. Talk about awkward! But maybe this is good. You're welcome to ask Russ if he'd like to join us. Maybe we can soften him up about the will?"

Darci had finished her own call and was unabashedly eavesdropping.

"I don't think any discussion of the estate is a great idea, Farrah," Miranda said quietly. "But I might ask him anyway since this has now turned into a party. I'll see you in an hour or so."

Miranda ended the call and Darci wasted no time. "Did I hear *party?*"

"Yes."

"And you get a plus one?"

"Yes."

Darci smiled. "I'm free now that my intended is stuck at the hospital for half the night. Do I rate an invite?"

"What?"

"I love parties, and I've heard about your stepmom's talents in the kitchen. They rival mine in the gallery. Actually, this is perfect. I haven't been thrilled with my current caterer. This would be a nice chance to snag Farrah's business. Maybe *she* could do the Durani exhibition!"

Miranda was reeling from the boldness it took to basically wangle an invitation from a person one had just met, but she figured it wouldn't hurt to keep on Darci's good side. Not to mention Darci could latch on to whichever eligible bachelors Farrah had invited and let Miranda eat in peace. A win-win.

"Fine. You're invited. Give me your cell and I'll type in the address."

Darci nodded. "Fabulous. Okay, back to business for a few minutes before I run home and find something gorgeous to wear. You've seen the space and heard the who's who and the what's what for the reception. I guess we can call it quits once you tell me whether this is what y'all had in mind for Kamyar's works."

Miranda pushed all thoughts of the evening ahead out of her head and was absolutely honest. "I think the Becker Gallery will be perfect and I'm sure the Durani family will be really pleased with all the arrangements."

She and Darci headed back to the bench where Russ was still sitting, gazing at a work that appeared to have been finger painted by a manic five-year-old. He glanced at the two women and stood, shaking his head in sheer disgust. "I don't get it. Really. I thought the world of art had gotten beyond this kind of junk. This sells?"

Darci grinned at him and for once spoke slowly enough so that the Dragon could translate. "You're very astute. It *is* junk. But I've got a buyer who's about to shell out two-hundred grand for it so I'm keeping that opinion to myself."

After handshakes all around, Miranda and Russ left the gallery. Miranda was exhausted and irritable from her conversation with Darci and unsure about whether to ask Russ to come over to the Nolan house. She stayed silent until she and Russ were in her car, then turned to him. But before she had a chance to say a word, he said, "She's a trip, isn't she. And no, that was not a question. She's annoying and tiring and she also has the best eye of anyone on the planet for what works in that gallery. It's like watching someone with multiple personality disorder run for president. Believe it or not, when she's holding an exhibition she's quite professional and almost as snooty as an auctioneer at Sotheby's. Did she drive you completely crazy?"

Miranda nodded. "She did. But she had some truly brilliant ideas for how to best show Kam's work. Abra and Yusuf will be thrilled." She inhaled.

"But?"

"Oh, well. Semidifferent topic. It's just… my stepmother was supposed to be having a small family dinner but it's turned into one of her bashes and Darci just wangled an invitation. Farrah wanted me to ask you but I'll admit, I'm hesitating."

Russ scowled. "Why? Afraid the fine folks there won't be able to deal with the deaf guy and you'll be embarrassed?"

If Miranda hadn't been tired and cranky after teaching and dealing with Darci she might have provided a more diplomatic response. Instead, she angrily burst out, "What is it with you? I was hesitating because I didn't want you to have to deal with what you call 'fine folks' who, knowing Farrah, will be some of the most boring, egotistical people on the planet. And now they'll be joined by the tempestuous Ms. Becker. But you, Russ Gerik, are too touchy to even contemplate the possibility that I might be shielding a friend from having a miserable time. You *really* need to get over yourself!"

Miranda stopped, horrified that she'd let her temper rule her words. She glanced at Russ, sitting silently in the passenger seat, his Dragon software picking up each word. She tried to figure out how best to apologize.

He stared at her for a long moment while they waited at a red light. Finally he said, "It's green. You can go."

"Uh, thanks."

He suddenly began to laugh. "You're not so bad in the biting-off-heads department yourself. I'd say that got me back for my comments the first day I met you."

Miranda groaned. "I am *so* sorry. I mean, it's true what I said about Farrah's guests and my reasons for debating about asking you, but telling you to get over yourself was uncalled-for. I blame it all on the blue paint dripping into my brain, and trying to sidestep Ms. Becker's verbal traps."

Russ shook his head. "No. You were right. I had no business jumping to conclusions and I can get pretty touchy. I'm the one who should apologize." He grinned. "And the blue is quite decorative."

She chuckled. "Courtesy of Yasmin Durani, who was madly flinging paint on everything and everyone today. I could tell she was having the time of her life."

"If it makes you feel any better, I ended up with rainbow-colored hair more than once when Kam was on a roll. I used to hope he'd be in the mood for black ink illustrations only." He paused, then asked, "So? *Am* I invited? If nothing else, I'd love the chance to taste the results of Farrah Nolan's prowess in the culinary arts."

Miranda glanced over at him as she navigated her way through a convoy of slow-moving sedans determined to use a non-existent middle lane. "Seriously? You want to go?"

He smiled. "Well, someone needs to keep you from blowing blue-painted steam at all these boring, distinguished fine folks, not to mention Darci, who needs to stay happy for the Durani exhibition. Who better to do that than the man who needs to get over himself?"

CHAPTER FOURTEEN

FARRAH NOLAN HAD been right. Her new recipes were delicious and Miranda had quickly achieved new heights of sheer gluttony. She helped herself to a third serving of the "little cheese appetizers" and the small stuffed mushrooms and the healthy crisp veggies waiting to be dunked into the unhealthy but delicious dip and tried to gauge how many calories she could consume and still fit into Miami Montreville's black leather spy suit in a couple of weeks.

Miranda waved at Dave Brennan, Brett and Cort and two men she didn't know. George Miller was happily chatting up Darci and hadn't approached Miranda apart from a "Hi. How are you?" when she and Russ first arrived. Russ was currently in a corner conversing with Miranda's dad via the Dragon and some major hand waving.

She turned from the hors d' oeuvres table with the intention of joining Russ and Tim but was stopped by George and Darci. George handed her a bourbon on the rocks and asked if she had any idea as to when she and Russ would be through with the inventory.

"Is there a court date for the contested estate?" he added, leaning toward her.

Miranda set the glass down on the nearest table, picked up the lemonade she'd just refilled and wondered if it would be considered rude to simply scream, *Go away!*

Instead, she politely responded. "I have no answers, George. Trying to organize the last seventy years of someone's life is tricky and time-consuming. Russ and I are sorting and labeling to make it easier for a real appraiser to find anything valuable. But I'm also busy working at the children's theater and trying to fit in some classes. As to court dates? I haven't heard a word."

"Classes?" Cort had joined their conversation just in time to hear Miranda's last comment.

"Yep. Classes."

"In what?" Darci asked. "I thought you were teaching classes, not taking them. Or did you sneak into a mini-summer-graduate course somewhere?"

"I *am* teaching. I'm also trying to keep my

own skills up and I found a place that has a vocal coach as well as dance for adults. Plus, I took a crash course in…"

"In what?" Cort asked. "Diving? Scuba? Mountain climbing? Hang gliding?"

Miranda chuckled. "Nothing quite so strenuous. I recently graduated from the crammin' three weekend course in ASL at The Cooper School. Actually, they *were* strenuous— just not physically. My brain was in constant overdrive."

"ASL?" George asked.

"American Sign Language," Darci said drily.

George seemed puzzled. Then he glanced across the room as the light dawned. "Ah. I get it. Russ Gerik?"

Miranda kept her temper and did not reply, *None of your business*. Instead she calmly explained that yes, she had taken the lessons partly to communicate with Mr. Gerik while they worked at Virginia's but also because she had a non-hearing child at the children's theater and she hoped to encourage their board of directors to reach out to more non-hearing children. Plus Jesse was a cool kid and she liked "chatting" with him as best she could.

There were nods all around except from

Darci, who sniffed. "Sounds lovely, Miranda. I'm sure that *one* child really appreciates your efforts." Her amusement grew. "I'm sure Russ appreciates them far more."

Cort came to the rescue. "My soon-to-be sister-in-law isn't totally deaf but she lost a lot of hearing after a major illness, so our whole family is looking into schools. We figured it'd be easier at family gatherings to keep her in the loop. So you liked this Cooper School?"

Miranda nearly hugged Cort in gratitude. She began to explain the methods used, at least by Dr. Vinny, and managed about two sentences before she was interrupted. This time the culprit wasn't Darci. It was Farrah, playing the good hostess and ushering her guests toward a huge round table in the center of the dining room laden with heavier fare that no one really needed after devouring appetizers for the past hour.

Miranda quietly told Cort to give her a call and she'd provide him with the particulars on the Cooper School. She headed toward her father and Russ, who were ignoring Farrah's efforts to herd any and all strays to gather, but Farrah grabbed her arm before she'd managed more than three steps.

"Miranda? Tim and your friend are being

rude. They've been talking only to each other since y'all got here. Please get them to join everyone, would you? It looks so uncomfortable having these little clutches when I'm about to serve the main courses. Tim will listen to you."

Miranda stifled a sigh and nodded, reluctantly accepting the assignment. She'd barely reached her father when he stood up and gave her a quick hug. "I know. Don't tell me. We need to be good boys and go join the others."

Miranda grinned. "You know your charming wife well, don't you?"

He smiled. "I love her and she has many wonderful traits, not the least of which is her ability to wander into a kitchen and come out with a meal rivaling the best French chefs, but her insistence on being the perfect hostess does occasionally drive me batty. I wince every time I realize she talked me into buying a table worthy of King Arthur and his knights."

Russ had followed most of the conversation on the Dragon. "What's up?"

"We've all been summoned to the center of the dining room to gorge and presumably engage in one huge discussion on whatever topic gets voted most interesting." Miranda pointed to the chairs that had been swiftly placed around the table by George and the two nameless bachelors. "Whoa! It looks like a séance."

"Come on, kids," Tim said. "Food and Farrah wait for no one."

Darci hadn't endeared herself to Miranda at the gallery but Miranda's opinion about the woman nearly made another abrupt switch to best friends forever when Darci echoed Miranda's last statement.

"Whoa! All we need is a happy medium and we can have a séance!"

Farrah didn't seem offended. She took a sip of wine and proclaimed, "That's a great idea! Maybe Miranda could summon Miss Virginia's spirit and find out where she stowed those priceless works of art?"

Russ's Dragon was too far away to pick up Farrah's comment, but the look on Miranda's face told him something was not right. He handed her the device and whispered, "What's wrong?"

She quickly used the Dragon to text an abbreviated version of Farrah's suggestion. His eyes narrowed and he spoke up, saying, "Excuse me, Mrs. Nolan, but that's a myth. Rumors only. That house has been searched

on numerous occasions and there's not a hint
of anything other than sentimental value to
those who loved Miss Virginia."

Farrah plowed right on. "Well, maybe Virginia wrote something in one of her diaries
about where those paintings could be hidden?"

"Diaries?" Brett asked. "I thought she only
wrote about the concentration camp."

"No one knows," Farrah said. "But the
journals are the only things Miranda and Russ
have managed to organize so far." She looked
directly at Miranda. "Now if y'all could just
get Virginia's kitchen pulled together like
that, I'll bet you could find some amazing old
things like madelin tins or cherry pitters or
a really good antique coffee grinder. I could
use all of the above."

Miranda vowed to keep any future discov-
eries a secret from Farrah and the world. As
she pondered the merits of gagging her stepmother with a scarf, she said, "Virginia did
leave some diaries. But there are no 'Aha!'
revelations pointing the way to nonexistent
treasure. I do think an historian would find
the diaries interesting and I plan to donate
them to the Holocaust museum if they're ever
legally mine." She glanced at Russ, who nod-

ded. "Russ feels the same." She shook her head. "It's very sad. Virginia had a horrible life in the camps. It's amazing she was still so gentle and kind."

Miranda wasn't sure if she'd deflected the talk away from treasure, but her father winked and added, "Virginia and Farrah would have gotten along beautifully. Both of them make Julia Child look like a lightweight in the kitchen. Which reminds me—I have an announcement to make. Farrah is negotiating with one of the local cable stations to host a food show!"

The ruse worked. "Farrah! That's awesome!" Darci squealed. "Will you be cooking or are you having guest chefs? Tell us all about it! Maybe we could do an episode at the gallery? Part of an exhibition? I've got this wacky artist who lives in Atlanta who does nothing but paintings of food, but they're really good. This could be a marvelous way to show them!"

The conversation quickly turned to the ever-popular topics of food and reality television shows featuring celebrity chefs, and then it shifted to a news story that had been taking Birmingham by storm—the possibility of a casino right outside the city. Every one of

Farrah's guests had an opinion on the merits of legal gambling versus the consequences for persons who already had addiction issues. The only other mildly personal question came from George, who mumbled around a full mouth of broccoli casserole. "Miranda, you mentioned dance classes. Could you give me the name of the studio? I have a college-age sister who's been looking for a place to take adult ballet."

"Magic City Academy. Lots of info on their website but I'm actually taking some classes in the morning so I could pick up a brochure if you'd like."

"That'd be great. Thanks. So, tell me, I seem to remember some talk about your career at Farrah's last party. Are you still doing a spy movie?"

Darci gasped. "You're doing a movie? When, where, what!"

"The when is right after the Fourth. The where is Manhattan and the what is *The Agency,* which is supposed to be this super-duper spy outfit that makes all the other initialed services look like elementary school monitors."

"Fabulous!" Darci exclaimed. "Do you make a pot load of money?"

"I'm not in the star bracket, Darci, so I'm not making out like the proverbial bandit. It's a living and if it does well then residuals will be very helpful. But I'm *really* excited about doing this. The script is great and my character has a blast doing bizarre stunts." She grinned. "I hope the studio has insurance."

The talk shifted back to whether Farrah would have a script for her TV show or if she'd wing it. Miranda mused that if Farrah asked Darci to be her sidekick she wouldn't have to worry about any awkward silences.

Miranda scooped up a spoonful of the homemade raspberry sherbet and refrained from voicing that particular opinion. She glanced at Russ, who was eyeing the Dragon with wry amusement.

"What?"

"The battery died."

Forget to charge it? she signed. *Want me to find an outlet?*

"I didn't forget," he said quietly. "Just didn't get a chance between the gallery and coming here. Frankly, I'm not terribly concerned. The conversations with the few folks I had earlier didn't thrill me—apart from a great discussion I had with your father about the history of Sharia law in Afghanistan and the perversion of that law by the Taliban. We also discovered we're both model-train nuts."

Miranda grinned at him, then signed, *There are times when talk is overrated. This evening is a great example.*

He nodded.

Miranda dug her fork into a creamy pasta dish, then stopped before taking a single bite. What was it *really* like not to be able to hear that talk, even if the conversation wasn't funny or interesting or intelligent? She suddenly needed to know. Using her imagination as an actress went only so far.

Miranda placed the fork back onto her plate, pulled out her cell phone and stuck in the earbuds. She smiled at the guests. "Uh, folks, I don't want to appear rude but I need to learn this song so I'm bowing out of the conversation for a bit."

It wasn't a complete lie. She did need to learn the song. Perhaps for an audition next fall—or a year from next fall.

The earbuds acted like industrial strength interceptors. They didn't allow even white noise to seep through. For the first few minutes, the absolute silence was restful. She was able to focus on her own thoughts and on the visuals around her, picking up the emotions from people's facial expressions instead of listening to words that she now suspected were filled with lies or subtext. Her olfactory senses kicked into high gear. She could smell the nutmeg and cinnamon flavors in the cold squash casserole. She could taste the white mustard in the potato salad and the basil and thyme in the pasta.

After approximately fifteen minutes of total silence, Miranda realized she was starting to breathe harder. She was sweating even though the Nolans' air conditioner was set to sixty-eight. Her palms were wet and she was having difficulty swallowing that nutmeg-and-cinnamon-scented casserole. Her stomach veered from a cramping sensation to a roller coaster dip. Her eyelids were even starting to twitch. She felt hemmed in by the room itself, as though she'd suddenly fallen into a world walled off from the rest of humanity. She had to stop herself from jumping out of the chair and running into the street.

How did Russ and Jesse live with this? Hour after hour, minute by minute. It must be worse for Russ since he'd been much older when he lost his hearing. Miranda believed she would've been institutionalized in less than a day.

Russ glanced at her as though reading her thoughts. He reached over and patted her hand, then signed. *Not as easy as it appears, is it?*

How did you know?

He winked. "The volume on your phone's keypad is at zero."

She bit her lip, embarrassed that he'd caught on to her attempt to experience his world. But he signed, *Thanks.*

They smiled at each other. The silence that separated them from the rest of Farrah's guests was comfortable and peacefully intimate. Miranda continued to keep the earbuds in while they finished the meal.

After the Italian crème cake and coffee were served, Russ signed to Miranda, *Farrah wouldn't ever be my choice in a wife, but I'd hire her as my personal chef any day of the week.*

Miranda grinned before finishing every bite of a large slice. After she placed her fork on the plate, she glanced over at Russ, who nodded and signed, *Time to split.*

She removed the earbuds and announced, "Not to be party poopers, everybody, but I've got to get up early for Saturday dance classes and Russ has some deliveries scheduled for the morning. I'm his ride tonight, so we need to make tracks. Farrah, this was beyond delectable. If you want backers for that TV show, all you'll need to do is let them taste this cake. Or anything else you served tonight. I'll be home a bit later on. I'm going to grab Phoebe out of the yard and let her ride with us, maybe run her around the park after I drop Russ off."

She and Russ rose and waved goodbye. Russ headed for the front door and Miranda took off for the guest bedroom, where she'd left her purse and keys.

Farrah followed. "Miranda, I'm sorry if talking about Miss Virginia's diaries upset you. Tim didn't originally tell me it was a state secret and I thought everyone already knew you'd been reading them."

"It's okay, Farrah. I tend to get a little emotional about Virginia especially when she becomes the topic of conversation. But there was no harm done."

"Oh, good." Farrah paused for a moment before adding, "This young man, Russ. He seems a bit odd. Kind of aloof or detached. Are you two an item? I don't mean to interfere but he doesn't seem your type."

Miranda inhaled and counted to ten. It

didn't help. "Russ is not odd, aloof or de-tached. He's not going to come across as the life of the party when ninety-nine percent of the people here don't sign or don't slow down enough for his voice-recognition software to translate. Plus, not to sound cranky, but I don't have a 'type' and it makes me crazy when that excuse is used by casting directors bumping me from good roles or anyone in-quiring about my dating habits. I know this is a celebrity cliché but Russ and I are really just friends."

She grabbed her bag and was out of the bedroom before Farrah had a chance to re-cover. Russ was already at the front door. Miranda gave him the keys and signed that she'd meet him at the car once she released Phoebe from the backyard. Russ and Tim shook hands and Miranda gave her dad a hug. She thanked Farrah for the exquisite meal, then called out, "Nice seeing everyone. Bye."

"Y'all are leaving so early," Darci said. "Got a romantic night planned?"

"Maybe someone does!" Miranda quipped with a perkiness she didn't feel, mentally putting Darci back onto her "avoid like the plague" list. "As for me? I need to come up with brilliant dance steps for brilliant kids before crashing."

She promptly performed a short but perfect vaudevillian-style shuffle off to buffalo and made her exit to the sounds of applause and light laughter.

CHAPTER FIFTEEN

THE SATURDAY MORNING adult advanced dance classes were so tough that Miranda had been forced to use every ounce of technique she owned to master the combinations in contemporary and ballet. She was exhausted by the time she got to tap and was relieved to be able to take it easier.

The only problem was that Miranda finally had space to think about the insanity of the past couple of weeks. Much of the confusion swirling in her brain seemed to be centered around Russ Gerik. Or rather, Miranda reflected while executing a few shim-shams and cramp rolls, the recent comments about Russ Gerik. Comments which had come from four different women.

Candy Cassidy had been simplicity itself. *"Break Russ Gerik's heart and I'll break your legs."*

Darci had been snide and almost creepy.

"If he ever gets to that point I might consider giving him another run."

Farrah hadn't exactly embodied the soul of tact with *"Are you two an item...he doesn't seem to be your type."*

Abra had been fairy dust and flowers. *"You and Russ are perfect for each other!"*

Miranda had to wonder what Abra saw that no one else could see—including Miranda and Russ. They disagreed about the politics of war. Neither was willing to give up the inheritance. Miranda was a singer and Russ had been abandoned by a mother hoping to become a star. He'd also never be able to hear her sing. Miranda couldn't forget the look on his face when he'd watched her perform for barely a moment during the first day of the theater camp.

On the other hand, they both loved dogs. A plus. They shared the same taste in art and neither was willing to suffer dishonesty. Perhaps the most important trait—whatever it was—had been the something that had made both Russ and Miranda love, and be loved, by Miss Virginia.

Miranda wasn't ready to deal with her feelings about Russ and she didn't really want a myriad of opinions thrust at her by women she barely knew, even though she'd felt an immediate bond with Abra and was aware she needed to establish a better relationship with her stepmother. Not to mention the fact that once she was back in Manhattan *no* one's opinion would matter—including her own.

The tap instructor yelled, "Once more!" Grateful for the distraction, Miranda focused on the routine, determined to nail every step. She finished class, walked back to the dressing room, changed and was out and heading for the afternoon session at Virginia's in less than twenty minutes, which meant she was about fifteen minutes early.

No cars were in sight. Miranda wasn't sure if Russ had been able to pick his car up from the shop earlier. If not, he would have just walked over and gone inside.

The front door was unlocked so she assumed Russ had already gotten the key from a paralegal. She didn't see him in the living room and she didn't hear any sounds from the kitchen, but Russ might've gone out back to play with Spero.

Miranda dropped her bag and headed toward the kitchen. She'd barely made it halfway across the room before she heard a scuffling noise behind her. Fabric was thrown over her head. Someone grabbed her arms and dragged her back a few feet, then shoved her inside the closet. The door slammed shut and was locked with a click. Miranda felt claustrophobic and sick to her stomach until she was able to struggle out of what turned out to be a tote bag, wrenching her neck and shoulders in the process. She took several huge breaths in the musty space and started coughing.

"At least it's canvas and not plastic," she muttered, trying to keep terror at bay. She waited a moment until the nausea and the urge to faint had passed. Then she started screaming for help as loudly as she was able.

A few moments later, she let her voice rest. "Miranda, what are you doing?" she scolded herself. "Who exactly is going to hear you? Russ can't. And the neighbors are too far away. You are so dumb. Why didn't you get Phoebe after class? You had the time. She would've bit the intruder and charged out of here to bring help!"

She tried to control the second onset of panic that hit when she realized she might be trapped for days. After a few minutes of hysterically banging on the walls, kicking the door and digging through the old coats in the hope of finding something useful, like a crowbar—"or a rocket launcher" she muttered—she stopped. "This is stupid. You are not a stupid person. Now stop and think and quit acting the maiden in distress." She almost smiled. "You're about to play a superspy. What would Miami Montreville do?"

Talking aloud gave Miranda the calm she needed to consider her options and bringing up her future alter ego reminded her of a past character. She'd played a hostage in a TV movie about a bank heist. The show had veered more toward comedy than high drama and the writers had come up with various wacky ways for Miranda's character to escape, but the solution had been simple. Pick the lock. Miranda—always diligent when researching a role—had found at least five different ways to escape. The easiest was the credit-card technique. Unfortunately, her cards were in her bag, along with her cell phone. But the second best method was very low-tech, very old-fashioned and usually got the job done.

Miranda reached up and pulled a bobby pin out of her bun. It wasn't normally the way she wore her hair but the metal pins kept flyaway strands off her face during dance class.

It took some doing, but she was finally able to maneuver the pin into position and open the door. "Gotta love old houses with lousy locks!" she muttered.

She quickly ran to her bag and grabbed her cell phone.

Within seconds she was talking to Officer Hernandez.

"I almost hate to ask," he said.

"Oh, yeah," Miranda replied. "Another break-in."

"I'll drive over but it's going to take at least twenty minutes. Is that okay? Should I see if another officer is closer?"

"That's fine. I'd rather wait and see a familiar face."

"I'll be there soon. Stay outside. Better still, go to a neighbor's if anyone is home."

She hung up and went outside to wait. Ten seconds later she called her dad's house and asked if Farrah would mind popping Phoebe into her car and bringing her over to Virginia's. She skipped any explanations about burglars and closets.

"I'd get her myself but I'm waiting for, uh, Russ, and I don't want to leave the house."

"No problem," Farrah said. "You caught

me just as I was leaving, so I'll be there in a few minutes, dog in hand. Or leash, anyway."

About five minutes later, Farrah pulled into Virginia's driveway and Miranda was reunited with her buddy. "I can't stay, Miranda, I'm meeting a client in about twenty minutes."

"That's fine. I'm just grateful you didn't mind bringing Phoebe. See you later."

Farrah waved and drove down the street. Miranda immediately felt safer having the small but protective dog by her side.

Six minutes later Miranda spotted Russ rounding the corner of the block with Spero ambling happily at his side. He picked up the pace until he was on the sidewalk in front of Virginia's house. The dogs immediately began their greeting dance.

Russ took one look at her and asked, "What's wrong?"

How do you know something is wrong? she signed.

"Because you have as much color in your face as the curb here."

Ah. Good point. Miranda walked up the driveway and sank down onto the porch steps. *We had a visitor.*

"Again?" Russ quickly pulled the Dragon out of his pack and handed it to her.

"Again. Only this time I was here. The door was unlocked and I figured you'd arrived early, so I went in. About two minutes later I was stuffed into the hall closet with a tote bag over my head. My neck twisted twenty ways to Sunday trying to remove the silly thing and I think I need a large aspirin." She pretended nonchalance and held out the bag, which she planned to give to Hernandez as some kind of evidence. She stared at it and mused, "It's a nice bag. Sadly, it's generic. Not a single logo to be seen. Looks pricey, though. I guess it could start a new trend. What the well-prepared burglar carries to stun his victims."

"Miranda, you're rambling. Are you in shock? Are you hurt? What can I do? Maybe hot coffee? You're scaring me."

Miranda stared at him. "I don't know." Her brain silently said, *Liar. What Russ can do is hold you in his arms for the next few minutes and keep you safe.*

For a moment it seemed Russ might do exactly that. He reached out and took her hand in his, then moved closer.

Hernandez pulled up into the driveway.

The moment was lost. Russ dropped her hand as he watched Spero and Phoebe immediately encircle the officer.

Hernandez finished patting the dogs and joined Miranda and Russ on the porch. Miranda shook his hand. "Why do we keep bothering to lock and arm this place? Seems a waste of both our time and the burglar's."

Hernandez smiled. "If nothing else, at least you know he or she has been here."

"Well, sadly, this time so was I."

"What?"

"I got here early and thought Russ might have already gone inside."

"Why did you think I was here?" Russ asked. "Didn't you get my text?"

"Oh, shoot. You called?"

He nodded. "I did. I wanted to let you know that even though I'd be late, you could still meet the paralegal du jour and start working."

"I didn't even check my messages this morning. I drove straight here from class and figured I'd spend some quality time on the porch just drinking in the atmosphere. But the door was open. It didn't occur to me that anything was wrong, although by now anything out of the ordinary should be a good clue to take off, screaming."

Miranda gave Hernandez the rundown, trying to pretend the whole event hadn't turned her insides into oatmeal. "Maybe we should leave a little bowl on the hall table with a note reading, 'Don't forget to leave a guest card.' We could offer free dinners or something."

Both men ignored the absurd suggestion. Hernandez gestured toward the house. "Let's go inside, if you're up to it?"

"I'm okay now."

Miranda took one step into the front hallway and immediately turned back around. "Well, well. What do you know. For once, the burglar didn't leave empty-handed."

"Uh-oh. What do you see? Or not see?"

"A box of journals from 1954. I labeled them myself. They're gone." She stifled the urge to let loose with a peal of laughter, certain it would dissolve into hysteria. "The thief is doomed for disappointment—unless he's a master chef."

"How so?"

"Because I'd mislabeled them. They're recipe books I was saving to give to my stepmother." She bit her lower lip.

Russ glanced at her. "Miranda? You're losing color again. You sure you don't need to sit?"

She shrugged. "I'm about as fine as I can be after being locked in a closet with a bag thrown over my head. Y'all know something? This whole 'come back to Alabama and inherit a house and hunt for missing art treasure in between teaching kids and avoiding thieves popping in every other day' isn't really working for me lately."

Russ bit his lip and stared at the ceiling. Hernandez smiled. "My wife would say you are a woman in serious need of a spa day."

"Your wife would be right. I like her already." Miranda closed her eyes, thought for a moment, then opened them and said, "I'm not a lawyer. My dad is, but his area is international law so we don't discuss burglaries. I'm not up on the latest legalities of interrogation—apart from what's on television shows—but I'm wondering if we can take a good look at the people who knew about these diaries."

"You want me to question some folks who might have motive and opportunity for this latest break-in?"

Miranda nodded.

"Well, I'm not an attorney, either, but if you have names I'll take them and see what can be done. They can always say 'no comment.' If anything interesting turns up I can start asking for warrants." He shook his head. "No offense but this entire business with the house has gotten ridiculous."

"None taken. Look, do y'all want to adjourn to the kitchen for some iced tea? I'm dehydrated from dance classes and the ordeal in the closet and I also need to give Phoebe some lunch."

Russ helped her brew the tea, retrieve the ice trays from the freezer and feed both Phoebe and Spero so neither dog would get jealous. Once Miranda was sipping out of a frosty glass, she felt better. She was still angry and scared, but she was thankful that the villain had chosen to lock her inside a closet rather than beat her up or shoot her.

"Ready to name names?" Hernandez asked. "Provide a little context as to why you think these might be persons of interest?"

Russ interrupted before Miranda could respond. "I'm taking the dogs into the yard to toss the Frisbee. No point in having Miranda slow things down for my software to catch. Y'all good with that?"

Miranda and Hernandez nodded. Russ opened the back door and was nearly knocked down by two anxious canines who clearly understood the word *Frisbee*.

"Ready?"

"Sure," Miranda said. "I should give this some context first. To begin with, everyone on this short list was at my stepmother's party the night of the first break-in, when she babbled on about Auttenberg's paintings. They were all aware I was staying to chat with my dad before coming here to meet Russ. Same thing for last night, when the diaries became a prime topic of conversation at another of Farrah's dinners. I also announced I was taking class this morning, again leaving the house free for someone to search."

"Got it. Go on."

Miranda hesitated. "I hate this. It feels pretty vile to accuse people. But, okay, let's start with Brett King and Cort Farber. They were the ones writing out Miss Virginia's respective wills, so they might have access to information about those paintings, assuming they really exist. Both men were also here when the alarm system was installed. They seem nice but, as we all know, greed can trump nice at any time."

"Anyone else?" Hernandez asked.

"George Miller. He's a Realtor and he's

pushy. Can't seem to get it through his head that once this house is ready to be sold he is *not* going to be named the agent—by either Russ or me. Miller was also here when the crummy alarm system was installed."

Hernandez glanced up from his notepad. "Did Miller seem interested in the diaries?"

Miranda thought about the question for a moment. "Truthfully? Just about everyone at each party was interested."

Hernandez stared at her. "You're holding back."

"Not really."

"Miranda? It's okay. No one is going to be thrown into jail today—unless we get lucky. And I'm not telling anyone who named names. Go ahead."

"Well, *maybe* Darci Becker. She knows the worth of the paintings but I just met her the other day and I don't think she knew about the artwork possibly being here. I'm also pretty sure she was at the gallery this morning. Saturdays are generally busy for art dealers."

"What about Russ?" Hernandez asked quietly.

Miranda gulped. "I didn't mention Russ. There's no way he would have done this."

She sounded defensive even to herself, and Hernandez picked up on it.

"Look, I like him, too, but he does have a lot to gain here. You're rivals for an estate that may be worth a huge sum of money. Forget the idea of a real search. Who's to say he doesn't already know where this artwork is hidden and isn't trying to scare you into giving up your claim?"

She groaned. "I really, really don't even want to contemplate that Russ could be capable of that. For whatever it's worth."

Hernandez picked up the notebook, took a last swig of iced tea and pushed his chair back. He smiled. "Truthfully? I don't believe he is. I just want you to be aware, Miss Manhattan Not-so-Tough Girl, that not everyone in the world can be trusted. Now I'm going to make a few polite inquiries as to where these people were this morning. Don't get your hopes up. It may not come to anything. Meanwhile, you and your friend Russ need to get back to the hunt, or at least the inventory, assuming you can tear him away from the dogs."

Miranda escorted the officer to the front door. "Thank you—for checking this place what seems like every other blasted day, for listening to me and just your general kindness." She took a breath. "Plus I appreciate your calling Russ a friend and not implying anything else…unlike several other people in Birmingham who are ready to carve our names in trees everywhere."

Hernandez grinned. "I didn't need to imply a thing, Miranda. You did that all on your own."

CHAPTER SIXTEEN

MIRANDA HEADED FOR the backyard, where Russ was playing with the dogs. She'd planned to join them but suddenly her legs wouldn't carry her any farther. She sank into one of the chairs on the deck and stared out across the yard. She felt confused and ill as names of possible suspects swirled through her mind. Miranda wished Ted Hernandez hadn't pinpointed the one suspect she was determined to erase from the list. She groaned. Could she rely on her intuition—or a growing friendship—that someone who had the most to gain wasn't trying to scare her away?

When she saw Russ rolling on the ground with two of the most trusting creatures on earth, her heart answered the question—a leap of faith. This man was honest. She could easily imagine Russ flat out telling her she had no right to the house since she'd been away for six years or pointing out all the ways he'd helped Virginia in that time, but he wouldn't sneak up on her and shove her into a closet. They'd met less than a month ago, but she was certain that Russ Gerik would never lie to her or deliberately hurt her.

But someone was lying.... Someone who had no qualms about hurting people. She started shivering.

Russ caught her staring at him and abruptly stopped the game. He gave the Frisbee to Spero, then joined Miranda on the deck.

"Miranda. It's okay."

"What?"

"I know you're very frightened and I simply want to tell you it's okay to feel that way."

How can you tell? she signed.

"You haven't moved an inch in the past ten minutes, you're swallowing almost nonstop and there's an expression on your face I saw more than once on soldiers back in Afghanistan. Good grief! You got locked inside a small space and you didn't know when you'd get out or what else might happen. No one expects you to behave as though this is normal. It's all right to show you're scared."

Miranda tried to nod but her neck still hurt even attempting a slight movement.

He winked at her. "Plus, I had a ton of combat training before I ever stepped foot in

Kabul. I can take down any other burglars who are crazy enough to show up today with a single karate chop before breakfast, lunch or dinner."

Miranda managed a weak smile. She signed, *Thank you.*

Russ grinned. "Speaking of lunch, would you like some Chinese food? Always helps in a crisis. I texted Won Ton Wong's while our dogs were flying through the air. Delivery guy should be here in about five minutes which should be just enough time to stop Phoebe from chasing Spero around the yard again. I'm pretty sure she doesn't even want the Frisbee. She likes to herd and Spero is more than willing to comply and play sheep. Anyway, does a little sustenance sound good?"

Miranda was finally able to laugh. *Yes! Thanks for the distraction and the offer of food.*

Russ whistled for both dogs, who joined them on the deck and lapped up two bowls of water, then patiently waited for someone to open the back door and let them inside for their well-deserved naps.

Russ led the way to the living room, where

he'd left the Dragon. "So? What did Hernandez have to say?"

"He's going to question the usual suspects," Miranda responded.

Russ raised an eyebrow. "Exactly whom are you accusing?"

She ran down the list she'd just given Hernandez. Russ nodded after each name but stopped her when she mentioned George Miller.

"I'd put him at the top of the list merely on principle—the guy's slimy."

Miranda chuckled. "Do we want to tell him that no matter who wins the estate battle, he's not setting a toe inside this house?"

"Ah, gee, it'll break his heart." He chuckled. "Believe it or not he and I were in high school together. Only guy in class who knew exactly what he wanted to do in life but even then he was voted 'most likely to end up annoying potential clients.' Wouldn't surprise me to hear that he came over on an annual basis and bugged Virginia to sell this house and name him as her agent."

"I would've bought tickets to watch Virginia deal with anyone who tried to make her sell. This house was so…her. Plus, where would she have gone? Can you see her trying to bring thirteen cats into a retirement home?"

Russ and Miranda both burst into laughter. Russ solemnly declared, "She's the one person who could've gotten away with it."

The doorbell rang and Miranda jumped to her feet.

"What?" Russ asked.

"Delivery," she said. "Which reminds me, what do you normally do? I mean about knowing when someone is at your door?"

Russ accompanied Miranda to the door, while explaining that he had a light that flashed whenever the bell rang, adding, "I'm trying to get Spero to chase his tail in circles when he hears a knock but I can't figure out how to do that without turning him into a maniac every time a squirrel throws a nut and hits the door."

Russ refused to allow Miranda to pay but graciously accepted her offer to give the delivery boy a very generous tip. "He needs the money for a new tire for his bike," Russ explained. Once the food was on the table, Spero and Phoebe flopped next to each other and promptly went to sleep, even with the tempting chicken scents wafting from the boxes. Miranda eyed them with no small amount of envy.

"Chopsticks or forks?" Russ asked.

"Forks."

"Wimp."

Miranda lifted her chin. "I'll have you know I am one tired lady. I took three impossible dance classes and was burgled and stuffed into a closet all in the same morning. I spent last week nurturing the creative beast lurking within small children. I need nourishment and I don't want to wait for it. I'm ashamed to admit I never mastered the technique and hot sauce will land on the ceiling if I try to deal with chopsticks."

Russ slid a fork across the table. "You *are* a whirlwind of activity, aren't you? Do you ever slow down and take a moment? Or are you always running around expending tons of energy. Much like Phoebe."

Miranda eyed Russ, who looked quite innocent. *Had the remark been intended as a dig? "Activity" meaning too busy to visit friends like Virginia? Too busy to connect with family? Too caught up in work to try and establish a relationship?*

Russ waited, obviously expecting her to comment.

She slowly said, "I've been accused often of trying to do about twenty things at once, to the extent that I forget to stop and notice others around me. When I didn't make it to my dad's wedding, he called the next week." Miranda hesitated. *Could she—should she—admit this to Russ?* She tilted her chin and continued. "Dad said he often wondered if I kept so busy because…I was afraid I'd die young, like my mom, and never get to accomplish all the things I wanted to—just as she didn't."

Russ remained silent for a moment, then he reached across the table and gently placed his hand over hers. "I'm sorry. I should learn to think before making comments when I don't know the background of someone's life."

"It's okay. Believe me, I've wanted to smack myself more than once for stating opinions or asking personal questions—" she smiled "—including the day I first met you."

Russ returned the smile. "Well, maybe we're both abnormally honest people who say what we think—or we haven't learned the art of diplomacy yet."

"For abnormally honest you can read 'perpetual foot in mouth disease,' in my case."

Russ grinned and moved out of emotional

territory. "Well, let's exchange the foot for something more nourishing. This should help revive you. General Tso's chicken, spicy bean curd and peppers, veggie lo mein, egg rolls— all from the kitchen of Won Ton Wong's."

Miranda dove in without hesitation. "For this I could endure a burglary on a daily basis. Almost. Now, don't take offense but I have yet to find a place here in Birmingham that serves anything truly hot and spicy. Actually the best place outside of Manhattan was this little café in Vancouver. I was there on tour and was always hoping to go back but for some reason I kept getting sent to Oklahoma or Kansas or Indiana. All lovely states except for their tornado season but none of them had Chinese food that compared to Vancouver or my favorite spot in Manhattan, China Tan's. I miss that place and I was just there a couple of weeks ago."

Russ paused then quietly asked, "So you're sticking to Manhattan? As your home, I mean."

Miranda, startled, glanced down at her food before replying, "I guess that depends on what happens here."

Russ finished a bite of egg roll. "Tell me

this, then. What will you do if it turns out you inherit this house?"

"What do you mean?"

"Exactly that. Will you sell it? Will you rent it and keep it for the day you decide to retire and enjoy a leisurely Southern life? Will you fly down from Manhattan now and again and use it as a weekender?"

"Wow. That's...direct."

"Well, didn't we both just admit to diving in and speaking our minds?"

"True. As to the house? My only answer is that I don't know yet." Miranda paused. "What about *you?* Do you want to live here?"

"Yes. If I inherit I won't sell. I'd probably quit my job at the furniture store and just hunker down and work on renovations."

Miranda thought *Hunker down as in "hide." Funny. Russ obviously believes I run away in what he calls a whirlwind of activity. I see him slowly turning into a recluse.*

Aloud she simply said, "I'd say we both have time to consider options. As far as I can tell nothing has been done to get this whole inheritance issue settled any time before next Christmas, if then."

"True. I often wonder exactly what the lawyers do that takes so long. Meantime, at least we get to enjoy the backyard for our pups—and try to make the right decisions."

Miranda nodded.

Nothing more was said about future plans. They spent the next thirty minutes enjoying the tasty Chinese food.

After Miranda placed her fork in the sink she turned to Russ. "I am replete. I am happy. My neck even feels better. Thank you."

He smiled. "Don't you want to read your fortune?"

What's the point? she signed, not quite joking. She grabbed the Dragon. "I can see it now—'House much loved. More thievery to follow.'"

"Now, now. That's not a fortune. That's plain fact. Here, try this one. Handpicked by Russell Gerik."

She broke the cookie and popped half into her mouth before unrolling the tiny piece of paper. Her eyebrows lifted and she handed the paper to Russ. He handed her his.

The two fortunes were exactly the same. "You must make a big decision soon."

Russ pursed his lips. "I'm assuming Mr. Wong's cookie is nudging me toward deciding what to do with the job offer."

Miranda decided to take the plunge. Russ

wanted direct? She'd give him direct. "I don't want to get into a big debate about U.S. military policy but I have to ask—why don't you go back to teaching?"

"Because Samford filled my job two years ago when I told them I wasn't ready to return. Understandable."

Miranda shook her head. "Russ, it's not the only game in town. Community colleges or less-than-well-funded four-year schools would love to have you. I taught part time at a community college in Queens, and I can truthfully say those are the kids—and adults—who want to learn. They don't have parents who can afford to send them off to school just so they can party. They're the students working low-paying jobs at fast food joints at all hours so they can get an education."

He didn't speak for a few moments. Finally he said, "I honestly don't know what to do. The defense job sounds really interesting."

Miranda inhaled and headed for deeper waters. "You can tell me to butt out, Russ, but it seems to me that by taking the job you're only trading one retreat for another."

"What?" He stared at her.

"You currently deliver furniture and you

don't talk to anyone. You order from the same Chinese place so often you know that the delivery kid needs a new tire. Although, that I get, since I don't cook and my idea of kitchen décor is take-out menus plastered next to the wall phone." She forced herself to continue, unsure of his reaction. "I'm honestly amazed you got the Dragon because it's been easier to withdraw from everyone around when there's no way to know what they're saying."

Russ looked down at the floor. Miranda stopped talking.

After an agony of waiting, Russ spoke. "I don't want to admit this, but you're right to some extent. I've been in the back of a furniture van for the past two years, hoping to avoid running into anyone I know who feels sorry for me or might be embarrassed because they don't sign. Part of that revolves around issues of post-traumatic stress disorder, which can affect anyone who suffers a major injury during war, even if that someone is just a lousy interpreter. In my case, survivor guilt was added to the diagnosis." He looked at the ceiling for a moment. "I'm sorry. That sounds whiney. Was it what the kids call too much information?"

"Aren't we friends by now? Or at least

friendly rivals? After all, we've endured one of Farrah's dinner parties, an afternoon at the Becker Gallery and a burglary about once a week!"

He smiled. "We're friends. You didn't even mention diving through old journals together, which reminds me—we should probably read whatever we have time for this afternoon, before our thief decides to make a repeat visit."

"We should rig up a trap. You know, glue on the floor or something." Miranda sighed. "First, though, I *do* get it, Russ. You went through a horrific experience and you have every right to find a cave and turn into a hermit. But I can't help thinking that if you take this job, you'll never leave that cave. Twenty years from now you'll still be avoiding people and your only involvement will be with reams of documents."

Russ's jaw went rigid.

Miranda took a breath and prayed she wasn't about to destroy their tentative understanding. "We've been reading the diaries of a woman who spent seventy years as a virtual recluse...a woman who missed out on seventy years of life. She had excellent reasons, but I'd hate to see that happen to you."

Russ's eyes narrowed and Miranda thought, *Now I've really done it.*

Finally, he asked, "You truly believe I'm turning myself into Miss Virginia?"

"Not completely…yet. But how often do you see the Durani family? How often do you do *anything* outside of your job that has you talking to other people?" She started to ask if he even saw his family but suddenly remembered Candy and Darci's words about the mother who'd abandoned a young Russ to become a singer and a father who died. "That day at the Trussville Fair, when you were telling me about Kam's illustration and giving me a short lecture about sign language I could tell that you have the soul of a teacher. For you not to be in front of a classroom when good teachers are so badly needed seems to me to be worse than hiding."

"Wow. You just don't hold back, do you?"

"I'm sorry. Tell me to shut up. Tell me to mind my own business. Because if you don't I'll keep on saying exactly what I think."

Russ's face turned an unbecoming red. For a few moments Miranda couldn't tell if he wanted to ask her to leave or strangle her. Then he started to laugh.

"You, Ms. Nolan, are a meddler. A blunt,

nosy, meddling noodge who is the only person in two years to let me have it with both barrels. First you tell me to get over myself and now you're verbally whapping me over the head, saying I'm about to follow in the footsteps of a very lovely but very sad lady. Right?"

She gave him a tentative smile. "Uh. Yeah. That about nails it." She paused, then jumped back into the deep end. "While I'm being a nosy noodge, I have a suggestion."

"I'm almost afraid to hear it, but go ahead."

"Well, when do you have to tell the defense contractors if you'll take the job?"

"Middle of July."

"Okay. You know a mess of languages, don't you? Including Spanish?"

"I do. Why?"

"The school where I took the ASL classes is in desperate need of a Spanish-speaking instructor. Very part-time. Just three weekends for their beginner course."

He lapsed into silence for a long moment. "Interesting. That sounds like it might be good for me. I assume classes are small?"

"Yep."

"So this would be a way to teach without, pardon the pun, signing my life away—

a chance to find out how I work with people and not furniture or documents."

Miranda started to breathe again, relieved he hadn't ripped her head off for meddling. "It would also be a wonderful thing to do. We're talkin' brownie points in heaven for this."

"Brownie points," he said wryly. "Something I can always use. Okay, I'll give this a shot. In fact, if you'll give me this Dr. Vinny's number I'll text him right now and try to set up a meeting. I might be a hermit, but I'm not one to procrastinate."

Miranda gave him the number, then excused herself to wander into the living room and begin pasting labels on a box that held lamps sans shades.

Less than ten minutes later, Russ joined her. "I like your Dr. Vinny. And he apparently likes you because when I dropped your name he texted back to say he trusted your recommendation."

"Wow! So, you're going to do it?"

"Sí! Empiezo a enseñar en dos semana." He grinned. "For you pitiful English-only speakers, roughly translated that means 'I start teaching in two weeks.'"

CHAPTER SEVENTEEN

SIXTEEN SQUEALING CHILDREN bounced up and down in sheer glee after hearing that they were about to create the Most Extraordinary Super-duper Unbelievably Amazing Kick Line in the Universe. Miranda wasn't sure she could explain *why* it was so wonderful, but she was also fairly certain none of the six- or seven-year-olds would even consider asking such a tactless and unnecessary question.

Aided by her two high-school-age counselors, Miranda managed to herd the dancers into a Rockettes-style kick line, with the shortest child in the middle. The biggest obstacle was ignoring the cries of "I'm taller 'n you!" and "Look, Miss Randi! See how high I can kick!"

"Hang on, crew! No joining of hands or arms around middles yet. Got that? Just let us figure out where you're going to stand and exactly what the height is going to be for the 'all kicks.'" She grinned. "It doesn't matter if you can kick your leg over your head. This is the Most Extraordinary Super-duper Unbelievably Amazing Kick Line in the Universe and that means *everybody* has to kick to the same height, otherwise you look sloppy. We don't want sloppy, right?"

Sixteen heads bobbed in agreement. "No" to sloppy.

Once the children had been led to their spot in line, Miranda showed them the proper way to kick, with backs straight and heads lifted. They spent the next eight minutes working on that as Miranda and her assistants patiently repeated that height didn't matter. Proper form and unity was what counted.

It wasn't until Miranda was gently placing little hands behind the backs of their fellow kickers that she realized something was very wrong with Jesse Castillo. He winced when Miranda guided his arm to the right position next to Amos MacIntyre. Jesse was wearing a long-sleeved sweatshirt so Miranda signed, *Is it okay if I roll this up?* Jesse bit his lower lip but nodded yes.

The instant she saw the bruise on his arm, right below his elbow, she knew. Someone had twisted that arm so forcefully it had nearly broken. Miranda felt a rage she'd never before experienced. She signaled to her assistants to carry on, took Jesse's hand and with a calm exterior hiding the fury burning inside headed for the hall leading to Bonnie's office.

Jesse tugged at her hand. She stopped. *Am I in trouble?* he signed.

She leaned down and gave him a quick and gentle hug. "No!" she said, then signed, *We're going to try and make things better for you, okay?*

He nodded.

Once they reached Bonnie's office Miranda asked him to stay with Miss Candy for a moment while she spoke to Miss Bonnie alone. Candy raised an eyebrow and Miranda whispered, "Possible abuse." Candy's expression remained placid but she turned from Miranda, winked at Jesse and pointed to the little cabinet across from her desk where she kept her "emergency stash." There were carob bars, trail mix for kids without nut allergies, licorice and fruit twists and gummies of all shapes and sizes. Jesse eagerly accepted a cherry-flavored all-day sucker and settled down to watch Candy type. He was in good hands.

Miranda knocked on Bonnie's door and entered after hearing a cheery "Come on in."

Bonnie glanced up from a pile of scripts on her desk. "Problems? I heard you were teaching the most extraordinary adjective-and-adverb-filled kick line today. Are they getting rowdy?"

"No. They're great and the kick line is going fine. Sadly, Jesse is *not* fine although he's a trouper. Bonnie, I want you to take a look at his arm. Possibly his back, as well, if we can check without embarrassing him. I'm almost a hundred-percent certain he's been abused."

Bonnie's eyes reflected Miranda's anger. "Willow Terence, foster mother with the IQ of a peanut?"

Miranda shrugged. "I don't know. I assume so, but he *does* have some foster siblings. I haven't met them so I have no idea if they're angels or demons. I did, however, share ASL classes with Willow. She didn't strike me as the abusive type, just, as you say, not the brightest bulb in the pack, but then, most abusers don't run around with a tattoo on their forehead reading Villain, now, do they?"

"Well, either way, he needs to be removed from the situation. Bring him in and let's see what we can find out firsthand before I call his social worker."

Miranda opened the door and waved for Jesse to join her. He politely returned the un-used portion of the lollipop to Candy, then ran to Miranda's side.

Would you show Miss Bonnie your arm? she signed.

He closed his eyes and rolled his sleeve up. Bonnie took one look and asked Miranda, "What about his back?"

Jesse's eyes were still closed and since he couldn't hear Miranda quietly said, "I could swear that's a cigarette burn on the inside of his elbow. Right there near the bruise that looks like it came from a major twist. I'm no expert but it seems to me if someone burns once they'll burn again and try to do so in spots that aren't visible under shirts." She took a breath. "Ms. Terence also happens to be a smoker." Miranda knelt down by Jesse. He opened his eyes.

Jesse? Did someone grab you really hard? she signed.

He began to cry. Soft, slow tears that broke Miranda's heart. He nodded.

Miranda glanced at Bonnie. "I don't even

want to ask about that burn mark. What do you think?"

"No. It's enough," Bonnie said. "He doesn't need to relive those moments. Do you want to ask him who did this?"

Jesse was clinging to Miranda like a fabric sheet in a dryer. "I don't think so. Not right now anyway. Maybe it's better to wait on that and just make sure he's out of that house. Apartment. Whatever. I wish I could take him back to my place after classes, except that my place is currently my dad's so I don't really have the right to impose. Maybe I could arrange with Russ to do inventory today instead of tomorrow so Jesse could stay with us while we work for a little while. I just hate the idea of Jesse being with strangers."

"I'll see if any of my social-worker friends can help. Call in a few favors." Bonnie's tone suddenly hardened. "But what's most important for now is making sure he's safe. Go ahead and take him back to class and I'll track down everyone I know who has some pull at the DHR. End of day we'll meet here. If all else fails, I'll take him home with me. I'm an emergency foster."

Miranda and Jesse made it back to the special Saturday rehearsal in time for Jesse to join the kick line. Miranda gave him a spot at the very end and told Braydon Jenkins that they'd be holding hands instead of placing them behind their backs. With the understanding some children innately possess, Braydon followed instructions without asking questions. The kick line was a roaring success, and Jesse was smiling again.

After rehearsal, Miranda and Jesse walked hand in hand back to Bonnie's office where Candy had a coloring book and some juice waiting.

Bonnie ushered Miranda into her office.

"The good news is that Willow Terence doesn't actually have custody over our young friend," Bonnie said. "In fact, she's a temporary foster. So no one has to go to Family Court to get him out of there. The bad news is that everybody who has experience dealing with special-needs kids is either out of town or taking care of a few children at once. But I talked to the folks at the DHR and managed to get myself designated as Jesse's emergency foster for tonight and Sunday."

Miranda gave a sigh of relief, slumping back in her chair. She absently chewed on the fruit twist Candy had given her just before she entered Bonnie's office.

"I'm hoping you'll also come spend the night, Miranda. Jesse's social worker agreed that he needed someone who signs around so he won't be scared. You can even bring Phoebe and I won't complain about all the fur."

Miranda grinned. "I foresee immediate bonding. I'll be lucky to have a dog I can call my own once Jesse sees her. You are awesome, Ms. Hamil."

"True." Bonnie winked at her. "But so are you. This will be great. Kids love you. You love kids. Jesse loves you. You love him. Slumber party at Bonnie's!"

"What about this afternoon? I'm supposed to do inventory at Miss Virginia's house."

Bonnie waved her hand. "Covered. I managed to call Russ, too. He's got no problem with you taking Jesse to Miss Virginia's house even though he can't be there. He said he knew Virginia would approve, as well. "

Miranda jumped up and hugged Bonnie tightly. "You're an angel."

Bonnie turned red. "I've been called many things, but that's not usually one of them." She smiled. "Thanks. Okay, brace yourself for the nasty part. Jesse needs to see a doctor—we need photos to keep him away from

Willow Terence for good. Pictures would probably help in removing her other kids, although I'm not sure how that works. Hopefully by end of Monday Jesse will have some special-needs fosters who can take him in for the next couple of months." She squinted at Miranda. "I'm forgetting something... Aha! Got it. Russ told me he'd call the law office and tell whoever's up for the day to come by with the key so y'all can get in. That's one nutty situation you guys have."

"Agreed." Miranda sank back down into her chair. "So, in between making all these arrangements, were you able to get the full scoop on Jesse's background?" she asked.

"I did. It's really tough, Miranda. Heartbreaking in the first degree. Jesse's dad was in the military, serving in Pakistan. He was killed a few years ago by a suicide bomber. The timing couldn't have been worse. Jesse's grandparents had died only six months earlier in a car wreck. Jesse's mother sank into about the deepest depression possible and when she heard that her husband was gone... well, I don't know why no one helped this poor woman, but she couldn't cope."

Bonnie paused and grabbed a tissue.

"Miranda, his mother decided to commit

suicide. No idea if she also intended to kill Jesse but she chose a method of dying that included her son, who had just turned five."

Miranda's stomach filled with acid. She didn't want to hear this. "What happened?" she asked flatly.

"She drove her car off the highway at the top of Shades Crest with Jesse strapped into the passenger seat. The driver's-side air bag was disabled, but she apparently forgot there was one on Jesse's side. The air bag saved his life but cost him his hearing. He broke a lot of bones, was in a body cast and had to stay in the hospital for about six months." Bonnie cleared her throat, grabbed extra tissues, then, shoved the box toward Miranda.

When Miranda felt capable of speech she asked, "Where did he live after he got out of the hospital?"

"When he was finally ready to be released no one could find relatives who would take him in. But he was placed in a foster home that sounded ideal. The foster mom signed, so she was able to teach Jesse. He stayed for a year until the woman found out she was having twins and told social services she couldn't keep the kids anymore. The dad had a job that kept him on the road a lot. So, long story short, Jesse was given to Willow Terence, who shouldn't be in charge of a goldfish, much less a child."

Miranda remained quiet for a few moments, absorbing the tragedy of Jesse's story. Finally she asked, "Do you know if it's true that Jesse can speak? Willow seemed to think he wasn't bright or was just being ornery."

"Well, he was five and talking in complete sentences at the time of his accident. There's no physical reason for his not being able to speak. During his stay at the hospital, a tutor taught him to read since Jesse wasn't able to go to school, but he hasn't spoken a single word since the night that car went over the railing." Bonnie wiped her eyes one last time, then waved Miranda away. "Now go tell the young Mr. Castillo that you'll both be staying at my place. Give me about five minutes and I'll meet you outside and then we'll visit the doctor's."

"Can we do a tour of a store or two?" Miranda asked. "There are a few things I think he'll need for the next two nights."

Bonnie chuckled. "Fairy godmother time?"

"Toothbrush and clothes time. Every kid can use a new toothbrush and jammies, not to mention something to wear for the rest of the weekend."

"It's a plan."

Miranda paused before she opened the door to Candy's office. "By the way, I didn't realize you knew Russ well enough to call him. What's up with that?"

Bonnie chuckled. "I took his Intro to Cultural Anthropology class about eight years ago. The man's an awesome teacher. Made me consider becoming an anthropologist and getting a second degree. But I couldn't quite abandon a career in theater and focus on social conflicts in modern society."

Miranda laughed. "Social conflict and theater. Is there a difference?"

"Go away, Miranda."

Jesse was waiting anxiously to find out where he'd be spending the next few days. Miranda was able to sign that she could stay with him, although Miss Bonnie was officially in charge. Jesse jumped in glee until he was told he'd have to check in with a doctor and talk to the police, but Miranda let him know that she'd be with him the whole time.

Jesse nodded, ran to give Candy a quick goodbye hug, then grabbed Miranda's hand.

Miranda smiled, then gulped. She was

about to be a foster co-mom for the weekend… She felt much the same way she had
when she entered school for the first time in
kindergarten—excited, grown-up—and just
a bit terrified.

CHAPTER EIGHTEEN

TWO HOURS LATER Miranda and Jesse pulled into the driveway at Miss Virginia's, ready to spend the rest of the afternoon inside.

Bonnie, Miranda and Jesse had been a close trio at the doctor's office, where a police officer had questioned Jesse using sign language. It was not a pleasant experience for anyone involved.

After the X-rays were taken and the observations recorded, the police had headed off to Willow's apartment for a meeting with Ms. Terence. Bonnie left to attend a meeting with the theater's board of directors and rearrange her house for her guests. Miranda and Jesse went shopping before swinging by the Nolan house to pick up Phoebe.

Dog spotted boy, boy spotted dog and an immediate bond was forged. Miranda was doubly grateful for Phoebe's presence when they reached Virginia's house, remembering the last time she'd entered. The paralegal from

Brett's office was then thoroughly scrutinized by Phoebe, who barked her approval. Miranda had Jesse wait with the paralegal while she and the dog proceeded to make a quick tour of the house like security guards doing rounds. Once Phoebe had indicated no threats were to be found, Miranda felt comfortable about bringing Jesse inside. Jesse actually let go of his new bag so he and Phoebe could hug and roll on the floor. Miranda rescued the tote before either of them could squash Jesse's new supplies. He was now the proud owner of a pack of toothbrushes depicting cartoon characters, a large notebook designated for writing whatever Miranda was unable to convey through signing, several school shirts and sweatshirts, undershorts, sweatpants and school pants, sneakers, socks and a new backpack. Miranda carried the bigger "cool" bag that was filled with a bright red superhero baseball cap, two toy trucks, construction paper, a dozen bottles of watercolor paints and a build-your-own snap kit that assured the owner it could turn into a running robot if the snapper pieced it together correctly.

Miranda took both bags into a spare bedroom for safe-keeping and began cutting tags and putting the new clothes and essentials into the backpack for the upcoming trip to Bonnie's. She returned to the living room in time to watch Jesse and Phoebe engaging in a lively game of tug-of-war with Phoebe's favorite rope toy. Miranda tapped Jesse on the shoulder then wrote on the first page of the notebook, "If you want a snack, I've got some fruit, nuts and cheese in the kitchen."

Jesse's expression revealed his dilemma: leaving the dog versus the lure of a little sustenance. Miranda grinned and wrote, "I also have doggie biscuits. If you like, you can feed them to her while you eat."

Jesse signed, *Would like.* He and Phoebe continued to build their friendship over snacks. Only when the sated puppy flopped at Jesse's feet and fell asleep did he look up at Miranda. He signed, *What do I do now?*

Miranda had this covered. "Do you like to paint?" she wrote. "Mr. Fraser said you'd added some nice butterflies and clouds on the flats for the show. I've got materials if you want to play artist."

Jesse's eyes lit up.

Miranda led him back to the living room and gave him the paper and watercolor paints. Phoebe managed to wake up long enough to follow them before winding herself into a little canine ball and going back to sleep.

What should I paint? Jesse signed.

House across the street? Colorful. Flowers.

Jesse ran to the window, took a good long look, then ran back to the spot on the floor that was clear of boxes or furniture. He immediately began to create his masterpiece and Miranda returned to the kitchen to make a little dinner. She wasn't the greatest cook, as she kept telling Farrah, but chili was easy and she didn't want Jesse to have to endure take-out. A home-cooked meal would make Jesse feel like he was in a real home.

She was in the middle of chopping onions and peppers when she heard a small crash coming from the living room. She started to put down the knife but had second thoughts considering that whoever had broken in before had not been caught. She hurried out of the kitchen to see if Jesse was all right.

He was kneeling on the floor with a once-white T-shirt in his hand and a horrified expression on his face. One of the plastic bottles of paint had spilled onto the floor and he was trying, without success, to clean it up. He looked at Miranda and began to cry. Phoebe anxiously nuzzled his leg but even the comfort offered by the dog didn't help his distress.

She quickly placed the knife on a high table, then ran over and knelt down by his side. *It's just paint. It's okay, sweetie. You're not hurt, right?* she signed.

He shook his head but continued to cry. Then he spoke. "Are you going to hit me?"

Miranda wasn't sure if she was more shocked that Jesse had chosen this day to finally give voice to his thoughts or at the awful memory behind his words. She was able to sign, *Of course not! Why would you think that?*

He chewed his lower lip. "I dropped a whole bottle of red nail goo stuff on the carpet at Miz Willow's. She was really mad. She…smacked my face and she grabbed my arm and pulled it. It hurt."

Willow Terence. Miranda had an urge to drive to the woman's apartment and splash that "red nail goo" over her dyed blond hair. She stifled any murderous urges, reminding herself that the police and social services would handle Willow. It was far more important to reassure Jesse he wouldn't be hit again.

Jesse, Miranda signed. *That was wrong of her. Even if you'd done something bad, that was wrong of her. Hitting another person is never a good thing. And what you did wasn't bad at all. It was a little accident. Everybody drops things. Everybody spills stuff. People drop things and things break. It's okay.*

He looked deep into her eyes. He'd obviously been able to understand the majority of her words but was still extremely upset. "But I got paint on your floor *right here*. And my new shirt!"

She wrote in the notebook, "Paint will wash off. But guess what? If it doesn't, you can use that as your painting shirt at the theater. And if we can't clean the floor I'll buy some hardwood stains and finishes from the store and redo it. Which I should do anyway."

Jesse appeared astonished that he wasn't going to be punished. Miranda handed him a tissue then politely turned away while he wiped his tears and blew his nose. She stared at his painting. It was her turn to be astonished.

"Jesse!" She tapped his shoulder to get his attention. *This is wonderful!* she signed. *You're awesome! Wow. A budding artist!*

He beamed at her. She motioned for him to continue his painting while she cleaned up the spill.

Once the floor had been taken care of, Miranda was glad to focus on chopping veggies. Her emotions swung from pleasure and excitement over hearing Jesse speak to anger at Willow and anguish over the very real fear that had prompted him to ask, "Are you going to hit me?"

She revisited the conversation she'd had with Bonnie regarding Jesse and his tragic past. There was an almost magical symmetry knowing that a child orphaned by hate shared a talent for art that Kam Durani—loved by his family and also killed—wouldn't be able to fulfill. Miss Virginia would be thrilled that this magic was taking place in her house.

She peeked back into the living room for a moment. Jesse was intently filling in details of the flowers growing in the yard of the Howard family across the street. He was occupied and happy.

She pulled her bag off the coatrack near the front door and dug out her cell phone, then went back to the kitchen to keep an eye on the stove while she called Russ. They'd planned to do some work at the house Sunday afternoon but that needed to be postponed. Miranda didn't care if fifteen burglars showed up at the door with tote bags in hand.

Jesse deserved a fun day and watching Miranda and Russ read dusty tomes was not any child's idea of thrilling.

She texted the events of the day to Russ's phone and within two minutes received his response.

Carnival Patriot Park. Sunday afternoon. Petting zoo. Ferris wheel. Rides & booths. Will win plush animals for U and boy at ring toss.

Perfect! she texted back. She hurried into the living room and showed Jesse Russ's text. His eyes widened. Then he broke Miranda's heart.

"What's a petting zoo? And a Ferris wheel?"

She smiled and helped him to his feet, then led him to the small room she and Russ had been using as an office. She turned on the computer and found the carnival's website. Jesse spent the hour before dinner plotting out every ride he wanted to go on, which animals he'd pet, which booths he'd visit and what he'd eat.

Dinner was a rousing success. Miranda didn't ask what Jesse had been eating at Willow's but she sensed meals came out of boxes, cans, sugary juice pouches or the nearest fast-food grease pit. He eyed his salad as though it was about to take flight and she wondered if he'd ever tasted one before. After dinner she and Jesse played with the trucks she'd bought earlier and snapped the robot together.

A paralegal (from Dave's office this time) arrived around seven-thirty to pick up the key and lock the door. He stayed for a moment or two to pat Phoebe, admire Jesse's artwork and make arrangements with Miranda for the next scheduled session. After he left, she packed up Jesse's gear, Phoebe's supplies and her own overnight bag and they all drove to Bonnie's house.

Jesse was a bit shy around Bonnie but when she presented him with homemade hot chocolate for a pre-bedtime treat, he grinned and even began chattering about how he couldn't wait to go to the carnival the next day. Bonnie's eyebrows shot into her bangs when she realized Jesse was finally speaking but she didn't launch into questions. She simply said she wished she could go with the group but had previous plans, so she hoped Jesse would give her a full report when they got back.

By eight-thirty, the seven-year-old was

nodding over a second cup of cocoa. Miranda signed *bedtime,* then made sure he used a new toothbrush and washed his face. Bonnie stayed in the living room and let Miranda take over the parental joys of tucking him in and accepting a good-night hug.

Phoebe hadn't let Jesse out of her sight from the moment they'd entered Bonnie's house. The dog jumped onto his bed and eyed Miranda with a look that plainly stated, *I love you, but Jesse needs me more right now,* then she snuggled next to Jesse's side with her head resting comfortably on his stomach. Jesse was thrilled. Miranda backed out of the room, stood in the doorway for a few moments and waited until she was certain he was asleep.

RUSS ARRIVED AT Bonnie's house promptly at 1:00 p.m. Phoebe and Spero exchanged excited yips then turned their attention to Jesse, who took one look at this second dog and began to giggle. Spero appeared more than pleased at having the chance to be hugged by a small boy.

"Bonnie's going to murder us both for keeping two dogs at her place all day long," Russ said, "but I figure she'll put up with it for Jesse. Besides, she owes me for giving her an A when she really deserved a B plus."

Miranda snorted as Russ handed her the Dragon. "Bonnie loves dogs. I'm fairly certain she also loves you and would have, even if you hadn't committed academic malfeasance."

Jesse's admiration for the man who'd brought the second dog soared to hero status when Russ signed, *Good morning, Jesse!* and asked, *Ready to meet lambs, baby chickens and miniature horses?*

Jesse glanced up at Russ. He shyly signed, *Are you deaf, too?*

I am, Russ signed.

Jesse was surprised and pleased. He looked at Miranda and said, "I'm not so weird after all, am I?"

Miranda's heart constricted. No child should ever believe he's "weird." She choked back the well of emotions that were about to overwhelm her. Instead she grinned at Jesse and spoke into the Dragon. "Not so weird at all, Mr. Jesse Castillo. But even if you were, you'd be in good company. Most theater people and artists are considered weird—just in a neat way!"

Jesse was clearly fascinated by the Dragon

and wanted to spend a few minutes talking nonsense to see if it would pick up his words. Russ was finally able to persuade Jesse that he could play with the device as long as he liked after they returned but if he wanted to eat real funnel cakes and cotton candy, the time was now.

Russ looked around for an outlet. "The battery is low, plus I have no desire to lug it around on roller coasters and carousels." He smiled. "Jesse or I will figure out whatever you attempt to sign, Miss Crash Course." He plugged the Dragon into the socket near a hall table and the trio took off.

Miranda didn't want the day to be one long junk-food fest, but she did want Jesse to get the full carnival treatment. It was fun to hop from booth to booth with Jesse and Russ as they devoured funnel cakes, cotton candy, hot dogs, candied apples and caramel corn. She did, however, draw the line at the stick of fried butter—even though both Russ and Jesse begged.

Jesse patted every lamb, guinea pig, bunny and miniature donkey at the petting zoo and proudly posed with a llama for a photo Miranda assured him would be seen by every member of the Masquerade Theater camp. He was thrilled with the ring toss—where Russ won a stuffed panda for him—and the peach basket toss—where Russ won a stuffed bear dressed in a tutu and tiara, which was obviously meant for Miranda. The day's best moment came after Jesse won a bracelet at the baseball toss. He presented it to Miranda as he signed, *For the coolest lady I know!* The booth's caretaker was both savvy and sentimental—he offered to engrave "From Jesse to Miss Randi," which earned him hugs from both parties.

They waited until the heavier foods had settled before hitting the rides. The creators of the Ferris wheel, roller coaster and Tilt-A-Whirl had been smart—the seats were precisely the right size to enable two adults and a small child to ride in comfort. Miranda was just sad that neither Russ nor Jesse could hear the carousel's tinny organ music blaring out of the numerous speakers surrounding the painted horses.

Following the fifth ride on the Ferris wheel, Miranda and Jesse's favorite, Russ checked his watch and glanced down at Jesse, who was clearly fading. "Four o'clock. I don't know about anyone else but I'd say it's time to head out, let everyone rest for a bit and clean up. Then we can hit the 'meat and three' diner over on Green Springs." He winked at Miranda.

I agree, Miranda signed. Her mouth watered at the idea of a meal at one of the uniquely Southern diners that serves an entrée and three veggies.

The child was valiantly attempting to stay awake but was rapidly losing the battle. As they were leaving the fair, he stumbled on a small crack in the sidewalk, and Russ scooped him up. "Piggyback ride," Russ whispered. Jesse was asleep, head resting on Russ's neck, within minutes.

Phoebe and Spero were patiently waiting for their return, positioned just behind Bonnie's front door. The dogs instinctively muted their normal exuberant greeting once they spotted the sleeping child and followed Russ as he carried Jesse back to Bonnie's guest room. They waited until Russ had gently deposited the boy on the bed, then hopped up and snuggled next to him like bookends.

Russ collected his Dragon from the hall table and joined Miranda in the living room.

"That is one cute, sweet kid," he said. "And smart. He was signing faster than I could teach him."

Miranda nodded. "He's *way* ahead of me. Of course, his need is more urgent. I gather he learned some signing in the hospital and his original foster mom taught him for a year before she had to give him up."

Russ grew serious. "What exactly is the situation with the current foster—Willow, right?"

"Bad. She's been abusive. He's not going back, but no one seems to know where he's going next. Bonnie has custody for now so that's a good thing."

Russ's expression hardened. "Don't they check these people?"

"They do. But things got messed up because Willow wasn't the official foster—her ex was. He left and Willow somehow took over. I guess the Department of Human Resources hadn't had complaints from Jesse's foster siblings and I'd imagine kids are more frightened of change than sticking with a bad situation. When I met her she didn't seem horrible or mean, just not terribly bright. But I doubt she's been giving Jesse real meals even though the state pays for them. I'd say he's a good fifteen pounds lighter than he should be and that matters at his age. Something tells me Willow uses the money for cigarettes."

Russ clenched his fist. "This makes me furious. Anyone who'd abuse a child needs to be locked up and fed moldy bread for about twenty years."

"I'd bring the key and be more than happy to toss it into the nearest lake."

Miranda started at the sound of crying coming from the guest room.

"It's Jesse!"

"What?"

"I'll bet he's having nightmares. Too many funnel cakes?" Miranda smiled but immediately rose.

"Go on. I need to do some stuff at home anyway." He whistled for Spero, looped the leash around the dog's neck then headed for the door. "I'll be back around six-thirty. We can all go out and have a meal. Bonnie's welcome to come with us if she's home by then. Meantime, go play mom." He winked.

It wasn't until thirty minutes later, after the comforting hugs had put Jesse back to sleep, Miranda thought about Russ's words. "Go play mom."

She wondered what it would be like to substitute *be* for *play*.

CHAPTER NINETEEN

RUSS TOOK JESSE and Miranda to a Southern-style, family-friendly diner about a mile from Bonnie's house. Jesse's eyes widened at the sight of the menu and Miranda wondered again if the boy had been eating much beyond fast food. While the trio waited for their order, she sat back and let Russ and Jesse take over the conversation strictly through signing. She discovered she'd been wrong. Jesse wasn't intermediate level with ASL. He was advanced. He'd been kind enough to hold off from near monologues with Miranda, aware that while she could teach him some awesome dance moves, she was light-years behind in signing.

Jesse and Russ were enthusiastically exchanging views on what Miranda discovered was the topic of model trains. "Lionel and HO," Russ politely explained. "Jesse has never seen one so I'm giving him the basics. Know anything about 'em?"

Miranda chuckled. "Seriously? My dad is still in mourning for the set he sold in college," she said, pausing to let the Dragon translate. "I was dragged to model train shows on an annual basis when I was a kid. I like them but am not an expert on sizes and speed or much else and have no intentions on becoming one. But you two go ahead and wax eloquently to one another about your beloved choo-choos." Miranda was truly happy to watch Jesse "chattering" with his hands. She knew he didn't often get the chance.

Her attention strayed to the booth next to theirs once she noticed the four teenage boys who also appeared to be signing. Within a few seconds she realized they had no hearing issues. They were mimicking Russ and Jesse. Except *mimicking* was too nice a word. *Mocking* was closer to the mark. Miranda was glad neither Russ nor Jesse could hear their laughter or catch the rude actions. She hoped Russ had overstated his lip-reading skills, but it wouldn't be hard for anyone to understand "stupid dumb deafies," followed by a few curse words.

It struck her that she was very naive. It had never occurred to her that intolerance and hostility toward people with hearing disabilities even existed. She'd thought sympathy would be the normal first reaction.

The boys continued their obnoxious charades and Miranda's temper rose. So had Russ's—apparently he'd been trying to ignore them, but that was at an end. He growled. "That's enough. A few noses need busting and a few eyes need blackening."

She signed, *No!*

"Why?"

"It won't do any good, Russ. It'll just get us thrown out of here and you'll be arrested for assault."

His eyes narrowed. "I may not care."

Miranda stood. "Let me try to handle it peacefully. Please. I don't want you landing in jail while Jesse is traumatized." She grabbed her bag and quietly pulled out her cell phone…the one with an excellent digital camera. She recorded a video of the boys' wild signing, then leaned down and spoke to the boy closest to her. First he laughed. When Miranda whispered something else, he turned white and immediately signaled to his companions to stop, yelling, "Outta here. Now!" His leadership skills were excellent. All four boys slapped money on the table and exited the diner in less than a minute.

Miranda smiled sweetly and slid back into the booth.

Russ stared at her in sheer amazement. "What did you say to him?"

"Oh. Not much. I told him I was so entertained by his crew that everyone in the known universe should get the chance to see them, too. He thought that was funny until I told him he and his buddies had inadvertently signed they were in the midst of a major drug deal that was going down in the next five minutes. Anyone that ignorant is bound to be somewhat concerned that the cops will be busting in and hauling them off to jail. Wouldn't surprise me if at least one of those clowns already had an arrest or two under his belt."

Russ howled. "Talk about brilliant on your part and totally stupid on theirs to believe you!"

She nodded. "The same techniques work with emotional, intolerant bullies and temperamental divas. The only way to fight back is to keep your cool, not let them know they're getting to you and then embarrass the fool out of them." She grinned. "But it's not really as satisfying as pouring iced tea over their heads would have been."

She paused when the waitress brought platters of food to the table, thanked her and quickly took a bite of a squash casserole. Jesse was wolfing down his chicken as though it were his last meal on earth. Miranda gently touched his hand and signed, *Slow down. Take all the time you need.*

Russ was staring at her. "Ever done that?"

"What? Pour something over someone's head?"

Russ nodded.

"Actually, yes," Miranda said, blushing.

His eyebrow rose. "So you *do* have the proverbial redhead's temper?"

"On occasion."

"Care to share?"

She smiled. "Okay. If I must. One particular event comes to mind from my days in high school. I was at a party after a football game and noticed this jerk was being verbally abusive to a new kid. A freshman. He was shy and awkward and obviously out of his element and I'm pretty sure several of the seniors only invited him to make fun of him. Anyway, I happened to overhear some unsavory statements so I marched up to Mr. I-Own-the-School and poured the contents of my glass over his head. Sweet tea. With ice.

Someone captured the moment on their camera and by Monday Mr. I-Own-the-School was being laughed at throughout the hallowed corridors." She paused before adding, with a grin, "It was rumored that he'd been planning on asking me to prom that year. Imagine my surprise when he never did."

Russ couldn't stop laughing. Jesse asked him what was going on and he signed, *Flashing back to school days and crazy things Miss Miranda used to do.*

Miranda winked at Jesse and signed, *And still does.*

Her cell phone suddenly rang. She grabbed it, glanced at the screen, then answered the call.

"Hey, Darci."

"Hey, Miranda. I see that you have caller ID. I'm impressed."

"It's standard, Darci, as you well know. So, you're calling—why?"

"Because I've had to change the dates for the Durani showing. It's not cancelled or anything; just postponed."

"Anything wrong?"

"No, no," Darci said. "It's just that I need to reschedule until late fall. Turns out I'm going to be out of town for a few weeks and

I don't want to have this one be a rush job. It deserves more and, really, autumn is better for exhibitions. Everyone's bored after summer vacays and they're ready to take the time to actually look at the works presented."

"Well, autumn is a better time for me since I should be done with the movie shoot, but I'm not the one who needs to give the okay. Have you checked with the Duranis?"

"Yeah. I called them a few minutes ago. They're good with the new dates. I was about to call Russ but thought it'd be easier if you deal with him."

"He's right here. I'll tell him about the proposed change."

"He's there.... How interesting," Darci said, chuckling softly. "Are y'all on a date?"

"If taking a seven-year-old boy out for dinner can be considered a date, then yes."

"Who's the boy?"

"One of my kids from the children's theater. I'm playing foster mom for the weekend."

Darci snickered. "Russ playing dad, huh? I'll reserve any comments so you'll remain civil toward me. I'll merely say good luck."

"He and Jesse are getting along famously," Miranda said.

"Well, lovely.... Aren't you going to ask why I'll be out of town?"

Miranda was puzzled. "I didn't think I knew you well enough to be that nosy."

Darci chortled. "Girl, I dove into your business five minutes after meeting you. You're simply more polite. But you might find my reason interesting."

"Okay then, I'll bite. Why do you have to leave town?"

"Because an Auttenberg painting showed up in some little town in Upstate New York called Jamesville. I'm off to see if I can snag it for the gallery."

Miranda's eyes opened wide. "Now *that is* interesting. Are you sure it's authentic?"

"Yep. Been verified by experts and all that jazz. There's some question as to how the painting made it from Europe to the U.S. but apparently the man who owns it, one Noah Mandler, is the son of the folks who helped Virginia Auttenberg get to America. That family was quite close to Mrs. Auttenberg and I'm hoping Mandler might have some information on where Benjamin's other works might be hidden."

"Wow! That's more than just interesting— it's fantastic!" Miranda paused, then added,

"It's also a rather spooky coincidence that this painting turns up just when Russ and I are searching for clues about any Auttenbergs that might have been hidden at Virginia's."

"Not really. To be honest, y'all piqued my interest about his works and, as a very conscientious gallery owner, I did some digging and calling, which was how I learned about this particular piece in Jamesburg."

"Hmm. Maybe I should hand over a diary or two to you? With your investigative skills you might be able to figure out a clue that's eluded Russ and me."

Darci laughed. "Something tells me if there really is an Auttenberg to be found, y'all will be the ones to find it."

"You'll be the first dealer we call."

Darci was silent for so long Miranda thought they'd lost the connection. Finally Darci quietly said, "Miranda, you'll never believe which Auttenberg it is."

"I haven't actually heard of many."

"Well, you've heard of this one. It's *Performance*. The piece we know was *definitely* painted at Terezin."

Miranda was thunderstruck. "Really? This is amazing."

"Yeah, my words exactly. I can't wait to put it in a prime spot at the gallery."

"Well, I sincerely hope it all works out. I think Virginia would be pleased to know that her husband's work will be shown to folks who appreciate not only the art but the feeling behind the piece's creation."

"Agreed. Uh oh. My other line is buzzing. Catch ya later." Darci hung up.

Russ and Jesse were both demolishing cheese biscuits. Russ stopped buttering and placed his knife back on his plate. He pointed to the phone. "Darci?"

"Yeah. With some very unexpected news."

"Tell me."

She told him about the change in the Durani exhibition and the Auttenberg piece *Performance* showing up in Jamesville.

Russ looked a bit perturbed. "Doesn't it seem odd and a bit too coincidental that this piece shows up in the middle of our search? Think there's a connection to the break-ins?"

"I thought the same thing at first. But that would make Darci our burglar and I doubt that's the case unless she knew all about Virginia before we told her. She just said her interest was sparked by all the talk of Vir-

ginia's journals so she set out to find an Auttenberg—and did."

"Well, when Darci puts her mind to something, she generally succeeds—even if she
has to fly to New York." He shook his head.
"Auttenberg's *Performance*. In a word—fantastic."

"I can't wait to see it! But as to the Birmingham connection, I still think the diaries hold the key. We simply need the time
to read them." Miranda smiled at Jesse, who
was rubbing his eyes. "Maybe every day after
my classes?"

"Unfortunately, that poses a problem."

"Which is?"

"I'm booked solid this week with deliveries for Rocky Ridge."

"No big deal. We'll put another hold on it.
They've been unread for seventy years. They
can wait a bit longer."

He nodded. "Meantime, let's get Jesse
home before he falls asleep on the table." He
signaled to the waitress. "Three desserts to
go."

JESSE WAS SLEEPING long before Miranda
knocked on Bonnie's door. Bonnie opened it
quietly and let Russ carry Jesse inside while

Miranda motioned to both dogs to refrain from jumping onto Russ and Jesse in excitement. Phoebe and Spero followed Russ back to the guest room at a sedate pace, apparently making sure he turned down the covers correctly. Miranda brought up the rear of the small parade and tucked Jesse securely under the down comforter. Phoebe promptly hopped up on the bed and resumed her place at Jesse's side before Miranda whispered, "Not yet, muttlet. You and your buddy need to go out."

Phoebe knew the word *out,* and she slid quietly off the bed.

Thirty minutes later the dogs were taken care of, Phoebe was back on the bed and Miranda was saying good-night to Russ and Spero, who appeared disappointed he couldn't spend the night with Jesse.

Thank you, she signed.

"I should be thanking you. Great day. Great kid. I'm definitely up for more of this."

Before she could respond, Miranda was interrupted. "Miss Randi!"

"Uh-oh. Looks like Jesse needs me."

Russ nodded. "Go," he said, then signed, *He's not the only one.*

Russ headed toward his car, motioning for Spero to follow.

Miranda closed the door and stared around Bonnie's living room, stunned and in a haze of confusion and hope.

Outside Bonnie's house, Russ turned back just before he reached his car. He stood for several moments in front of the door, hand raised, mirroring Miranda's confusion—and her hope.

CHAPTER TWENTY

MIRANDA SPENT THE next five days trying to concentrate on her teaching. In between perfecting the Most Extraordinary Super-duper Unbelievably Amazing Kick Line in the Universe for the upcoming show and explaining the intricacies of a heel ball change questions were bouncing through her mind.

Had Russ really signed, *He's not the only one,* as he was leaving? If Miranda's ASL translation was correct, what had Russ meant? Was he referring to the kids at the theater? To the dogs? To Bonnie trying to deal with social workers and police to get Jesse into a better home? Was there the slightest chance this was a roundabout way of telling her he cared about her? That their relationship had shifted from adversaries to acquaintances to friends to…what exactly? What if Russ was playing her—manipulating her into giving up the inheritance? Miranda dismissed that thought in a hurry. She was the actor, not

Russ, and she felt certain he was honest, albeit not always the most communicative in any language.

By the following weekend, Miranda had worked herself into a frenzy of angst, wonder and tingling anticipation. She and Russ hadn't arranged any inventory sessions and she hadn't tried to text him so she felt nervous after a week's absence. Saturday afternoon, she and Russ arrived at Virginia's at the same time and Miranda began blushing and perspiring the moment she saw him. The immediate arrival of the day's keeper-of-the-keys forestalled an awkward greeting. Russ waited until the woman had left before exclaiming, "I have had an amazing morning!"

Doing? she signed.

"Teaching ASL to Spanish speakers at The Cooper School."

Oh! That's right. That started today, Miranda signed. She waited while Russ removed the Dragon from his backpack.

He nodded. "It did indeed and I want to extend my appreciation to you, Ms. Nolan, for making me get in touch with Dr. Vinny. He's smart, obviously cares about his students and I was immediately impressed."

Russ told her all about the class while they

watched the dogs run around the yard. "Honestly? Within about five minutes I'd started seriously considering your other suggestion—about me applying for a position at a community or state college. I'd forgotten how much I liked teaching and I didn't even feel the need to hide under the desk. Of course, all my students at Cooper are deaf, too, which made it easier to teach again."

Miranda grinned. "Toe in the water, Gerik. Toe in the water. Then you add stepping into the sunlight."

He laughed. "Working on it, Nolan, working on it. Speaking of work, are you ready? Or are you too pooped? I assume you had your dance classes today?"

It was clear that Russ wasn't going to bring up anything personal. *I'm fine,* she signed.

Inside Virginia's living room, Russ headed for a large box Miranda had labeled odds and ends. Miranda sank down onto the floor by the piano and dumped out the contents of a smaller box. Phoebe curled up on her feet, fell asleep and began emitting soft doggie snores. Miranda was grateful for Phoebe's comforting presence when she opened a journal at random. It appeared to be the first one Virginia had written in America. Within seconds Miranda realized it might be the most tragic. She patted Phoebe as she began to sift through the horror that had been Virginia Radinski's early life in Terezin.

The journal, written in the broken English of someone still struggling with a new language, was dated 1951, six years after Virginia and the other survivors had been liberated from Terezin. A short enough time to write about the events in detail, long enough so that the pain wasn't fresh, even though that pain was clearly evident in each word.

I write this in English, the language of my new country. I will always love Czechoslovakia but I have too many bad memories. I hurt when I think of my lost country and I am thinking if I write in English, maybe it lessen my hurt?

Today is May 3, 1951. Benjamin was buried six years ago today. If one calls act of a bulldozer spreading dirt over bodies a burial. The bullies who guarded us were scared. Word had spread that German troops had surrendered to Soviet forces earlier that week. Red Cross workers, they come to Terezin along with Soviet troops. Guards wanted to

get rid all of evidence of their maltreat-
ment and cruelty and shove our dead into
large ditch. Benjamin, too. I feel anger
still over no proper burial. We could not
sit shivah. The bodies were burned in
defiance of traditions. I can dwell no
more on this. Benjamin has been gone
for more than six years. My son longer.
My new Christian friends in the United
States believe in heaven and resurrec-
tion. I hope this becomes true. I want to
see my family when I die.

Miranda sat straight up, stunned and sick-
ened. She forced herself to read a little more,
allowing herself one small pat on Phoebe's
furry head, again thankful to be in the presence of a sweet, breathing creature incapable
of hate. The words blurred on the page, partly
from Virginia's spidery European penman-
ship and partly from the tears Miranda barely
realized had been falling from her own eyes.
Virginia had spared herself and the reader
nothing. She wrote of daily atrocities in Terezin, a camp that had been considered better
than places like Dachau and Auschwitz and
Buchenwald until long after the war when the
truth was revealed.

Miranda had already done her research on Terezin. The camp had imprisoned enough musicians to create two very fine orchestras. Composers, actors and painters had called Terezin their place of residence and their prison since the day it was first created. Virginia and Benjamin Auttenberg had been brought there in 1941. Four years later Benjamin was murdered and shoved into a mass grave…only a few days before the Soviets arrived. Two young composers—friends of Virginia and Benjamin—had also been killed. Miranda recognized one of the names—Franz Rosenberg—from the first journal she'd read where Virginia had described running into Franz's widow in Birmingham. Miranda forced herself to continue reading.

Benjamin and Franz heard in odd communication that flows like river between prisoners that the beautiful children— our babies—who performed for the Red Cross when the Nazis pretend to outsiders Terezin is cultural—those children were killed at Auschwitz. Thousands murdered. Thousands! Many of our people wanted to sit shivah to honor their memories. Benjamin and Franz and

Izzak said they would sit shiva alone.
They understood people were frightened.

I write "heard" but is not true. Benjamin and Franz can not hear more than
muffled sounds. The butchers experi-
mented on them. They sealed them into
chambers with high altitudes. They do
this and the men lose hearing but re-
gain maybe a week later? One evil man
who claimed he was scientist delights in
stealing hearing from musicians, from
composers. I believe if Benjamin lived
this man would experiment to destroy
sight from an artist's eyes and Benjamin
would be blind.

The guards scream at Benjamin and
Franz and Izzak. Izzak still can hear and
he falls to the ground. Benjamin and
Franz are reciting the blessing with the
Keriah, the rending of garments. I know
the name of the guard. Ernst Konig. I see
his face in nightmares. He shot Benjamin
in front of us all. I became hysterical.
I was screaming. Konig did not understand my words but he saw the meaning. Why he did not shoot me I do not
know. My friend Abram Sabatka picked
me up and carried me like some rag doll

from Benjamin's body. Konig laughed and laughed. He allow us to pass like we mean nothing.

Miranda stopped. She thought she knew her World War Two history. She'd stage-managed a production of *The Diary of Anne Frank* in college and researched the Franks and the Gies family who had hid them. She'd learned everything she could about the atmosphere surrounding the Jews in Holland and had been horrified that so little had been done to try to help so many souls in anguish. Now, seeing the story through Virginia's eyes created a racking, physical force within her. She could feel Virginia's anguish and her fear. She could hear the screams of the women who watched their men murdered as they stood by—helpless.

"I can't take more of this today," she whispered. Phoebe perked up her ears.

Russ glanced at her and immediately noticed all was not well. "What's wrong?"

Miranda tried to smile but her mouth felt frozen. Instead, she crouched down and hugged Phoebe until the dog squirmed away. She motioned to Russ to bring the Dragon, gave him the diary and stayed silent while he read through it.

Russ flinched. When he finished the sections Miranda had just read, he handed it back to her and said, "This makes Dante's version of hell appear tame."

Miranda nodded. "I always thought I was fairly tough. I made it through my childhood without a mom from age five. My dad was so broken by her death he shut himself off for years. I went to New York when I was twenty and lived by myself like a big, brave girl. I even kicked a mugger one time on the subway platform when he was too stupid to realize my bag only held scripts and music and a pass for dance classes. But this? Virginia faced death on a daily basis. She saw her son and her husband and her friends murdered. She knew hundreds of children who were killed. Somehow, she survived. I can't bear to read another word and yet this was her life for *years*. No wonder she would allow only the neighborhood children to visit."

She glanced up at Russ. "I'm surprised she allowed you into her life. Wait. That isn't going to read right on the Dragon. I meant I'm surprised that she allowed *any* adult into her life. You must have found a way to make her feel safe."

"I tried. I knew she was a Holocaust survivor, but I never knew exactly what had happened. I refrained from asking. I was sure it would cause a lot of pain."

Miranda couldn't hold back her tears any longer. She let them flow freely down her face, not caring whether streaks of mascara flowed with them. Finally, she wiped her eyes and blew her nose.

"I'm sorry. It's just…the past few weeks have been stressful, and reading this—I think my emotional quota in angst and sorrow has been reached for the decade. Maybe *I'll* go into hiding. Or maybe we should just give these diaries to a Holocaust museum and never open one again."

She took a deep breath. "You know what else? This sounds awful but Virginia piled a ton of guilt on my head. I was her lifeline for twenty years. What kind of burden is that to give to another person? That's the other harsh reality about hiding. It's ultimately selfish. I loved this woman dearly but the fact that I was her sole purpose for living from the time I was seven on is almost frightening. How do I deal with that?"

"Puff only picked up about half of that, but I got it." Russ gently brushed a strand of hair away from her eyes.

Miranda's breath caught. She stared at Russ. He stared back.

A small paw suddenly batted Miranda's hand. Phoebe, taking on the role of doggie therapist, was doing her best to make "Mom" less sad.

Russ laughed. The moment was gone. But so was much of the tension.

Miranda exhaled and spoke slowly. "I'm serious about not being able to take much more today. Between burglaries and teaching and classes and crazy foster mothers and Farrah's dinner parties and feeling remorseful and constantly saying more than I should, but knowing full well I can't keep quiet, I'm a wreck."

Russ sat back and began to absently pat Spero, who'd awakened when Phoebe decided to comfort Miranda. A wicked gleam appeared in his hazel eyes. "Are you afraid of heights?"

"What?"

"Heights. As in way more than twenty feet or so."

"That's what I thought you asked. No, I'm not. Why?"

"I have a plan," he said.

"Okay, now I'm confused."

He grinned. "Not for long. Grab your bag, Miranda. We're off."

"Where to?"

"Emerald City."

CHAPTER TWENTY-ONE

MIRANDA GAZED IN admiration at the inside of Russ's car. It was filled with every bell and whistle needed to keep a driver safe from any accident apart from the unlikely possibility that Air Force One might land on the roof. She'd seen this model advertised and marveled at the ability of a machine to warn the human driver about objects in front, beside, behind or even above the vehicle. The car automatically slowed if it was approaching another car's bumper. A pedal on the floor nudged the driver's foot if a collision appeared imminent. Another device warned the driver if someone was weaving from lane to lane in the blind spot. Although Russ could've driven without the extra devices, he clearly didn't want to take any chances.

She mused that the only thing the car wasn't designed to provide was a shock to warn a non-hearing driver that an ambulance or police car was tearing down the street at midnight.

Russ glanced at her and winked. "It does *not* provide a bolt of electric current in case of emergencies but that's about all it doesn't do. Well, come to think of it, it doesn't brew coffee, either, but I'm hoping for upgrades next fall."

They were in sync. She smiled at him but didn't try to sign her agreement. He didn't need the distraction even if the car could practically drive itself.

Russ was keeping quiet about their destination and she knew there was no point in trying to sign *where?* again.

He inclined his head toward the middle dashboard. "If you want to listen to the radio, it won't upset me."

She quickly signed, *I'm fine.* Her life was generally filled with noise. It was nice to experience a silence that provided comfort and solidarity between two people.

Thirty minutes later, Russ pulled into a parking lot and pointed to a huge, colorful sign on the front of a small building. Large green-and-white letters spelled out *Emerald City.* A giant depiction of Oz himself in his preferred means of transportation took up the rest of the space.

Four people dressed in casual clothing and one man wearing a uniform stood next to a wicker basket and a large, currently deflated, hot-air balloon.

So we're off to meet the wizard? Miranda signed.

Russ's eyes twinkled with amusement. "Worried you'll end up over the rainbow?"

I was in the chorus of Wicked *on Broadway a couple of years ago,* she signed as best she could. *I have no fear of going over the rainbow. This looks great. I'm a little anxious but excited.*

The man in uniform greeted Russ like an old friend, and then he turned to Miranda. "I'm Tony." He gestured toward the balloon. "Your first time, right?"

"Yep. I needed a de-stresser and Russ thought this might be the way to go. Of course, he didn't tell me the going would be into the heavens!"

Tony laughed. "You'll love it. Did he explain you also get to help with the rigging for the launch?"

"No, he left that little detail out. Then

again, since he kept the whole excursion secret he left *all* details out."

"Are you okay doing that? Any broken fingers or carpal tunnel?"

"I've got healthy hands," she told him. Tony handed her a pair of heavy gloves to help with the crew work and a pair of earmuffs for the ride. She noticed that Russ had already donned his gloves and was patiently waiting for Tony to give instructions to the other passengers regarding the launch setup.

Tony introduced Russ and Miranda to the two other couples, who seemed delighted that more folks were accompanying them. Within minutes all six passengers were busy tying ropes to what Tony called the "uprights" then staying a safe distance from the balloon and the propane tanks that were filling it. Twenty minutes later the clumsy and ultimately comic attempts to board the basket began. Russ climbed over the side with ease, then extended a hand first to Miranda, then to the two other female passengers, sparing them the embarrassing view of their partners trying various techniques to hoist a leg over and not land face down in the basket.

Russ chuckled. "There's just no way to do this with any kind of grace."

Russ placed Miranda's hand on the side of the basket near his and before she had a chance to wonder if she'd end up in Oz, Kansas or California, the balloon was slowly ascending. Miranda could feel the tension from the past few weeks drain away with every foot the balloon rose. She made a mental note to tell the producers of *The Agency* they needed to add a hot-air balloon ride to the script. Perhaps send Miami Montreville floating across Indonesia, even if Jakarta was only a fake sound stage in Brooklyn. It could be a neat way to escape the bad guys and give Miami a respite from her numerous brushes with knives and bullets.

Conversation aboard the balloon was minimal. The noise from the hot-air burners was intense and Tony wasn't there to serve as a tour guide, but as a pilot ensuring the safety of his passengers.

Miranda had always thought that Birmingham was beautiful. It had been nicknamed the Magic City at the start of the 20th Century because of the almost mystical speed at which it had grown. Miranda now gazed below and realized the name could also define the magical view. Russ pointed out various sites on the ground as the balloon sailed over them, including the statue of Vulcan, the Botanical Gardens and the ghostly old Sloss Furnace buildings with its outlying sculpture garden. For Miranda, the biggest thrill was watching a herd of deer running out of a wooded area to stop at a river just as the sunset spread its colors across the sky and the water below them.

Russ put his arm around her shoulders and gently hugged her. Miranda felt a complete rapport with him. She wanted the ride to go on for hours. For the first time since she'd come home to Birmingham she felt every ounce of tension fade off into the skies.

Even when the ride was over, the magic still held for all the passengers. No one spoke apart from Tony, who quietly and simply showed the group how to undo the rigging and get the balloon ready for a well-needed rest.

Once the ropes were undone and the balloon lay flat on the ground, Tony escorted his passengers to the transport van that would take them back to the Emerald City office, about ten miles north from where the balloon ultimately landed.

They remained silent for the trip back to the starting point. Russ held out his hand to

Miranda to help her out of the van, then continued holding her hand as they headed toward his car, which was parked at the far end of Emerald City's lot.

About twenty feet from the car, Russ suddenly stopped. He let go of her hand and encircled her waist with both hands, picking her up and twirling her high in the air. She was stunned, confused and delighted with the move. He slowly set her down, grinned and explained, "I'm filled with the jubilant spirit of the air!"

Before she had a chance to respond, Russ leaned over, took her in his arms and placed his lips on hers. Her senses began whirling higher than the balloon. His arms tightened as she responded, and she caressed the muscles of his strong shoulders, then softly tousled his hair. When they broke apart, there was no strain or stress. Only smiles and a promise of more.

Russ stared into her eyes. "I'm giving up my claim."

"What?"

"To Miss Virginia's house. It's yours."

Russ! You don't have to do that. Yes, I want the house but you have as much right as I do. Why are you doing this?

He remained silent for so long Miranda wondered if he'd understood her. Finally he smiled. "Because I want you to stay—here in Birmingham. I know you've got a career elsewhere, but I also know I don't want you to leave. Look, you aren't the only one who's been dealing with remorse about Virginia. Once I got back from Afghanistan my visits were sporadic. But the few times I saw her she'd try to tell me about her friend in New York and how proud she was of her Broadway 'star.' I actually resented you before I met you because you had a successful career and you had your hearing. Why should you get her house?

"When I met you I tried to despise you and make you feel guilty for not coming home even though Virginia knew you were working nonstop. I told myself you didn't deserve the house. Then I watched you with the Duranis and with Jesse—and even with your diplomatic handling of Darci—and I had to change that image I'd determinedly built in my mind of the girl who didn't care about anyone but herself. I began to see why Virginia loved you. I'm probably saying too much and not making a lot of sense because the most important thing I want to say is I want you to stay." He took a breath. "And if that means giving up a house? Then so be it."

Miranda motioned for him to wait until she could grab the notebook and pen from her bag. Then she wrote, "My life has been in turmoil for the past month. I'm scared to make any decisions that could change my life or someone else's, especially when that someone is a person I care about. And I *do* care. But…"

He read what she'd written before quietly asking, "But?"

This was not something she wanted written on an impersonal notebook. But her signing wasn't up to her feelings so she plowed on with the pen.

"I've had to change how I see you, as well. You were so distant when I met you, so angry and I begrudged your friendship with Virginia. Lately, I have this huge mixture of emotions tugging me in every direction imaginable. About the only thing I'm sure of is what I vowed when I first arrived in Birmingham and sat in front of Virginia's house. I need to curb my impulsive tendencies. So at this point I'm not sure whether to listen to the girl who keeps yelling 'Go back to Manhattan, Miranda!' or the girl who keeps whispering, 'Stay.'"

CHAPTER TWENTY-TWO

A FRANTIC BONNIE HAMIL seized Miranda's hand the instant she dropped her bag backstage. "You are looking at a desperate woman!" Bonnie cried.

Miranda grinned. "I have never known you to be anything else before a show. I'm assuming you need a combination stage manager and wrangler?"

"Absolutely. You're wonderful and I love you and I'll see you after the show. I have to go play theater director and act dramatic but responsible for all the parents and guests." She gave Miranda a quick hug and took off at a run toward what passed as the lobby.

Miranda stowed her bag and spent the next hour dealing with chaos and crises.

She exchanged lighting cues over the head set with the young teenagers in the booth, told the parents acting as house managers when it was time to "open the house," and helped line up various groups to prepare them to head onstage. She attempted to keep them from peeking through the curtain to check out where friends and family might be seated. She ended up peeking out with them after her maneuvers to shoo them away from that curtain failed and she smiled when she spotted Russ, her dad and Farrah sitting together about six rows back.

She provided encouragement to children who'd never been onstage before and were terrified to perform in front of an audience and traded jokes with the teens who were nervous but didn't want to admit it. She led breathing sessions for everyone to get them through that stage fright—admitted or not. She applied make-up to the children who hadn't mastered the technique of eye liner and braided hair. She found bobby pins to hold hats in place and safety pins to keep small rips that hadn't appeared until two minutes before an entrance from turning into large rips that could lead to humiliation in the middle of a song. She snuck into the lobby for about six minutes to return a call from her agent, Brooks, who'd phoned to tell her that he couldn't wait for her to shoot the film and the buzz was that *The Agency* was going to be a blockbuster. Brooks had also made sure the actress subletting her apartment for the past month would leave the place in great shape. Apart from that distraction, she stayed with the children.

Halfway through the show, Bonnie spirited Miranda away from soothing an eight-year-old with a skinned knee.

"We got trouble, my friend."

"What now?"

"Alicia will not be performing 'Defying Gravity' this evening."

"Why not?"

"Because she's silently dealing with strep throat," Bonnie said. "According to her mom Alicia was determined to make it here. Thankfully, mom convinced her that we do *not* need an epidemic of strep."

"Poor kid. Been there, done that and wasn't thrilled. It's painful. So, who's her under-study?"

"You."

"Beg pardon?"

"This is children's theater, remember? Un-derstudies do not exist."

"Bonnie Hamil! I figured that was for small parts. Not for the star spot in Act Two."

"Surprise!" Bonnie chuckled. "You sang the song for six months touring *Wicked* so

I know you know it and our kids will be thrilled you're performing. Seriously, do you mind?"

"You know me. It's fine. Just shove me onstage when it's time in case I'm in the middle of convincing a seven-year-old that life will not end without a third layer of red lipstick."

Miranda blessed whatever instinct had prompted her to join the vocal warm-up earlier in the evening and managed to find a quiet spot to do a second warm-up about five minutes before she headed onto the stage. Miranda had to admit that while she was extremely sympathetic to Alicia's plight she was excited to have the chance to sing a song she loved.

The audience loved it, as well. She received a standing ovation. Smiles shone on every face.

Every face except one. Russ Gerik.

THE CONTRAST BETWEEN the party Miranda had attended for *Illumination* and the get-together put on by Masquerade Children's Theater was striking. A ginger ale–lime sherbet punch replaced champagne. Pizza was the main dish and music wasn't playing from a live band because the live band was made up of a group of sixteen-year olds who were too busy sampling deep-dish pepperoni and thin crust mushroom with triple cheese slices to mess with anything else.

In both Manhattan and Birmingham, however, Miranda could sense the identical emotions from the performers torn between the high of knowing they'd done a good job (amplified by family and friends hugging, squealing and taking massive amounts of photos) and the sadness that inevitably arises knowing the show is over. Bonnie was trying to overcome the separation anxiety by handing out letters to parents with information on the classes starting in fall and dates for auditions for the annual holiday show. The theater would be closed from July through late October for work to be done on as many renovations as funding and time would allow.

Miranda made the rounds of congratulations and hugs, weaving through hordes of children and their families until she found Jesse, who was standing far too sedately with his emergency foster parents. Miranda introduced herself and asked if she could borrow Jesse for a few moments so he could receive hugs and "you're awesome!" fist bumps from Miranda's family and friends. Once permission was granted she took Jesse by the hand and led him to the far corner of the scene shop where Russ, Tim and Farrah had been joined by Abra and Yusuf Durani. Their daughter, Yasmin, who'd been excitedly pointing out every fleck of paint she'd splattered onto the sets, stopped when she saw Jesse and immediately ran to his side, signing *You're the best! Congrats!*

More squeezing and squealing all around. Abra gave Miranda an extra hug before exclaiming, "I knew you had to be good since you've performed in New York, but wow! You were amazing."

"Oh, thank you!" Miranda said. "It was an unexpected treat for me when Bonnie told me I was needed. I mean, give me a song and I'm there. But, more important, I wanted y'all to meet Jesse, and I need to thank Yasmin for helping him backstage when I couldn't. She's one super guardian!"

Miranda made the introductions. Jesse was obviously thrilled at meeting Abra and Yusuf, who signed *hello* and expressed their excitement at seeing him perform. He shyly acknowledged the *You were wonderful!* Farrah and Tim signed—Miranda had coached them in a few phrases only the day before when she told them she'd love for Jesse to have supportive folks in the audience. The group spent another fifteen minutes chatting about the show before Jesse's foster parents came to collect him. Russ spent the entire time signing with Jesse and the Duranis. He continued to ignore Miranda, who tried to figure out what she'd done to make him act as though she didn't exist.

She found out after the party was over and Russ met her at Virginia's. He was obligated to meet her there since they both had keys, an arrangement they'd made with both law firms the day after their balloon ride. Cort and Brett had even met with Judge Rayborn and received his approval. Miranda and Russ had left Spero puppy-sitting his pal Phoebe during the children's show and Miranda quickly realized that picking up Spero was Russ's sole motive in knocking on Miss Virginia's door.

He called the dog to his side and was about to loop the leash over Spero's neck, briefly stating, "good night," when Miranda's temper flared. There was no Dragon in sight, but she quickly managed to sign *Whoa! Wait one second, Mr. Gerik!*

"What?"

Why are you acting like I'm as nasty as that

dead squirrel Phoebe rolled in last week? Explain. Or are you going to continue to pout?

He pulled the Dragon out of his backpack and held it out.

"*You* are leaving for Manhattan in two days. Thanks so much for telling me about this film."

Miranda was astonished. "I thought you knew. Heck, I thought everyone in Birmingham knew. I'm surprised it hasn't hit billboards and local TV the way Farrah has been spreading the word. She asked me about it at her dinner party that day we went to Darci's gallery."

Russ's jaw set. "If you'll recall," he said tersely, "the batteries in this device died and I spent most of the meal in silence."

She hesitated a second before saying, "Russ, I don't really remember at what point in the evening someone asked me about the film and I'm truly sorry you didn't know about it. I admit it's a pretty big deal. Scratch that. It's a huge deal. But I've been way too busy getting the show prepared and finishing inventory and taking care of Jesse to really think about it. I'm confused. Why are you so upset?"

"Why am I upset? I've just discovered that

Miranda Nolan, star of stage and screen, has obviously been having a grand old time playing at relationships during her short trip to Alabama. Apparently she's now ready to resume her *real* life and her overly bustling career in New York. Is that a good enough reason?"

"Hang on there. You're implying that because I'm going to be working out of town for a lousy three months or so, suddenly I'm playing at relationships? You've got to be kidding!"

"Are you really trying to say you'll be back? That you're not planning to audition or interview or do whatever else your agent sets up to further your career?" He paused. "From what Farrah told me tonight this is the kind of role that could land you immediate work in other films. So, nice knowing you, Ms. Nolan, and I hope Phoebe loves being stuck inside an apartment ten hours a day before she gets a crummy walk. You're one stellar actress. You made me believe we could have some kind of future with each other. Or was that to get your hands on the inheritance? Were you playing me so I'd relinquish my claim to the estate? Give the house to you so you could turn around and sell it."

"No! That's not true!"

Russ ignored her. "Brett had planned to start the paperwork a few days ago. After all, we had this great trust going, didn't we? Even the nutcase judge thought so when he gave his permission for the two keys. But now I'm relieved he couldn't get to it. Know this, Miranda—my part of the claim is still intact."

"Russ! You're acting crazy!"

He remained silent.

Light dawned. "You *really* don't think I'm coming back. Wow. Look, Russ, I've already told Bonnie I'll be down for the fall classes. That's late October. I told Darci I'd be here for Kam's exhibition. I'm not auditioning while I'm in New York, and—you may not want to believe this—but I truly…care about you." She stopped herself from saying *love*. He obviously didn't want that word coming from her at this moment and she wasn't sure of her own feelings, either. "I wasn't kidding when I said I wanted to stay."

She thought Russ would calm down and believe her. But instead, he blurted out, "You sang tonight. Apparently it was wonderful because I saw the faces of the audience around me and I watched that standing ovation and felt the vibrations of several hundred people clapping their hands. I also saw your face while you were performing and when you took your bow. You want me to believe you're going to give that up? For what? For a children's theater in Birmingham, Alabama? For the possibility that you and I…"

She stared at him for a long moment then she simply signed, *Yes.*

He didn't say anything.

"There are places for me to perform in Birmingham. I don't have to be on Broadway to have a career I'm happy with."

"If you mean that, you'll pick up the phone right now, call your agent and explain that you're not doing the movie." he said.

"What!"

"Do I need to repeat that?"

"No, Russ. I got it. And the answer is no. Good grief. I signed a contract. That's a *commitment.* I don't break commitments."

He shook his head. "Right. And you honestly expect me to believe that once you're diving into work again in Manhattan you won't stay? I'd say your commitment is to being selfish."

Miranda was so frustrated she was yelling, even though the Dragon could pick up her words at a softer volume. She'd never thrown anything at anyone in her entire life but suddenly she debated picking up the nearest object and hurling it at the wall. "Since when is it selfish to keep one's promise? Why aren't you listening to me?"

"Because I can't!" Russ shouted back. "And there's no point in yelling! I can't hear! Remember?"

"This has nothing to do with your hearing issues. You're not *listening! You're* the one being selfish. So, I'm supposed to act irresponsibly and hurt a group of people who trust me to do a good job for them by—what? Calling and say, 'Oops, sorry! Russ Gerik is acting like a toddler the first time his parents leave him with a babysitter and he's throwing tantrums, so gee golly, y'all just need to hire someone else tomorrow morning." She took a breath and tried to lighten the mood. "Sorry, Russ. I grew up with a lawyer, remember? I learned from the cradle that one honors a contract unless there's a clause requiring serial killing or kidnapping politicians or smuggling drugs from Mexico."

Russ did not smile. It was clear he didn't believe a word she'd said. "Fine. Go do your movie. Run off and overload yourself with career boosters. Have a great time. Just know that I will hang on to this house 'til my last breath to keep it out of your hands so you can't turn around and sell it."

He grabbed the Dragon and the leash and pulled a worried-looking Spero toward him as he opened the door. "Meantime, I'll look for you on the big screen."

Miranda snatched the Dragon back before Russ realized what she was doing. "And I'll look for you in the nearest cave because that's what this is really all about! You're going back into hiding." She took a breath, lowered her volume and handed the device to him. "If you ever decide to come out into the sunlight, let me know."

CHAPTER TWENTY-THREE

THE UPTOWN A TRAIN had been stalled for more than forty minutes. Thankfully, the air-conditioning was still blasting and Miranda's car was mostly empty so she didn't have to get too close to sweaty passengers or listen to loud complaints about New York transit. Miranda leaned back in her seat and idly tried to recall if she'd set her DVR to record *The Maltese Falcon* while she'd been out then mused that she didn't really care. The adventures of Sam Spade couldn't compare with the fun she'd had that evening, meeting with the other four actors who'd been killed in *The Agency* for a "zombie farewell."

They'd chatted about upcoming jobs, excitedly discussed the perks they'd receive if *The Agency* turned out to be next year's big blockbuster, and joked that Miranda might not really be in the zombie club since her demise in the film had been one of those soap opera endings where no body is seen, which left the possibility of her character returning for the sequel. Then they'd sworn off shop-talk to discuss their personal lives. All five had agreed that filming played havoc with relationships. Miranda had ruefully admit-ted that her own romance had gone bust be-fore she'd even arrived on set but noted that at least her dog still loved her. She'd found the best dog-walker/pet sitter in Upper Manhat-tan so Phoebe could keep a normal schedule

After dinner, the group had hit a small cabaret. She'd had a great time, but Miranda was ready to get home and grab some much needed sleep. She hadn't originally viewed having to remain on the A train for an extra hour as the highlight of the night.

Miranda suddenly realized she was relieved the train was stuck. For the first time in three months she had a chance to think. Shooting the movie had been strenuous. When she wasn't dodging fake bullets or emitting wild martial-arts cries (which tended to coincide with wild martial-arts moves) she was learn-ing lines or massaging arnica balm on her bruised arms and legs. At home, she would give Phoebe her last walk for the day, grab the food she'd picked up at the local deli or the Chinese restaurant around the corner then plop down in front of the TV to watch something mindless that didn't involve bullets or martial arts.

Each evening she checked her answering machine for messages. She'd checked her cell phone—which wasn't allowed on set— and she'd checked her email. Tim and Farrah had enthusiastically told her about how much they liked little Jesse. They'd been allowed to have him over to their house with his temporary foster parents. Abra and Yusuf Durani emailed or called with updates on Kamyar's show. Darci Becker had called twice about the same topic. Bonnie had managed to set up a Skype program and invited Jesse and his foster mom over to sign on Bonnie's screen so Miranda could see him. Dave Brennan had called three times to let her know that the court date regarding the two wills had been postponed to October, then November, then early December and that as far as he knew, Russ was still in it to win it.

She hadn't heard from Russ. He hadn't sent an email, hadn't sent a text, hadn't written a note saying "I'm sorry I didn't trust you and *of course* you're coming back and I miss you so much it hurts" on elegant stationery or even on a crummy page torn out of a spiral notebook.

Miranda, for her part, did miss Russ so much it hurt. She would have assumed being insanely busy would have helped push thoughts of Russ out of her head but the scriptwriters for *The Agency* had apparently been stalking her in Alabama because they kept adding scenes that brought back recent memories.

They'd filmed in an art gallery, having Miami Montreville meeting with a double agent determined to extract sensitive information about a mission. Miranda had immediately thought about her conversation with Darci Becker and Russ's amused disdain for the "new, new" Impressionist paintings. During the few moments she had for a coffee break, Miranda reviewed some of Darci's comments about Russ and relationships and wondered if he'd gotten so scared about his feelings that he'd used Miranda's decision to honor her movie contract as an excuse to bail or if he simply had become too much a hermit to ever commit to another person.

When a fortune cookie opened to reveal the words "You have a decision to make soon" while Miranda was shooting a scene in a Chinese restaurant whimsically called *Wing Ding's,* Miranda began to wonder if Miss Virginia's house had been bugged. She had to use all her skills as an actress to keep her focus on rolling under tables to avoid the super villain who was trying to use sharpened chopsticks to stab her. What she'd really wanted to do was run to a forbidden cell phone and call Abra to ask whether Russ had taken the job with the defense contractor or found a teaching job with one of the local colleges.

The most bizarre situation was the fight in a hot-air balloon, which they'd filmed in a giant warehouse in Jersey City. Dangling over the side trying to escape the clutches of the villain (who'd failed with the chopsticks at *Wing Ding's*) should have kept her mind off everything but falling. There was not an ounce of romance involved in the scene which called for Miranda to struggle with the villain and finally toss the villain overboard while keeping the balloon intact. Nonetheless, as Miranda grabbed her attacker and, with the aid of the stunt director and strong wires, carefully twisted and turned and kept the audience in suspense, she could feel Russ's arms around her as they gazed down at the deer running through the woods.

"Miranda?"

She glanced up and blinked twice. What was Grant Spencer doing on the A train at nearly two in the morning?

"Grant. Hey."

"What are you doing?"

"Trying not to fall asleep before I get back to my apartment. You?"

He laughed. "The same. Believe it or not I bought a one-bedroom up on Arden Street last month. I'm about ten blocks from your place now."

Not for long, she thought. "That's great. I know you always liked the neighborhood."

He nodded. "So, what are you up to work-wise?"

"Remember the audition back in May? For the spy movie?"

"You got it?"

"I did. Just finished wrapping up three months' worth of action and not much dialogue."

He smiled. "I heard it was pretty stunt-heavy."

"It was," she said. "My bruises have bruises."

"So, you're through?"

That's what wrapping up means, Grant, flashed through her mind but she simply said, "Yep."

"Hmm. That's fortuitous."

"O-kay. How so?"

"We're about to finish previews for *Topaz in Delirium* and are headed to Broadway once we've dealt with a few issues, one of which is the casting of a very crucial role. A role that has Ms. Miranda Nolan written all over it. Can I just say, we're in dire need of a triple threat here? This is perfect running into you! I was actually going to call your agent Monday and tell him the producers are already on board with an offer of a contract."

"You're kidding."

"I'm not." He inhaled then said, "Look, I know I messed things up with you and I'm *so* sorry. For what it's worth, the little fling with Cyan did not work out and I was an idiot for going out with her. I don't know if we can ever get back to what we had, but I'd like to try. Also, you're one of the best performers on the planet and you'd be an amazing asset to *Delirium.* If you need even more incentive, word after previews is that this one is going to break records for Tony nominations and that particular role is sure to get a nod for Best Featured Actress."

Miranda was stunned. Memories began flooding her mind, beginning with her confrontation with Grant late last spring. That scene was instantly replaced with the memory of Russ twirling her around, kissing her and telling her he cared. Russ offering to give up his claim to the estate for her. That vision suddenly changed to their last argument. Miranda could still hear the anger in Russ's voice.

Other visions quickly vied with each other for the winning spot in her mind.

She heard herself telling Russ that her father had wondered if she kept busy because her mother hadn't had the chance for a full life.

Next, Miranda saw herself onstage in the final moments of *Illumination,* singing along with the rest of the chorus then bowing during the standing ovation. Accepting the roses and the high-fives from her fellow performers. That morphed into a vision of the future—Miranda giving an acceptance speech while holding her Tony Award. The image shifted. Miranda saw herself receiving a different type of prize. Jesse clasped a cheap bracelet around her wrist; a bracelet inscribed *From Jesse to Miss Randi*. She closed her eyes, picturing Jesse being carried in Russ's arms after a full day at the carnival, then watching as Phoebe and Spero settled themselves securely around the child to keep him warm and safe and feeling loved as he slept. Jesse desperately needed more than foster families in his life, no matter how well they signed. He needed a real parent. Miranda remembered the look in Russ's eyes when he said Jesse wasn't the only one who needed her.

Her mind flashed again—back to the warehouse theater used by Masquerade, but this time the image shifted to the faces of the audience that included her family, Abra and Yusuf and...Russ.

For once Miranda's brain supplied her with words other than "Ah." She tried keeping those words civil—after all, she was on a train with no opportunity to make a grand exit. Miranda looked Grant squarely in the eye and said, "No offense, but it appears you're not coloring with all the crayons in your box. I have no desire to resume a romantic relationship with you and I'm pretty insulted you imagine that could ever happen.

I have no feelings for you anymore. While I truly don't wish for you to be run over by a bus or anything, I also don't particularly wish to be around you. As to the show? It sounds wonderful and I hope for the sake of everyone involved that it wins numerous awards, but I'm not going to be part of it. I thank you for believing I could be an asset and I'll admit it's tempting but there are more important things in my life now, and they're not here."

The train lurched forward. The stall was over.

Grant was clearly dumbfounded at her response, but he wisely chose not to argue or plead. "Well, I'm sorry. I wish you luck in whatever you've chosen for yourself."

"Thanks."

Grant walked back to the other end of the car. His stop was the one before Miranda's but Miranda didn't bother to watch him exit the train. She was too busy focusing on the decision she'd just made and what she needed to do.

First, she'd sublet her apartment to an actor from *The Agency* who'd been despairing of ever finding a place in Manhattan. Then she'd pack all the clothes, electronics and small pieces of furniture she owned, rent a truck and drive to Birmingham. She would grit her teeth and stay with Tim and Farrah until she found another place. She'd get in touch with an accompanist she'd worked with years before and see if she was interested in doing some cabaret gigs. She'd teach acting, dance, voice or all three at the children's theater.

Miranda resolved to get the stubborn, wounded Russ Gerik to understand that she loved him. Convince him to trust her. If he refused to be part of her life, she would cry and the pain would pierce her heart for a very long time. That thought nearly brought her to tears, but she wasn't giving up without a fight.

She was also going to do whatever it took to adopt Jesse Castillo.

CHAPTER TWENTY-FOUR

MIRANDA QUICKLY DISCOVERED that her decision to adopt Jesse Castillo would receive interesting reactions. Beginning with her stepmother... Farrah answered the phone early in the morning when Miranda called to ask if her father could recommend a lawyer who could handle the adoption. She needed to let Tim and Farrah know she'd be driving home in a week or so and she had to make sure she could stay with them for the time it would take to find a house. Tim was out playing tennis, so Miranda told her stepmother about her plans.

"You want to what?"

"Adopt Jesse."

"Are you out of your mind?" Farrah asked. "Miranda, this takes impulsive to the nth degree. What in blazes are you thinking?"

"I'm thinking this is a boy who needs a mom desperately. A boy I bonded with the instant I met him. I should have made this decision back in June." She tried to add something light and cute. "Hey! Even the dog is crazy about him. If I don't adopt him, Phoebe will!"

Miranda's jaw tensed. Light and cute hadn't even worked in her own mind. She went on the offensive. "I'm sorry, Farrah, but what is your problem with this?"

"Look, I'm sure I'm being nosy and trying too hard to play stepmom. But I worry about you. You're only twenty-seven. If you adopt this boy, you'll be tying yourself down for the rest of your life. What about your career? Touring? How do you manage that? How are you supposed to raise a child alone in Manhattan?"

Miranda took a deep breath. "I'm not going to tour. I'm also not going to live in Manhattan. Bonnie Hamil has a job waiting for me at the children's theater as soon as they start up again, and there are theaters and cabarets in Birmingham. No, it's not Broadway and it's not major film although one never knows when some producer might decide that the Sloss Furnace would make a great location." She calmly said, "Beside the point. I've already sublet my apartment and I'm packing as we speak. I loved performing on Broadway, but sometimes one has to trade one way of living for another. I believe this is one of those times."

Miranda waited through a long moment of silence.

"This may be too personal, but what about Russ Gerik? Where does he fit into this new life? Or does he?"

Miranda sighed. "Honestly? I don't know. We had a pretty bad argument before I left. I couldn't get him to understand I was under contract and that I also needed time to think. He's a smart man. I think his whole 'you're off to do a movie and you're never coming back' masked something else. I'm just not sure what that is." She blew out a puff of air. "Talk about impulsive. He makes me look like an amateur."

"Did he ask you to marry him? I mean, before the fight."

"Not in so many words, but it seemed he was on the verge before Mount St. Helens erupted in the form of 'you're leaving me' and 'you're selfish for leaving me' and various phrases that all started or ended with 'you're leaving me.'"

Miranda expected a barrage of something along the lines of *Are you crazy? He hasn't*

*asked, he probably hates you now and you
want to adopt by yourself?*

Instead, Farrah laughed. "Been there! Your
dad was always Mr. Glib-and-Polished until
the night he *finally* proposed. It took him a
good four hours to be able to form the actual
words and I thought he was going to pass out
the instant he'd uttered them. We broke up
three different times before finally getting
it together enough to admit we adored each
other and wanted a life together."

Miranda nearly fell onto the floor in aston-
ishment. She suddenly felt a kinship with her
stepmom she'd never expected.

Farrah continued. "It sounds like your
mind is made up, at least as far as Jesse is
concerned, so I'll merely say this. I wish you
luck in getting back together with Russ if
that's what you want. And whether that happens or not, that child will have two instant
adoring grandparents." She paused, "I never
thought I'd be a grandmother at forty-two but
what the heck? If you can give up Broadway,
I guess I can give up pretending to be thirty!"

"Thank you. I mean that."

After a slight hesitation, Farrah added,
"Miranda, I know I can be pushy at times.
This whole stepmom thing is strange for me,

too." She laughed. "I can't promise to stop trying to teach you to cook, but I do love you. We're family."

DAVE BRENNAN, whom Miranda called next, asking if his office handled adoptions, was amused. "I like it. Of course, you do know that the issue with the house is still not settled and it might be many months down the road, so adopting in Alabama and raising in New York City as a performer could get a bit tricky. Not to mention the single-parent thing—although these days that's not as big a deal. The good news is Jesse would be harder to place—he's a special-needs kid and he's not a baby—which should work in your favor."

"Dave, I'm moving back to Birmingham and I'll have a job with the children's theater." She didn't tell him she was determined to patch things up with Russ. If that didn't work, then the term *single parent* would still apply. "I'll find a good place to live in the next few weeks, once I'm back."

"Great! Okay, you need to check with the Alabama Department of Human Resources and get an application going. There'll be visits and checks and classes and guidelines to follow, but it shouldn't take more than a few months. If you need an attorney at the end of all that, let me know. Good luck, Miranda. I think you'll make a great mom."

"Thanks."

Miranda called Abra Durani next. She'd been keeping in touch with Abra and Yusuf throughout the past three months, determined not to let work or distance interfere with maintaining their friendship. They'd discussed how pleased they were that Darci had asked Miranda to sing at Kam's exhibition and Yasmin's enrollment in the children's theater program. Miranda had regaled all the Duranis with her exploits on the set as Miami Montreville. The only topic that had been deemed off limits—through a non-spoken agreement—was Russ Gerik.

Abra was thrilled to hear about the plan to adopt Jesse. "Hang on a second, Miranda. Yasmin is here with me and I want to tell her. We're painting the kitchen."

"Blue?" Miranda asked.

"Yes! But a far more muted blue than her skies for your camp show." Abra laughed. "We decided this was a way for us to share the kitchen with our own unique talents. She paints, I cook, we eat."

Miranda grinned. "I like it." She waited

while Abra gave Yasmin the news about Jesse and was delighted to hear a loud, "All right! This is awesome!"

"I suppose you caught that?" Abra asked.

"I think all of Manhattan caught that. Tell her she's Jesse's official babysitter if this goes through."

"Absolutely. And of course, add us as another set of grandparents."

"Already done. Jesse adores all of you."

They chatted about the process of adoption for a few moments before an impatient Yasmin was heard. "Mother. I love Miss Randi and I love Jesse but the wall above the counter needs a second coat, *now!*"

Miranda laughed. "I don't want to hold up the process of genius, Abra, so tell her to bring on the blue! And I'll see y'all soon once I'm back in 'Bama."

Bonnie Hamil's reaction was thoroughly upbeat. "Cool! Actually, this takes cool to the level of freezing! I'm so glad! I knew even one day taking care of that boy would turn you into a mama!"

"I'm glad you're glad," Miranda said. "Since you know his social worker, can you give her a heads-up and help me get started?"

"Let me call you back," Bonnie said.

Within fifteen minutes, the phone rang. "Great news!" Bonnie said. "Not only did I ask if she'd mind getting the forms ready, but you *should* be named the official emergency foster once you've gone through some preliminary interviews. They're already starting the background check. I told his social worker that you do some decent ASL and that Jesse adores you. She's very efficient and caring and she's also not happy with the current fosters."

Miranda was immediately terrified. "Why? Please don't tell me there's been more abuse."

"No! Nothing like that. It's just that they're older—not really fun for a child of Jesse's age. I mean, I can't see them taking him to carnivals or up in hot-air balloons. They *do* sign but Jesse is way ahead of them," she said. "By the way, you'll get paid for Jesse's room and board once you're a foster. I'm not sure how that works after you become the legal parent. Mrs. Warren, Jesse's social worker, can tell you more. Let me give you her number."

"Thanks for the number but I don't need any money. It would feel odd, somehow, taking money for Jesse. Let the state give it to someone who needs it more."

Bonnie chuckled. "You're just saying this because I gave you such an exorbitant salary for the camp."

"Yeah, right. Actually, I've always been good about saving. I have residuals coming in from some TV shows I've done over the past couple of years, plus a national commercial. And don't spread it around, but my earnings from the movie will easily pay for the care of a seven-year-old who needs nothing more than paper and paint to keep him happy."

"Well, it's there anyway. Take it and tuck it into Jesse's college fund."

Miranda fell silent for a moment.

"Miranda? You there?"

"Yeah…just zoning into the future. College. Wow. If I can make this happen I'll be raising a child and sending him off to college. It's a lot to process. Am I nuts? I mean, I've taught kids. I like kids. Kids like me. But I've never had a child around for more than class time. Okay. I've just officially scared myself."

Bonnie howled. "You are nuts, I agree. But not for wanting to adopt Jesse. You've got a great instinct for what kids need and what they want, and you know how to merge the two. You're a natural. Heck, people become parents all the time with no clue about what they're doing and that's been happening for thousands of years. In most situations, common sense is the best answer. Now give Mrs. Warren a call."

Thirty minutes later Miranda carefully hung up the phone, then leaped into the air and began dancing around the apartment. Mrs. Warren had been moderately cautious but ultimately optimistic. By early spring at the latest, Miranda should be the official new mom of Jesse Castillo.

CHAPTER TWENTY-FIVE

MIRANDA GRABBED PHOEBE'S leash and headed for the door. "I promise, puppy, I'm finally done checking every crevice of this place for anything I might have missed. One more run and we're headin' south for good."

They took the stairs and were in the lobby in less than a minute. Miranda's down-the-hall neighbor, Carolyn, was just returning from walking her golden Labrador so a few moments were spent letting the dogs greet each other while Carolyn wished Miranda good luck in her move.

Miranda opened the door and was nearly dragged across the street by an excited Phoebe who began yipping and wagging her tail with even more than her normal enthusiasm.

A man was leaning against Miranda's rental truck.

"Hi, Miranda."

"Russ!"

She wasn't sure if she led Phoebe or Phoebe led her but within seconds both were running toward Russ, who was running toward them. The collision was light but the hugs were strong and their kisses stronger. Miranda was glad it was only six in the morning so the entire neighborhood wasn't out witnessing those kisses, but she was so thrilled to be in Russ's arms she wouldn't have cared if some kid out for any early stroll had captured the images with his camera and their public display of affection had gone viral by seven.

Phoebe had managed to wrap her leash around both Russ and Miranda, so Miranda took a few seconds to unravel them all before the three of them ended up crashing onto the ground. Then she and Russ stared at each other.

Wow. I didn't expect to see you, she signed. *And certainly not in New York City.*

"Let's walk and talk. There's a lot to discuss and Phoebe does not appear willing to wait. The Dragon is charged and ready."

Miranda nodded and they headed toward a small park a few blocks from Miranda's soon-to-be former apartment building.

"First, Ms. Nolan, let me say that I have two masters degrees and one doctorate. I taught for eight years at the college level and published two text books. I was told I stopped three major attacks in Afghanistan because of my skills translating for recalcitrant villagers. I'm saying this because with all these so-called brilliant accomplishments, I'm basically lacking in whatever 'smarts' would've stopped me from letting you take off before I could apologize for being a jerk. I should have trusted you enough to believe you when you said you'd be back. Which is why I'm saying it now. I am truly so sorry."

He smiled. "I'm also apologizing for not making it very clear how much I want to be with you. I've spent the past three months alternately kicking myself and holding back from flying up here in case you pointed me right back to the plane—which you would've had every right to do."

Dragon? Miranda signed.

"Sorry. Hang on. It's in my messenger bag."

Russ pulled out the device and set it up. "Working."

"Good, because I don't know how to sign, *I think we could both be awarded slap-on-the-head-fool status.* Russ, I pretended not to understand that you were offering a commitment when you told me you were going to relinquish your claim to Virginia's house. I needed to think. I needed to be by myself for a while and not impulsively say 'yes' even though my heart was begging me to do so. For once in my life I wanted to stop and consider what I was doing before making the big jeté. Trust me to mess it up by slowing down the *only* time in my life I should've been leaping into your arms."

He read the words then glanced down at her. "Go on."

"And I got here and I thought. And I felt horribly alone. About two days into shooting the movie I knew that you were far more important than seeing my name on a big screen. I almost flew right back to Birmingham. But I wasn't sure if you'd ever want to see me again. Plus—" she grinned at him "—I may be impulsive but I *am* responsible and I was serious when I told you if I make a commitment I stick to it. Whether that's signing a contract to play a superspy—or agreeing to a relationship with a stubborn man who didn't believe me when I told him I cared and was coming back."

"And?"

She stopped, then signed, *And I want that relationship very, very much.*

Russ leaned down and kissed her again, then they gazed wordlessly into each other's eyes before the dog began tugging at the leash, determined to make her silly humans pay attention to what was important—finishing her promenade through the park.

They walked in silence along the wooded path until they reached the dog run. Once inside, Miranda carefully closed the gate behind them then let Phoebe off the leash. The dog jumped into the air and landed gracefully. When she spotted a large Irish setter, a larger bull mastiff and one huge Great Dane she immediately gave chase, happily herding all three with authority. Miranda wished Jesse could see them.

Jesse. She nodded at Russ. "I need to tell you something."

He appeared anxious. "What?"

"I've already set this in motion. I'm adopting Jesse."

It was Miranda's turn to be anxious. Would this affect his feelings?

Russ laughed. "I know. I'm all for it."

She stared at him. "How did you know? The whole process only started three days ago when I called my dad, and *he* didn't know until Farrah passed on my message—he was out playing tennis."

"You're looking at Tim Nolan's tennis partner," he said, then kissed her again.

"Seriously?"

"Absolutely. Your dad is not only smart but a nice guy. A demonic tennis player but nice nonetheless."

"Dare I ask how you two became tennis partners?"

"Remember the night of the kid's camp show? Or at least the good part of the evening, before Russ Gerik made a fool of himself by turning into a stubborn jerk."

"We'll skip the latter part of the evening. I wasn't exactly in top form, either. So, at the show…"

"Well, during intermission your dad and I discovered we're both members at the Homewood tennis club, which is aptly named. Tennis only. No sitting around socializing while making business deals."

"I know it well. I've actually played there on more than one occasion. So? You and Dad?"

"I found myself agreeing to play with Timothy Nolan, international law expert and maniac on the courts."

Miranda chuckled. "Oops! Did Dad forget to tell you he's been on the faculty team since he first started teaching? I guess he also failed to mention that before he became a lawyer his dream was to be the next John McEnroe or Andre Agassi?"

Russ's laughter sailed into the trees of Inwood Park. When he'd calmed down, he wiped his eyes then said solemnly, "He left all that out when inviting me to play. Of course, I might have been somewhat less than forthcoming, as well. I didn't tell him I'd been champion of my college team or that I'd taught tennis at the downtown YMCA for years. But I repeat—Tim Nolan. Maniac. He'd knock me down in every set and smile that impish Nolan smile. Then he'd casually say I should play his darling daughter since I might be able to beat you. I gather that meant you're not planning to go pro anytime soon?"

Miranda lifted her chin. "I'll have you know I'm in awesome shape. I did my own stunts for the past three months. Jumped out of windows and landed three stories down on giant mattresses. Caught a helicopter as it was taking off over Central Park. Mixed it

up with bad guys doing major martial arts."
She grinned. "Of course, when it comes to
tennis, I stink. And no amount of physical fit-
ness would equip me for dealing with Dad."

"Well, Tim adores you, even though Wim-
bledon is not in your future."

Miranda grinned and signed, *I am rather
adorable!*

Russ planted a quick kiss on her forehead.
"I agree—but that's another discussion. Back
to your dad. Tim kindly gave me your itiner-
ary when I told him I couldn't take not being
with you any longer."

"I'm glad." Miranda smiled.

"Me, too. And with that being said and
too much time already wasted and—I know
this isn't the most romantic location…" Russ
put down the Dragon, stuck his hand into
his pocket and pulled out a small pouch. He
opened it and revealed a deep blue sapphire
ring, set in silver. "Miranda Nolan, I'm tired
of skirting and dodging. I love you. Will you
marry me?"

Miranda had never believed that real people cried during moments of happiness, but
her tears started to flow so hard she was unable to speak.

She quickly signed *Yes!* and Russ gently

placed the ring on her third finger. He leaned down and kissed her, then put his arms around her and held her in a secure embrace. The three other dog owners at the run quit drinking coffee and applauded. Even Phoebe appeared to know something important was happening and ended her chase.

After they finally broke apart, Miranda held the ring up and signed, *It's beautiful but also unusual. Where did you find it?*

"Kam made it back when he was in college. He was experimenting with jewelry and I personally thought this was the best of the lot."

Miranda scooped up the Dragon as she vowed to take every class Dr. Vinny taught. She hated that Russ was forced to read her words on a device, no matter how much of a boon that device was. Signing was far more intimate. She realized she'd soon be learning from Russ on a daily basis, a thought that made her smile through soft tears of joy. At least she was able to sign, *The fact that Kam made this makes it even more precious to me. Is it meant as both engagement and wedding ring?*

"It is. If you're okay with silver and not gold?"

I'd be okay with a cigar band or an ink

drawing around my finger! I love you. I'm so glad you finally asked me to marry you. She smiled. *Took you long enough.* She had to use the Dragon then. "I seem to recall you telling me once you didn't procrastinate."

"I didn't. Once I slapped myself silly for being stubborn and foolish, I was on that plane. I love you, too. I did say that before but I intend to repeat it as often as the next seventy years or so allow."

He leaned down and kissed her again. An excited Phoebe began running in circles around the two of them.

So, when did you get the ring?

Yesterday.

What? How did that come about?

"Blame our friends. I called Abra and told her I was flying to Manhattan to propose. She told me to bring Spero over so they could pet sit." He grinned. "Although for 'they' read Yasmin. Anyway, I'd barely brought in his toys and food when Yusuf handed me the ring and told me not to bother coming back for my dog if I didn't bring you." He paused. "And Abra called me a donkey-headed goat for not proposing the day I met you."

"Well, for the record, I behaved like a pig-headed chimp and I didn't make it clear I

planned to come back right after the movie."
She chuckled. "I'd say we have the start of a
great menagerie. Hopefully in the future we
can change the donkey, goat, pig and chimp
into harmonious love doves."

Russ placed the Dragon into his messenger bag. He took her hand in his and began
to swing it like a small boy walking his girl-
friend home after school. "I like this," he said
softly. "Hand in hand. Finally."

CHAPTER TWENTY-SIX

THE YOUNG MAN at the paint store had assured Miranda that Sunrise Serenade was taupe with a hint of mauve, which should work perfectly for the master bedroom. Miranda had almost asked him why the paint company had to come up with a nonsensical name instead of simply calling the color beige mixed with light purple, but as she stepped off the bottom rung of the ladder and moved far enough back to catch the full effect, she decided this particular company could be forgiven its whimsical names. Not only was the color exactly what she wanted, the finish was the right sheen and smoothness for the walls of the bedroom. If the other colors she'd bought—Desert Beach Party, a soft yellow with a hint of beige for the kitchen; Island Cascade, blue with a hint of peach for Jesse's bedroom; and Thanksgiving Delight Salad, cranberry with no hint of anything else for the living room and den—all turned out as well as Sunrise Serenade, she'd be a happy woman.

Miranda headed toward the room she and Russ were using as their temporary office. She needed to get away from the odor of drying paint—this particular October in Birmingham was still too hot for open windows. Her cell phone began ringing just as she was settling into Virginia's ancient office chair. Russ. He'd sent a text saying he'd be there within the next hour to take over painting duties. She smiled and texted back a parody of the seventies song "Feelings," changing the words to Ceilings. Nothing more than ceilings.

Bad! Very bad! Ouch! Russ replied. C U in a bit. Love U.

Miranda offered Phoebe a doggie treat from the big tin that mysteriously always seemed to be in the same room as Phoebe, then turned on the computer to return emails. Since coming back to Birmingham two weeks ago and taking up residence at Virginia's house (after receiving permission from Judge Rayborn) she'd discovered that dealing with wedding details was much easier by email, whether she was discussing menu options with her stepmother, ordering flowers or picking out invitations. Miranda was determined to keep the wedding small but had to fight all the folks who wanted it to be Birmingham's biggest event since the post-game party of 2012 when the Alabama Crimson Tide won the National Championship against Notre Dame's Fighting Irish.

At the top of Miranda's in-box were five emails from Farrah regarding the wedding cake. Miranda was staying with Farrah and Tim until the wedding, but Farrah continued to email rather than talking to Miranda in person. "I forget unless I see things in print," she'd said.

All five emails were invitations to tastings at bakeries. Apparently Farrah's incredible prowess in the kitchen did not extend to tiered Italian crème, decadent double chocolate delights or even traditional wedding whites. As Farrah explained, "I can guarantee great taste but not exotic decorations, which is why I use these guys for catering jobs when I need luscious desserts that also look good."

Miranda didn't really care whether the cake was a work of art, but in the spirit of keeping the peace she agreed to accompany Farrah on the wedding-cake tour next week. She was leaning toward Italian crème as the bride's cake with a raspberry-chocolate groom's cake on the side. Or maybe she should go with the white chocolate-pistachio-flavored for the bride's cake and the hazelnut chocolate for the groom's cake? She emailed Farrah, All of the above? And can we include some cupcakes for Jesse and the kids I've invited from the children's theater?

Darci had emailed to ask if Miranda needed an accompanist for her performance at the Durani exhibition. She sent Darci all the pertinent information.

She quickly deleted the emails from various home improvement, bridal and interior design stores. All the fashion and furniture details had been handled by Miranda or Russ within days of their arrival back in Birmingham.

She dealt with the rest of her unread messages before she was hit with the urge to snack on one of the gingerbread men she and Russ had bought in Williamsburg on the way down to Birmingham two weeks earlier.

She smiled as she thought about that trip. With Russ to share the task of driving, the sixteen-hour ride from New York City to Birmingham—which Miranda normally labeled a nightmare—turned into a fun mini-vacation. Russ's friends in Williamsburg, Virginia, had pet sat Phoebe so Russ and Miranda could explore the old Colonial village, starting with the shop that made musical instruments and finishing with the authentic 18th-century kitchen. They'd eaten gingerbread cookies, bought some to take home to Jesse and purchased two heavy gingerbread cookie tins.

Miranda grinned. "I figure I need to learn to make cookies. It's a mom thing. The other tin is for Farrah."

"She's going to love it. I gather you two are getting along better?" Russ asked.

"Surprisingly, yes. I decided to put aside my Cinderella stepmother complex and try to see Farrah as a real person and not some character in a bad play. I think she accepted she'd never turn me into a combination of Julia Child and TV master chef. It'll be interesting to see if we can hang on to this new understanding. Of course, we both dearly love my dad so that's already kept any minor personality issues from becoming major battles."

The Williamsburg detour was followed by Asheville, North Carolina, for a stop at the Biltmore House and Antler Hill Village and winery. The final and best leg of their journey had been sharing the experience of walking on Kiawah Beach in South Carolina in their bare feet. Russ had looked out at the Atlantic Ocean and scooped up some sand.

"We're coming back here after we're married. We can bring Jesse," Russ had said.

"Agreed. Maybe for Spring Break?"

"That could work. We just have to coordinate our schedules since I'll be teaching full time at Miles College, you'll be with the children's theater and Jesse will be at his school. Could get crazy."

"We'll work it all out. You are going to make such an amazing dad."

"I'm terrified." He grinned. "But very happy you'll be at my side while we navigate the waters of parenthood!" Russ had leaned down and kissed her while Phoebe danced around them in approval.

Miranda smiled, remembering how funny Phoebe had been during that trip, trying to herd seagulls while avoiding the ocean itself. She glanced down at the dog, who'd fallen asleep under the desk—on Miranda's feet. Phoebe awoke and wagged her tail, then headed toward the back to be let out. Spero, who'd also been asleep by Phoebe's side, immediately jumped up and followed. Miranda watched the two chase invisible squirrels around the yard and was about to join them for a little stick throwing when the doorbell rang.

Miranda hurried to the front door.

"Hey, Brett. How are you?"

He appeared startled. "Oh. Hi. I actually didn't think anyone was here. I didn't see your car but I figured I'd ring the bell just in case."

"Russ has it. So far mine's the only one equipped with a car seat for Jesse. So, what's up? I guess you need more documents signed? Is Cort with you?" She turned around without waiting for a response. "Come on in. We can go to the kitchen, since it's the least bad smelling of the rooms right now. I'm sure there's a pen in one of the drawers."

She led Brett toward to kitchen, chattering about how great Miss Virginia's house was going to look once all the painting was finished. He remained silent until she turned around. "I don't need a pen. I don't want a pen. What I want are the Auttenberg paintings."

Miranda blinked. "What?"

"You heard me. I never found them. So, I

assume you and Russ did. It's simple. I want them."

Miranda's mouth dropped open. A crazy person was standing in her kitchen. Maybe she'd misunderstood. Maybe Brett needed them for appraisal for the estate?

"Brett, I don't have any paintings. Russ and I have looked. We've read most of her diaries and we can't find a single clue. Assuming they even exist, are they needed for probate?"

"They exist. Virginia told me about them when I was drawing up her will. If nothing else, give me the diaries."

His tone was even but there was an edge that made the back of Miranda's neck prickle.

She took a deep breath and tried to stay calm. "Look, I'll tell you right now, there's nothing in the journals to indicate where an Auttenberg might be hidden. I really don't understand what the problem is."

"The problem is that I've been trying to find those paintings since the day Virginia entered the hospital. They're mine. I deserve them as payment for her will!" Brett pulled a gun out of his waistband.

Crazy was right. Virginia would never have offered priceless works of art to some-one she'd met once, who spent perhaps two hours with her as she dictated that second will. Someone who was now waving a gun around. Miranda's throat closed.

"Fine," she croaked. "Take the diaries. I'll give you a dolly to haul them out. I don't care."

Will Brett really leave once he has the journals? Nothing about this nightmare encounter was logical but Miranda felt certain that sending the man away lugging a load of boxes wasn't going to solve anything. Brett appeared to be willing to resort to extreme measures, including violence.

"I'm not taking the boxes, Ms. Nolan. They're staying here. So am I. So are you. If I find what I need…well, let's just say that would be the ideal solution."

Having Brett stay and go on a hunting expedition through Virginia's journals didn't sound pleasant, but Miranda figured it was better than having Brett shoot her. She nodded but couldn't stop herself from asking, "Why?"

"Why what?"

"You're an associate with a good firm. One assumes you'll make partner at some point. Why jeopardize your career, heck, your whole life, trying to get your hands on something that may not really exist and quite frankly that you have no right to?" Miranda's voice shook but she wanted to keep him talking.

Brett exhaled and pursed his lips. "I lost a lot of money at the racetrack. I'm in debt to some very impatient characters. Enter Virginia Radinski Auttenberg, who throws out all these hints about how valuable her journals are and I figured, why not me? Who's to know? I'd originally thought I'd wait until Russ got the house and I could make any artwork found part of the fee for my services. I had no idea he was Mr. All-Knowing about Benjamin Auttenberg. Then things went haywire with the other will and the shared inventory. Next thing I know you and Gerik start searching and everyone in town hears about paintings. I realized I don't have time to wait and there's no way either of you would let me have Auttenberg's works now that you're aware of the value. I'm sorry it has to be this way."

Not really, you psychotic creep! Miranda thought. She shook her head and tried to slow her racing pulse or at least hide her fear. "Well, then, get to it. We have all the boxes in the living room, except for the one I guess you stole. Remember? With the recipes?"

"Fine." He waved the gun at her. "It's time for some fast reading, Ms. Nolan. I'm not leaving until I can walk out that door with a couple of paintings under my arm."

There was no point in repeating that she and Russ had already read and searched and come up with nothing.

The kitchen door opened and Russ walked in, arms loaded with packages. Brett whirled around and pointed the gun at him. Russ's eyes narrowed in anger. Then his face took on an expression of horror. Miranda didn't know why until she glanced behind Russ. Jesse was happily marching through the doorway, carefully holding a bag with the store logo reading Trains, Boats and Planes.

Brett seemed to panic at the sight of a third person, even though that person was an undersize seven-year old. He wildly pointed the weapon at Russ and then at Jesse, who promptly began to cry and hug his package to his chest.

That was when Miranda experienced what parents throughout history have felt upon seeing their child in danger.

Rage.

Sheer, intense, burning rage.

Not an ounce of fear was left in her system.

This man was threatening her boy and there was no way she was going to allow that. She glanced at Russ and saw her emotions mirrored in his eyes. The only problem was how to get the gun without anyone getting shot.

The opportunity came within seconds when Brett motioned for Russ and Jesse to join Miranda at the opposite side of the kitchen. As Jesse ran toward Miranda, Russ neatly and quickly swung his packages at Brett's arm, which knocked the gun out of his hand. Russ dove to the floor to retrieve it. Miranda shoved Jesse behind her. In a move worthy of Miami Montreville, she grabbed the heavy gingerbread cookie tin she'd left on the counter and executed a blow to Brett's stomach before he had a chance to react. As he collapsed onto the floor, Russ sprang up, holding the gun.

"Enough," he snarled. "You stay down there. It's time to call Officer Hernandez and tell him we have a new occupant for the Homewood neighborhood jail." He signed to Jesse, telling him to go into the next room and close the door.

Once Jesse was safely in the living room, Russ asked Miranda to hold the gun. "I'm not taking any chances," he said, expertly tying

Brett's hands and ankles. When the wannabe thief twitched as though trying to get free, Russ smiled sweetly and said, "I wouldn't. That woman is more than ready to smash a cookie tin across your skull and I'm not about to stop her. And after she finishes, you'd get to deal with me."

Russ took the gun from Miranda's trembling hands. Miranda swallowed, grabbed her cell phone from the kitchen table and called Officer Hernandez. The instant she hung up she asked, "Since we have a moment or two before the police arrive, what exactly did Virginia say to make you believe those paintings were here?"

A defiant Mr. King grunted. "She told me that the house was the *least* valuable item named in her will. She also said her diaries were the threads of her life. Whatever clues she left are in those journals."

CHAPTER TWENTY-SEVEN

MIRANDA STARED AT the young lawyer who was now headed for prison. "You broke in here multiple times trying to steal Virginia's journals. You pointed a gun at two people I love—and me—and all you can say is she left clues!"

Brett shook his head. "I wasn't going to use it. The gun. Really. I'm sorry. I didn't think you'd be home and I panicked."

"That's the stupidest excuse I've ever heard. How you made it through eighth grade, much less college and law school, is beyond amazing."

Officer Hernandez knocked at the door before Miranda could ask any more questions. He and two other policemen placed handcuffs on Brett's wrists and read him his rights. Hernandez stayed with Russ and Miranda while the other officers escorted Brett outside.

Hernandez turned to Miranda. "I can't wait to hear how you and Gerik managed to disarm our suspect. I'm sure it's good. I'm also assuming it was moderately legal but even if it wasn't, I'm not sure I care."

Hernandez settled into a kitchen chair and pulled out his notebook. "Now then, could you please walk me through what just happened?"

"Is it okay if I bring Jesse in here? I want him to know he's safe now. He lip reads a little but it's not enough to be able to follow a police Q and A. I'm sure he'll love seeing your uniform!"

"I'd actually like to meet him."

Miranda hurried into the den and brought a still terrified Jesse back into the kitchen. He visibly relaxed when he saw that Brett was gone and he smiled when Officer Hernandez let him hold his badge, but he was still in need of some comforting.

Miranda let Phoebe and Spero back inside, then sank into one of the kitchen chairs and signed for Jesse to join her.

"Jesse and I have been staying here alone. I guess Brett didn't know that."

Hernandez nodded. "Go on."

With the child happily settled on her lap and both dogs curled around her feet, Miranda proceeded to give Hernandez the play by play of events that began when Brett rang the doorbell. The officer's mouth tightened when Miranda described Jesse's fear once the child realized he was in a dangerous situation.

"This guy's slime." Hernandez said. "Anyone who threatens a kid should be locked up forever."

"Agreed," Miranda said.

"Go on."

Miranda finished telling him how Russ how gotten the gun away from Brett. *He's my hero!*

Russ laughed. "Tell him how you thwacked the guy across the stomach after doing some pretty amazing stunts." He grinned at Hernandez. "I'm marrying a ninja."

"That reminds me. Congratulations! Thanks for the invitation. I'm RSVP-ing in person for both my wife and me, although I hadn't expected to give you an answer while arresting someone."

Miranda was finally able to smile. "Thank you. For the congrats, I mean. I'm really happy y'all are coming to the wedding. And thanks for getting here so fast and removing that man from our presence. I'm still trying to process that he burgled the place multiple times and waved a gun in our faces. He has absolutely ruined his life. That's sad."

Russ read her comments on the Dragon and said, "Sad is an understatement."

Hernandez rose. "If y'all would sign the statement, I'll get out of your hair. Hopefully Mr. King will plead out and we can all avoid a trial."

Miranda gently moved Jesse off her lap, grabbed a pen and wrote her name at the bottom of the statement. She watched Russ do the same then escorted Hernandez to the front door.

"Thank you again."

"No problem. I'm just relieved for all of you that this is over." Hernandez headed for his car, waving and calling, "Wedding. See you then."

Russ and Jesse were waiting for her in the den.

I'm exhausted, she signed. *I can't believe this just happened and Brett turned into a criminal because Virginia told him something valuable was here.*

"Insane" was Russ's sole comment.

Miranda grabbed the Dragon. "What? Brett? His so-called excuse for breaking, entering and threatening? The past half hour? The whole past six months?"

Russ smiled. "All of the above. Plus the idea that someone would commit multiple acts of burglary and point a gun at three people all for what? The off chance that he could find what no one else has been able to find, including you and me?"

Miranda shrugged. "I do have one more journal to go through. The last entry was made only a week before she died."

Russ nodded. "I'll let you do some reading. I'm going to hit the attic and set up the first part of Jesse's train. Using my hands to build something might help me calm down. I'm embarrassed and furious that Brett was my lawyer. Although, in my defense, I didn't hire him. Virginia contacted his firm, which *is* reputable even if they missed the mark when they hired the guy. Anyway, do you need anything before we head upstairs?"

Miranda smiled. "I'm good. I gather train tracks and other railroading objects are in the bag? That's why you guys were so long?"

"Guilty. We were going to bring home the actual model engine and a caboose but the one we wanted wasn't in stock. The owner will give me a call once it's in." He kissed her firmly on the mouth, which caused a delay in the construction plans, then he picked up Jesse's bags and headed for the attic.

Jesse glanced at Miranda and signed for permission to follow the man who was going to be his new dad. She signed back, *Sure. But be nice and maybe bring a couple of gingerbread cookies for Russ?* Jesse raced into the kitchen and blissfully grabbed about ten. Miranda didn't stop him. He paused at the foot of the stairs, then ran back and offered a cookie to her. She grinned at him, wondering how to sign *you're a charming little cherub,* although she assumed he knew that, in her eyes, he was too cute for words.

Miranda took a bite of cookie as she walked back to the den and turned on the floor lamp behind the rocking chair. She flipped through the first pages of Virginia's last journal until she found the date that mentioned the Brennan firm and the first will.

I called Dave Brennan and asked if he'd mind coming to the house as I did not drive. I promised tea and kolaches but Mr. Brennan appeared to be a kind soul who would have made the trip without what he called major perks! Once he and his young associate arrived I handed them my list for where I wanted my possessions to go and told them to be sure that my journals would not be destroyed. There is value there. A few hours later, I did the same with a young man from a different firm.

Miranda sat up straight. Virginia truly had written two wills and signed them both on the same day. The diary suddenly shifted from a memoir to a direct letter. Somehow Virginia had known Miranda would read her last thoughts.

If you read my other journals you already know that I endured much at Terezin. I lost my son and nearly went mad from the pain. I was forced to work as a tailor for the Nazis who guarded the camp and the officers who visited. Life is ironic. I lived because I had a skill they considered worthwhile. I was a lowly seamstress who was allowed to wear something other than filthy rags to do her work for these butchers while they listened to beautiful music. The same butchers who disposed of the creators of that music as if they were so much garbage. I lost my husband and my child. But I made it out and I made a life for myself in America. Some of my people were liberated, yes, but justice was denied. Please, Miranda, do what's right. For me. For Benjamin. For my baby."

Miranda was determined to find a way to get that justice for Virginia and Benjamin Auttenberg and all the victims of Terezin. She closed the journal, wiped her eyes and carefully placed the book in one of the four cartons that held Virginia's other diaries. Russ was going to load the boxes into his car and take them to Virginia's synagogue. If they wanted to donate the journals to the large Holocaust museum in Washington, D.C., that was fine. If they wanted to keep them and teach children in Birmingham about an evil past that still affected too many people that was fine, as well.

The sound of Jesse giggling echoed down the stairs. Miranda felt intensely grateful for the child's ability to retain his innocence and pleasure in simple activities. She was sorry that Russ couldn't hear him, but she knew he could see the happiness on Jesse's face while they planned the construction of what Russ was already calling Auttenberg Station.

Russ had left the Dragon charging on the hall table. Miranda picked it up and climbed the stairs to the attic in less than a minute. Jesse was carefully drawing his idea of what the train station would look like. Russ glanced up and smiled. "Casey Jones and I are going into business here. The J & R Railroad will be rolling within the month."

She tried to smile, but her lip quivered. She couldn't speak so she signed, *That's great! I can't wait!*

Russ stood and ran to her side. He put his arms around her and simply held her for a few moments. Finally he asked, "What did you find out?"

"That Brett King committed crimes for nothing. There are no clues. The value is in the diaries themselves and in honoring those who were slaughtered. Which I firmly intend to do."

CHAPTER TWENTY-EIGHT

"THIS EXHIBITION IS so smokin' hot, I may have to call my fiancé to come over with sirens blazing and hoses ready to douse the flames."

Miranda blinked. "I thought your fiancé was a surgeon? Are operating rooms that wild these days?"

Darci chuckled. "You're so behind the times, Miranda! The doc was May and June. It's October—I've moved on. My current fiancé is a captain at the Vestavia Hills fire station. Oh. You missed August, too. He was a professor Yusuf Durani introduced me to. Nice but dull."

Miranda coughed in an effort to hide her amusement. "Well, I suppose Darci Becker actually becoming Mrs. Anybody is not really in the works anytime soon."

Darci grinned. "Got to keep up my rep!"

Miranda grinned back. "I do agree with you about the show. This exhibition is hotter than hot. Kamyar's works are amazing and adding the Auttenberg you were able to buy a few months ago somehow pulls everything together."

Darci nodded. "I'm a flake in many ways but I'm a very talented one when it comes to anything artistic. Which reminds me, nice job tonight. Having you sing a few Cat Stevens tunes was a stroke of genius on my part." She squealed. "Ooh! Check it out! It's the critic from New York! He made it! We'll be in the *Times!*"

"Wow! That's a coup!" Miranda exclaimed. "How'd you manage to get him down here?"

"We used to be engaged." She ran off in the direction of a man standing in front of a piece entitled *Tuesday's Dead.* The critic had dressed in character, wearing an elegant charcoal-gray suit with a cranberry-colored silk scarf draped around his neck and black boots that shouldn't go with a suit but somehow added to the look of wealth. He and Darci exchanged platonic hugs then began a rapid-fire conversation, clearly about the painting.

Miranda chuckled. Her gaze switched to Abra and Yusuf, who were talking with Russ. Even from twenty feet away Miranda could sense the varied emotions from all three. Pride and pleasure at the sight of Kam's works clearly warred with the sadness of knowing he would never paint again. Kam Durani would never see those works hanging in a prestigious gallery and he would never hear the accolades that were his due.

The Duranis and Russ were joined by Tim and Farrah Nolan, who'd last been standing in front of Auttenberg's *Performance.* Miranda glanced around the gallery and smiled at the sight of an excited Jesse signing with Yasmin as they discussed one of Kam's paintings with the attitude of experienced art critics. It was evident the young pair were acclaiming the works as pivotal and groundbreaking and guaranteed to touch the heart of any and all who attended.

The latter was a given. Darci's taste in art was impeccable and she had a surprisingly generous spirit. She had invited the families of the soldiers killed in the blast that had taken Kam's life and paid for their travel expenses out of gallery funds.

Miranda loved all of Kam's artwork but she kept returning to *Silent Sunlight,* not only because of the beauty of the piece but for the memory it brought of the day she and Russ first broke down a few barriers. She was gazing at the piece when she was joined by an elderly gentleman who gestured toward the illustration and quietly said, "This is his best, I think. I've never seen anything that so expertly combines loneliness with peace."

Miranda nodded. "I totally agree." She glanced up at the man then squinted. He seemed familiar. "This might sound odd—" she smiled "—but have we met?"

"Not officially, but I did come backstage and shake your hand after your performance at the Alabama Shakespeare Festival about seven years ago. *Kiss Me, Kate.* You were swamped with admirers."

Miranda sighed. "And critics, if I recall!"

He laughed. "Not that many. It was a great show and you were excellent as Bianca. I could tell even then that you'd do well on Broadway. I also enjoyed your singing tonight, especially your rendition of 'Silent Sunlight.'" He extended his right hand. "Proper introductions. I'm Winston Rayborn."

Miranda's eyes widened. "Wait. As in Judge Winston Rayborn? The nut— Uh…"

His chuckle turned into a laugh. "Nutcase? I prefer eccentric but yes, I'm that judge. And I know quite well that you're Miranda Nolan, although I understand your last name is soon to change and I won't see you or your intended in my courtroom because of that. Congratulations!"

"Thank you! Funny how things turn out, isn't it," she mused.

He winked. "Not if one knew Miss Virginia. She was a hopeless and incorrigible romantic, and she loved you and Russ very much."

Darci swept up behind the judge and linked her arm in his. "Winston, darling! I'm so glad you came! Ready to buy?" The impetuous gallery owner hustled Rayborn away before Miranda had a chance to ask exactly what he'd meant about Miss Virginia. She almost called out asking him to come back but Darci was briskly escorting the judge toward Kamyar's piece called *Into White*.

Miranda headed toward some unusual pieces near the back of the room. She hadn't seen them at the Duranis' house.

Russ met her as she was weaving through the crowd. "You finally spotted these two. There's a story behind them."

Tell me.

"We'd been camped in this tiny village about a hundred miles from anything resembling a city. Everyone was on edge. Supplies were low. Kam didn't have paper or a canvas but he was determined to draw that village. We didn't have much food, either, but we seemed to have a great supply of army-issue blankets. Kam always managed to have some paints stuffed into his kit, so he decided to use what was at hand. *Et voilà!* He created *Moonshadow* and *Peace Train.*"

They're beautiful. Do you know if Abra and Yusuf are putting them up for sale?

"I'm not sure. I know at least five of Kam's pieces are going home with them. But they haven't told me which ones. Did Darci tell you that proceeds from the sales are going to the wounded veterans association of Alabama?"

Miranda smiled then spoke into the Dragon. "She did not mention whether or not her commission would be part of the donation."

"With Darci, one is never sure."

Miranda continued to stare at the two works. "I'm totally in awe that Kamyar was able to depict the village with such clarity. On wool! Wow."

Russ nodded.

Miranda suddenly stood absolutely still. Then she grabbed Russ's arm. "I have just been struck by a lightning bolt in a blue sky!"

"What?"

"See if you can wrest Jesse away from Yasmin and I'll say goodbyes to everyone. We're good here. We need to head back to Virginia's."

"Why?"

"I'm either brilliant or a complete fool. Possibly both. We'll see."

Jesse was reluctant to leave, but he was also showing signs of exhaustion, having been at the exhibition for several hours. After hugs with friends had been exchanged and waves waved, along with cries of "We'll see y'all next week at the wedding!" they were off.

Thirty minutes later Jesse was asleep with the faithful Phoebe curled up beside him. Russ turned to Miranda. "Mind telling me why we tore out of there like the cops were after us?"

Attic.

"Okay."

They climbed the stairs, opened the door—carefully avoiding stepping on any pieces of the J & R Railroad and Auttenberg Station—and ended up in the corner of the attic where Virginia's tailoring mannequin stood.

Miranda pointed to the mannequins. "It struck me when we were looking at Kam's paintings on wool. Art isn't always created on paper or canvas. *Fabric*. Beautiful pieces can be painted on fabric. Virginia told Brett the diaries were the threads of her life. She was a seamstress and a tailor. She wrote in her last diary that she was allowed to have 'good' dresses for the days she was forced to sew for the Nazis. Apparently they didn't want the person taking measurements to be dressed in rags." Her expression darkened. "So civilized of them. Anyway, what if Benjamin Auttenberg found himself in a similar position to Kam in that village? No paper. No canvas. Just paints or an ink source. Or what if Benjamin simply grew tired of having his works snatched up for Nazi generals to hang on their walls? Maybe he wanted to preserve something special for Virginia. Something he was determined no one could take from her."

Russ gently removed a wool dress from the mannequin it had adorned for over seventy years. He laid it on a clear space on the floor while Miranda opened one of Virginia's old sewing kits and hunted for a basting ripper. She found one in perfect condition and knelt on the floor next to a gray wool dress so shapeless it could have been a maternity shift. Turning the garment inside out, Mi-

randa carefully clipped the stitches that attached the cotton lining.

She sank to her knees then silently held
up the portrait that had remained hidden for
so many years. The model was a young Virginia Radinski.

"She was beautiful," Russ said with awe.

"Virginia was always elegant. She was already in her seventies when I met her but I
can clearly recall telling her she looked classy
and gorgeous, which is quite something for a
child to say. Kids assume anyone over the age
of eighteen is an old toad." Miranda tried to
smile. She pointed to the bottom of the portrait. "Look. He signed it. *Virginia. Benjamin
A. 1945.* This must have been done not long
before he was murdered. I wonder... Let me
check the other side of this dress."

She pulled the basting loose and discovered
a second painting. "Russ. This must be a companion piece to *Performance.*" She squinted.
"Tuning. Benjamin Auttenberg. 1945."

Russ stared down at the work, which depicted the children at Terezin quietly tuning
their instruments in preparation for a concert
for men who would later destroy them.

"It's even sadder than *Performance.* The
emotion pours through every brushstroke

and every line. You know, I think we should sell this one to Darci and the proceeds could go to causes that benefit children. A refugee camp in Afghanistan, perhaps? Maybe a little left over for the Masquerade Theater and The Cooper School?"

Russ nodded. "Great idea." He gestured toward the second mannequin. "I've been so struck by Virginia's portrait and this piece, I'd almost forgotten. Let's check the other dress."

Miranda rose, carefully draped the dress holding the two portraits over one of the few chairs still in the attic, then started undoing the stitches from the second dress, a faded beige wool, until she revealed a third piece of art.

Russ's jaw dropped. "It's Jesse!"

Miranda bit her lower lip. "It is. That black curly hair. The huge brown eyes that can't hide the imp even through the sadness caused by the cruelty meted out in an adult world."

Russ smoothed out the fabric. "Look at the title."

"Ariel Auttenberg. 1942." Miranda stared at Russ. "Ariel. Virginia's only child." She didn't bother to wipe away the tears flowing down her cheeks.

Russ knelt down on the floor next to her

and held her as she cried, rocking her against his chest. Finally he lifted her chin and calmly said, "We're keeping these. We'll frame them and put them up on either side of *Silent Sunlight*."

Miranda's eyes widened. "I thought Abra and Yusuf didn't want to sell it."

He shook his head. "They don't. It's their wedding gift to us."

She tried to smile. "I may start crying again, but if I do it'll be because even in the midst of horrors good people still exist in this world and we're lucky enough to know more than one."

Russ helped Miranda to her feet. He lifted her into the air and began to twirl her around before letting her slowly slide down exactly as he'd done the day they went hot-air ballooning. He stopped when her lips were in the perfect place to receive his kiss.

After they parted he quietly said, "We've all been told that when one loses one of the senses, another becomes stronger. Well, when I'm with you *all* my remaining senses are stronger. I love looking at you and inhaling that sweet scent of Miranda. I love feeling your soft skin against mine and most of all I love that tingle my entire body gets every time our lips meet. Which I intend to repeat as often as I can. Definitely at least once more this hour."

He kissed her again, setting her pulse racing.

"If it means anything to you, Russell Gerik, my own senses have been in overload since the moment I met you!" She glanced at the portraits of Virginia and Ariel and spoke to the air around her. "Thank you, Virginia, for willing us this house."

Miranda turned to Russ. "I forgot to tell you, but I met Judge Winston Rayborn today. The so-called nutcase? I gather that he knew Virginia quite well. I think the two of them decided to play matchmaker. They set something in motion…making sure you and I met and were forced to work together. Maybe she does haunt this house?"

Russ laughed. "Wouldn't surprise me. Virginia loved both of us and love as strong as hers doesn't die. Her love for Benjamin and Ariel lingered in her soul and it was freely given to you. She knew your love would be given to someone else and I'm so grateful that someone is me. If that's haunting, then I'm a believer."

Russ put his arms around her again. She

looked into his eyes and chose to sign instead of speak. *It has. That love has been given to you. And it will be yours for the rest of our lives and beyond.*

* * * * *

LARGER-PRINT BOOKS!

GET 2 FREE
LARGER-PRINT NOVELS
PLUS 2 FREE
MYSTERY GIFTS

Love Inspired

Larger-print novels are now available...